W9-CAM-391

Praise for

"Full of fierce girls, fabulously fun magic, humor,
and so much heart. I loved it!"

—Stephanie Burgis,
author of *The Dragon with a Chocolate Heart* and *Kat, Incorrigible*

"Antonia's lively first-person narration lends immediacy and suspense
to this compelling, complex adventure filled with capable, complex,
brown-skinned women. Clever, fast-paced fantasy punctuated
with surprising twists and plenty of girl power."

—*Kirkus Reviews*

"A gorgeous fairy tale that touches on the benefits of cooperation and
the beauty of discovering one's own particular brand of magic."

—*Booklist*

"A solid core of complexity underlies plentiful magical antics. . . .
Lovably imperfect heroines, dancing turnips, a sea monster or two,
and a political whodunnit keep the pages turning
until the satisfying conclusion."

—*Bulletin of the Center for Children's Books*

"A fast-paced and pleasant magical read that proves that the power
of friendship can help overcome many challenges. A strong choice
for middle grade readers who enjoy adventure, fantasy, and enemies-
to-friends tales."

—*School Library Journal*

RiVAL MAGiC

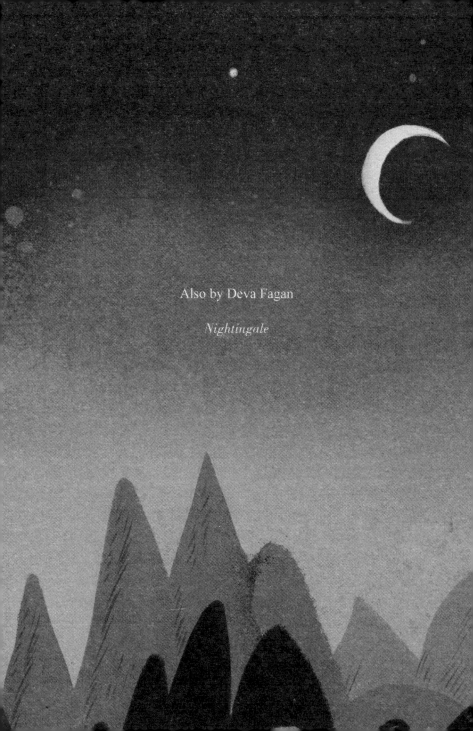

Also by Deva Fagan

Nightingale

RIVAL MAGIC

DEVA FAGAN

atheneum ATHENEUM BOOKS FOR YOUNG READERS

NEW YORK LONDON TORONTO SYDNEY NEW DELHI

If you purchased this book without a cover, you should be aware that this book is stolen property. It was reported as "unsold and destroyed" to the publisher, and neither the author nor the publisher has received any payment for this "stripped book."

A atheneum

ATHENEUM BOOKS FOR YOUNG READERS

An imprint of Simon & Schuster Children's Publishing Division

1230 Avenue of the Americas, New York, New York 10020

This book is a work of fiction. Any references to historical events, real people, or real places are used fictitiously. Other names, characters, places, and events are products of the author's imagination, and any resemblance to actual events or places or persons, living or dead, is entirely coincidental.

Text © 2020 by Deva Fagan

Cover illustrations © 2020 by Saoirse Lou

Cover design by Rebecca Syracuse © 2020 by Simon & Schuster, Inc.

All rights reserved, including the right of reproduction in whole or in part in any form.

ATHENEUM BOOKS FOR YOUNG READERS is a registered trademark of Simon & Schuster, Inc. Atheneum logo is a trademark of Simon & Schuster, Inc.

For information about special discounts for bulk purchases, please contact Simon & Schuster Special Sales at 1-866-506-1949 or business@simonandschuster.com.

The Simon & Schuster Speakers Bureau can bring authors to your live event. For more information or to book an event, contact the Simon & Schuster Speakers Bureau at 1-866-248-3049 or visit our website at www.simonspeakers.com.

Also available in an Atheneum Books for Young Readers hardcover edition

Interior design by Rebecca Syracuse

The text for this book was set in Bodoni.

The illustrations for this book were rendered digitally.

Manufactured in the United States of America

0321 OFF

First Atheneum Books for Young Readers paperback edition April 2021

10 9 8 7 6 5 4 3 2 1

The Library of Congress has cataloged the hardcover edition as follows:

Names: Fagan, Deva, author.

Title: Rival magic / Deva Fagan.

Description: First edition. | New York : Atheneum, [2020] | Summary: Apprentice wizards Antonia and Moppe must set aside their rivalry and unite their opposing skill sets to save Master Betrys, their island nation, and themselves.

Identifiers: LCCN 2019001933 | ISBN 9781534439054 (hardcover) | ISBN 9781534439061 (pbk) | ISBN 9781534439078 (eBook)

Subjects: | CYAC: Wizards—Fiction. | Apprentices—Fiction. | Identity—Fiction. | Friendship—Fiction. | Fantasy.

Classification: LCC PZ7.F136 Riv 2020 | DDC [Fic]—dc23

LC record available at https://lccn.loc.gov/2019001933

To anyone who thinks
they're not good enough.

You are.

RIVAL MAGIC

1

IT'S HARDER THAN YOU'D THINK to make a turnip dance. I mean, obviously you need to use magic. But it's not a difficult spell.

I learned the magespeak word for *turnip* almost six months ago, on my very first day as Master Betrys's apprentice. She says turnips are the perfect subjects for practice because they're plentiful and won't do too much harm if I accidentally send one zooming out her window across the plaza. I think the real reason is that she hates eating them and is trying to thwart Cook. There's no reason we couldn't be using carrots or quinces, except that Master Betrys hasn't taught me those words yet. I had to look them up myself, secretly, in her study, when she was out repairing Arles Nevin's enchanted clock.

But she did teach me the words for *animate* and *dance*. So I shouldn't have been having any trouble. And yet . . .

I tried my best to scrub the scowl from my face, to evoke the exquisite grace Master Betrys always displayed when casting even the most challenging incantations. I forced myself to ignore the ache in my shin from when I accidentally bumped into—well, kicked in frustration is more accurate— the kitchen table after my last failed attempt.

The innocent purple-white vegetable lay waiting atop the oak bench, bathed in the soft red glow of the banked hearth fire. I hadn't bothered to light a lamp. Everyone else was asleep at this hour, except for Master Betrys, who was out at a dinner party. And I didn't particularly want to be observed, especially if I failed again.

Master Betrys was expecting me to perform the enchantment tomorrow morning. And I would do it. I *had* to. In just over two weeks it would be my half-year anniversary as an apprentice. I was running out of time.

I still remembered my mother's words as she frowned over the banknote paying for my first half year of study with Master Betrys. *Six months, Antonia,* she had said. *I'll give you six months to demonstrate that this fascination of yours is of any practical use to our family. If not . . .*

I shuddered. I could already imagine the fine lines denting my mother's perfect brow, and the look in her bright green eyes. Not disappointment. You had to expect something from someone in order to be disappointed. If I failed as a wizard, my mother's eyes would say, *I told you so*. Then she would summon me home, and all my dreams would die. I'd lose the one thing that made me feel like there was a place for me in the world.

I shoved Mother out of my thoughts. I could do this.

I kept my arms loose at my sides, remembering how Master Betrys rolled her eyes at mages who indulged in what she referred to as "unnecessary theatrics." I took a deep breath and held it, setting the three words firmly in my mind.

Turnip. Animate. Dance.

Then I spoke them. Carefully. Slowly, but not so slowly that they sounded unpracticed and halting. I bent every scrap of my will at that cursed purple root. A tickling ripple of magic flared through me. For one brief moment I was part of something greater, one perfect stanza in the song shaping the universe. Glorious anticipation thrummed in my chest.

The turnip shivered. Slowly, slowly it bent one fibrous root. I'd specifically chosen a turnip with several rooty "legs." In theory it made no difference to the spell. It could have been an egg and it would find a way to dance, if the magic was strong enough. But I was going to take any advantage I could get.

My turnip clambered upright. It looked as if it might topple over at the slightest puff of breeze.

I said the words again, louder. The turnip executed a

wobbly pirouette. Good. I could do this. I'd show my mother she was wrong about me. I could already see myself, arriving home with my robes of mastery flowing all about me in a glory of blue velvet. And Mother, coming to meet me, her eyes shining with pride, the way she used to look at my brother. The way she'd never, ever looked at me.

That was when I heard the noise. I frowned, cocking my head. I could have sworn someone was *snickering*. I eyed the turnip suspiciously as it attempted another drunken pirouette. But animation didn't work that way. The turnip would only do what I specifically ordered it. And I certainly hadn't told it to laugh at me.

The sound came again. A giggle of mirth, barely muffled. I whirled around, searching the dim kitchen for the source. There. A shadow beside the pantry. A shadow with gleaming eyes.

I grabbed one of the fire irons. "Who's there?"

Master Betrys had told me not to heed the news criers, but I'd heard the stories. The rebellion was gaining ground, and I knew all too well the deadly lengths they would go to in their quest for independence. What if some rebel had decided Master Betrys was a loyalist, in spite of all her efforts to remain neutral? What if they'd come to burn down her house?

Or they could be here for me. Mother was an outspoken loyalist and a member of the council. Though I pitied anyone who actually tried to use me as a hostage. Mother wasn't the sort to negotiate. She'd probably be glad for a chance to be rid of me. Still, I wasn't going down without a fight.

I brandished my fire iron at the shadow. "Come out! Show yourself! Or I'm going to enchant every blade in this kitchen to slice you into—*ouch!*"

The ungrateful turnip had jumped off the bench and sashayed, very hard, into my ankle.

The shadow let out a hoot. "But I'm enjoying the show! It's even better than street puppets."

It was a girl's voice.

She was laughing at me. She thought I was ridiculous. And she was right. I snapped out two more words in mage-speak, a spell I knew well. *Candles. Ignite.*

Above us, the heavy iron ring suddenly blazed with light, as all twelve candles burst into flame. I could see my heckler clearly now.

She was around my age, twelve, but taller than me. Her olive skin was bronzed by the sun, making it a shade darker than mine. A patched and faded nightdress barely reached below her knees. She'd recovered from her laughter and now lounged idly against the door, arms crossed.

"Who are you?" I demanded, drawing myself stiffly upright. "What are you doing here?"

Her black curls bobbed as she gave a snort of disbelief. "I'm Moppe Cler."

"Mop?" I asked dubiously. "Like the thing you clean floors with?"

"No, Mopp-eh," she repeated, so that I could hear the very faint second syllable, like a forgotten breath. "And I'm here because this is where I live."

I blinked. She was wearing a nightdress, after all, which seemed an unlikely choice for a rebel or thief. "Where?"

She jabbed a finger toward a curtained alcove tucked into one corner of the kitchen. "Right there."

"Oh!" I said, finally understanding. "You're the new scullery maid!" I'd heard Cook telling Master Betrys she'd hired a girl to help in the kitchens last week.

She lifted her chin. "I'm an under-cook. Not a scullery maid."

An odd longing pinged in my chest. She looked so . . . confident. Like she was exactly where she wanted to be, like she knew exactly who she was. She looked the way magic made me feel. When it worked.

"Well, I'm Master Betrys's apprentice," I told her, taking a seat on the edge of the hearth, "and I have work to do. So you can just—"

"That candle trick was brilliant!" Moppe plunked herself down beside me. "Can you set other things on fire?"

Maybe the girl wasn't such a bother. I loved talking about magic, sharing the wonder and glory of it, but I rarely had the chance aside from my lessons with Master Betrys. I tucked my brown braids back over my shoulders. "Yes. I mean, not stones or water or anything like that. The spell only works on things that actually burn."

She frowned, cocking her head at the turnip as it continued its pitiful performance. "So why are you wasting so much time making a turnip wobble?"

My warm feelings chilled abruptly. "It's dancing," I said sharply. "Not *wobbling*. And it's harder than you think!"

I smacked my turnip, sending it sailing into the fireplace. It wobbled on through the embers as the scent of roast turnip filled the air. Heaving a sigh, I headed over to the storage crate to collect a new victim.

Even with my back turned, I could feel the girl's eyes on me. A flutter of nerves filled my belly. The whole point of practicing in the kitchen in the middle of the night was to *not* have an audience. But I couldn't let Moppe rattle me. I had to focus. Returning, I propped my new turnip on the table and intoned the spell once more.

"Turnip. Animate. Dance."

The turnip twitched. It began to roll back and forth, like a turtle tipped on its back. Only a very charitable person would have called it dancing. I snatched the thing up, ready to toss it into the fire to join its brethren.

Moppe arched her brows. "Are you sure you're saying the right words?"

"If you think it's so easy, maybe you should try it." I snorted. Barely one in a thousand people were born with the ability to understand magespeak, let alone cast magic. Surely no untrained scullery maid could—

"Turnip. Animate. Dance," said Moppe.

The purple root in my hand twitched, wriggling like a captive beetle. Startled, I let it fall. It jigged gracefully off across the worn kitchen floor.

"Ooh! It worked!" Moppe clapped her hands together, looking delighted.

My insides crumpled in shock. I'd been struggling for hours. Days. And now some kitchen girl marches in and casts it perfectly, her very first time? Was this a joke? A trick of some sort?

With a loud thump, one of the storage crates suddenly tipped over, loosing a tide of purple roots. Dozens of turnips scattered across the kitchen floor, some the size of my thumb, others nearly as large as my head.

And all of them were dancing.

All. Of. Them.

Moppe gave a stifled shriek. The turnips were getting wilder, bounding and spinning and leaping dangerously high. I yelped as one large root smacked into my chest. More hard blows battered my arms as I flung them over my face.

Desperately, I scrambled up onto the table. Moppe tried to follow, only to trip over a shimmying turnip and crash to the floor.

"Stop!" she shrieked. "Stop it! I take it back!"

"You need to use magespeak," I shouted. "The word for deanimate is—*oomph!*"

Oomph was not, in fact, the magespeak word for deanimate. It was the noise I made when a leaping turnip smacked into my mouth.

But Moppe was already shouting, "Oomph! Oomph! Can't you hear me, you nasty things? OOOOMMMPH!"

I yanked the rooty legs of the turnip that was trying to gag me. It squirmed, resisting my hold. Thumps and bumps struck the air, followed by a tinkling crunch that sounded distressingly like fine china being smashed to bits. I gave up tugging and bit down instead. The turnip gave a satisfying crunch, going limp. I spat it out.

One down. Only about one hundred more to go.

Below me, Moppe shrieked, huddling as a wave of prancing turnips bounced onto her, pelting her spine.

"Turnips. Deanimate!" I cried in magespeak, but it did nothing. I flung myself down along the edge of the sturdy table, reaching for one of Moppe's flailing hands. "Here! Get up on the table!"

Her fingers tightened on mine as I tugged her free of the turnips. She collapsed beside me a moment later, breathless and glassy-eyed. "Watch out!" I called, as a particularly large turnip bounded onto the table, rooty feet tapping an ominous tarantella as it advanced toward us. I seized the horrid thing with both hands and was about to toss it into the hearth when a voice thundered a single phrase in magespeak.

"Turnips. Deanimate!"

There was a sound like brief, hard rain as every single turnip fell to the floor.

Slowly, painfully, I dropped the now-limp turnip and surveyed the damage.

An entire cabinet of the best china had somehow ended up on the floor, smashed to creamy, flower-spattered shards. The butter crock was upended, and trails of gold were smeared across the countertops, leading to the inert bodies of several well-oiled turnips.

More turnips lay in pools of dark vinegar near the pantry. Others were strewn across the floor, across the pantry shelves, poking out of pies and loaves of bread. Three of the purple roots had even managed to lodge themselves in the twisted iron ring of the lamp above.

At the far end of the kitchen stood Master Betrys. She'd just arrived home from the dinner party and still wore her long velvet dress cloak, embroidered with stars and moons. It rippled around her as she paced forward. Her brown face was intent as she scanned the room, missing nothing.

Master Betrys was the most impressive person I knew. Even more impressive than my mother, and that was saying a lot. So impressive that I did not have even the *tiniest* urge to laugh when I noticed the small turnip dangling from her left ear.

Moppe, on the other hand, let out a high-pitched giggle.

Betrys lifted one hand, gloved in midnight-blue leather, to flick the offending vegetable away. Then she looked at me. "Antonia. *Explain.*"

It wasn't actually an enchantment, but it felt very much like a truth spell. I swallowed, preparing my defense, as I scrambled down from the table, followed by Moppe.

"I was, er, practicing. For my lesson tomorrow. I came to the kitchen because I didn't want to disturb anyone."

Master Betrys arched one eyebrow. She glanced meaning-fully around the kitchen, then to the door behind her, where I could see Cook, Dorta the maid, and Mr. Thesp the butler all blinking and muzzy-eyed in their nightclothes, very much disturbed.

I swallowed a sigh. "I'm sorry, Master Betrys. This is my fault."

"You did this? *All* of this?" She didn't sound angry, but then, she never did. It was part of what made her so intimi-dating.

I hesitated, glancing at Moppe. As infuriating as she was, I couldn't let her get sacked.

"Yes," I began, but Moppe cut me off.

"It was me," she said. "I said the words. Just like she did. I didn't think it would make them *all* start moving. Especially since she could barely manage the one."

"I was *practicing*!" I said through gritted teeth.

"Your name is Moppe Cler, yes?" asked Betrys, ignoring my outburst entirely.

"Yes," said Moppe, standing stiffly to attention. "Ma'am."

"Master," corrected Betrys. "You'll call me Master Betrys, if you're to study with me."

"Study with you?" I squawked. "But she's the scullery maid!"

"Under-cook!" protested Moppe.

"No," said Master Betrys. "She's my newest apprentice."

2

NEWEST APPRENTICE, I reassured myself the next morning as I stood outside Master Betrys's study. Not *new*, as in replacing the other one. I was still Master Betrys's apprentice. I wasn't giving up that easily. There was a question I had to ask of her, and I was running out of time. Before I could lose my courage, I rapped my knuckles against the door.

"Enter."

The door swung inward, admitting me into a comfortable room dominated by a massive mahogany desk. Shelves and cabinets lined the walls, with doors of glass to display the trinkets and tomes inside, gathered by Master Betrys on her many travels across the lands. She had led such an exciting life! Maybe someday I would do the same. Or we might travel together, searching out long-lost magical artifacts and discovering ancient grimoires. I would have loved to step closer and examine her treasures, but I could feel Master Betrys watching me from across the desk. I drew a bracing breath, then started forward.

"Stay to your right," she said crisply. "Don't step on the roses."

I froze, eyeing the pink floral design woven along the left edge of the lush carpet. It looked innocent enough. "What's wrong with them?"

"I've placed a few spells around the study, as a precaution," Betrys replied, as I picked my way gingerly to the right side of her desk. "I've had some . . . unwelcome guests of late."

"You mean thieves?" I asked.

"Of a sort. I caught that nuisance snooping around my study a few days ago."

She gestured to the nearest shelf, where a large golden cage sat between a bulbous lump of shiny red rock and an ancient-looking lyre with only one remaining string. In the cage perched a creature that looked very much like a ferret, except that it was pure white with silver markings. As if it sensed my interest, the creature raised its head, watching me with luminous blue eyes. Something about their intensity made me quiver deep inside, as if unseen whiskers were snuffling along my spine. "A ferret?"

"A furtive," said Betrys. "Or the Furtive. He seems to have an excessively grand opinion of himself."

"And why not?" came a squeaky voice from the cage. "I am the bearer of untold mysteries. The keeper of a thousand secrets, including yours, Julien Betrys."

I blinked in amazement. "It talks!"

"It does far more than talk," said Betrys. "The creature feeds on secrets. Someone sent him here in search of one of mine."

The Furtive blinked. Glittering whiskers shivered as he pressed his stubby nose between the golden bars. "Mmmm. And what would you give to know *who* sent me?"

"Nothing," said Betrys grimly. "I have a fair guess."

The creature gave a disappointed whiffle. "Then perhaps the girl will feed me?" The Furtive coiled his long pale body, round ears perking up.

"Take care," warned Betrys. "If the creature touches you, it will sniff out your secrets. Pull them from your thoughts."

I took a step back as the tickle of phantom whiskers returned. "Er, no. No, thank you."

Master Betrys's lips compressed to a thin line. She rose and strode over to the shelf, swept up a heavy velvet cloth, and draped it over the cage. The Furtive gave a shrill protest, then fell blessedly silent.

"That's better," said Betrys, returning to her desk.

"Is it enchanted?" I asked. My mind was already spinning, imagining the complexity of the spell required to create such a creature.

"Perhaps. There are many such beings in the world,

creatures that were once animal—or even human—who fell prey to a malicious or foolish wizard and ended up permanently altered. Flying horses, poet-hogs, mermaids, and the like. Once such creatures breed, it becomes nearly impossible to reverse the original enchantment. I've freed this one from his master's compulsion spell, but he could still cause considerable havoc, given his . . . gifts."

She sighed, pinching the bridge of her nose. "It's a good reminder that magic can have unforeseen consequences. But I hardly need lecture you on that count. Your rigor and attention to detail have always been admirable."

My cheeks warmed. I treasured Master Betrys's compliments. They were rare, but true. Like a handful of perfectly cut sapphires to tuck into the rattling treasure box of my heart. Which was why it was so important that she understand what magic meant to me. That it wasn't simply something I was studying. It was in my soul, just like it was in hers.

"It's not just rigor," I said. "I love magic. More than anything."

"Yes," said Master Betrys, with a wry quirk of her lips. "I had gotten that impression, given you've already read every single volume of Pendyce's *History of Magic*. Even the deadly dull one that's all plumbing charms."

"None of it is dull to me," I said. "There's that *zing* that snaps through you when you say the last word in a spell and it lifts up all crackling and ready. It makes me feel like—"

I caught myself. I'd already said too much. Master Betrys

probably thought I was a loon. Heat flushed my cheeks, and I stared at the tips of my shoes, pressing into the soft pile of the carpet.

"Like you're part of something greater?" She spoke softly. "Yes. I understand."

I jerked my chin up, meeting her gaze. There was no judgment, no scorn. My breath whooshed out, a gust of relief tinged with bittersweet yearning. No one had looked at me like that in years. Not since my brother, Florian, died.

Mother had certainly never understood. To her, everything was a row of numbers in one of her ledger books. Magic was only of value if it could add to the final tally.

Her warning echoed in my ears. *Six months, Antonia.* I only had two weeks left. I needed some sort of proof that I was making progress. Something that would impress even Mother.

Something like a letter of recommendation to the Schola Magica, back on the mainland of Regia Terra. At the Schola there were entire *libraries* of books about magic. Enormous codices full of words in the language of the ancients, the tongue said to have been used by the gods themselves to shape our world. There was so much I could learn! Sometimes the fierce need of it would twist me awake in the middle of the night, pinning me with hope and longing.

I'd been too scared to ask Master Betrys about it before now. Afraid she would say no. But there was no more time. I had to try. Before the newest apprentice made her rethink my position here. "Master Betrys, there's something I've been meaning to ask. I was hoping you might consider—"

A rap sounded at the door.

"Hold that thought," Betrys said, gesturing to the door. It swung open to admit Dorta. The maid took a tentative step into the room, bobbing a brisk curtsy. "If you please, Master Betrys, there's a visitor come to see Miss Antonia."

An icy knife of foreboding sliced up my spine. "Wh-who is it?"

"It's Councillor Durant, miss," said Dorta. "She's waiting for you in the parlor."

All my rising hopes began to plummet like wingless birds. I didn't have two weeks. I didn't even have two hours!

Mother was here *right now*.

I hesitated outside the door to the parlor, steeling my nerves. Maybe this was merely a social visit. Perhaps Mother was just passing through the neighborhood and decided to stop to say hello to her only daughter. There wasn't anything strange about that.

Except that Mother hadn't come to visit me *one single time* in the past five and a half months. If she wanted to see me— which wasn't often—she summoned me home. She must be here about my apprenticeship. I pushed the door open, then marched in to face my doom.

And a beautiful doom she was, as tall and glossy as one of the festival mares parading through the streets at the first landing celebration. Her dark hair hung in braided loops, caught up by a circlet of gold wrought in a pattern of roses and thorns. An unsubtle reference to the imperial flag of Regia Terra.

She sat in one of the plush armchairs, holding a cup of tea. As I curtsied, her green eyes narrowed, ready to catch the smallest stumble.

"Mother," I said, my voice a tight croak. "How lovely to see you."

She gestured to the hard-backed chair beside her, even though the room was furnished with several other armchairs. "Sit."

I perched on the edge of the wooden chair. Now that I was closer, I caught a faint whiff of roses. Anyone else would think it was her perfume, but I recognized the scent of her favorite pressed powder, the one she only used when she hadn't been sleeping and needed to cover the dark smudges under her eyes. For a brief moment a memory caught me. It must have been years ago. Mother was laughing, dabbing my nose with a sweet-smelling powder puff, telling me how not all armor was made of steel.

"Are you feeling well, Mother?" I began tentatively.

There was only the briefest of hesitations before she lifted her chin. "Of course, darling. But I'm not here to talk about myself. I'm here to discuss you."

She set her teacup on the table between us, beside a towering tray of cakes. She hadn't touched them. And with her watching, I didn't dare take one for myself. Not even the round of golden pastry oozing my favorite almond cream.

"You recall what I told you, Antonia, when you embarked upon this venture," she said, pouring a second cup of tea. She doled out a tiny glug of cream, then handed it to me. "I believe I made my expectations quite clear."

"Yes, Mother." I took the cup, forced to accept her words along with the tea.

"It's been six months."

An ember of rebellion flared. "Five and a half months."

Mother arched a perfect brow. "And what have you learned in five and a half months that's of use to the Durant family?"

If only I'd had time to prepare for this interview! Surely one of the spells I'd learned would impress even Mother. But giving her enchanted hiccups would probably just annoy her. And I doubted she'd follow me to the bathroom for a demonstration of plumbing charms. First Word preserve me, every single useful thought seemed to have dribbled out of my ears.

"I—I worked out a new variation of the Pinthou Principle to generate movement in vapor." It had been my proudest moment in recent memory. Master Betrys even said she might include it in the treatise she was working on, with credit. My own name, in the Schola journal!

Mother tilted her head. "And what exactly does that mean?"

I coughed. "Er. It means I can make shapes in smoke and steam."

She did not look remotely impressed. If I didn't change her mind, right now, my magical education was over.

"Wait," I said, "I'll show you!" I sputtered out the spell.

The steam rising from our cups began to writhe and twist, spinning up into the shape of a fluttering butterfly. This was the sort of spell I was best at. Fiddly and technical and not particularly powerful. I watched Mother, hoping she noticed how I'd even managed to get the patterns on the wings.

For a moment, I thought I had reached her. Something went soft around her eyes. My brother, Florian, had loved butterflies. One year he even filled a glass jar with buckthorn and raised a small brown caterpillar, waiting and watching as it spun itself a cocoon. He woke us early one morning, to see it emerge with glimmering green wings and fly away free into the dawn. Mother had laughed and kissed him on the forehead, and called him her butterfly boy even though he was a young man of fifteen. It suited him. He was always moving, always fluttering from person to person, vivid as a scrap of daydream, sipping any sweetness life could offer.

I was no butterfly. I could never replace him. I just wanted to make Mother smile again, the way he had. To show her how beautiful magic could be.

But as she watched my steam-spun creation, Mother looked more sad than happy. She swallowed sharply. "It's lovely, darling," she said. "But lovely isn't the same as useful." She slashed one hand through the steam, tearing the ghostly wings to tatters. "Enough foolishness."

If only I knew the spell to make myself into the daughter she wanted me to be. But the one spell that could really make Mother happy was the one that was impossible. There was no magic that could change the past, or restore the dead to life.

I fought to regain control of my spinning thoughts. If Mother had already decided to end my magical education, she wouldn't have bothered to come here. Between her work on the council and running the Durant Trading Company, she didn't have time to waste on failure. She'd have simply summoned me home.

Which meant there was still a chance she'd allow me to stay. But she wanted something in return. And I was tired of playing games. "If you think magic is foolishness, why did you send me here? You never do anything without good reason. Just tell me what you want, Mother. Please."

She regarded me over the brim of her teacup. "Tell me about Master Betrys. What do you think of her?"

It wasn't the response I was expecting. Nevertheless, I answered truthfully.

"She's brilliant. Her work on enchantments is revolutionary. She's the first person to propose a reasonable alternate to the Quelch Principle. And she's an amazing teacher."

"Gracious," said Mother. "It sounds as if she means a great deal to you."

For one brief moment, a traitorous thought flitted through my mind. How different my life would be if Master Betrys were my mother. I could fling myself into my studies without shame, without feeling like I was a negative number on the balance sheet, in desperate need of correction. I could talk about the things I loved without boring her. I would never have to parse her smiles to calculate how much of them was real.

Mother must have noticed my hesitation. A faint frown wrinkled her brow. A stab of guilt pierced me.

"I'm just grateful to be studying with her. She's the best wizard on the entire island of Medasia."

"Indeed." Mother's eyes glinted as if she'd just found a loophole in a trade treaty. "I understand that she is a direct descendent of Lyrica Drakesbane herself. A potent magical lineage."

That was strange. Mother usually didn't pay much attention to magical history. Then again, Lyrica Drakesbane had been more than just a brilliant wizard. She'd been the closest friend and confidant of Queen Meda, founder of the island province we called home.

"It places your Master Betrys in a pivotal position," she continued. "Especially given the current political situation. Tell me, Antonia, do you think that Master Betrys favors the Liberation movement?"

"Master Betrys is no rebel!" It was a ridiculous notion. Everyone knew the Liberationists were vile criminals. Heartless and cruel.

Mother gave an impatient twitch of her fingers. "I didn't say that. I asked if she favored the declaration of a free

Medasian state. She must have some opinion on the matter."

"Master Betrys hates politics. She says it's a messy, inconvenient, dangerous distraction."

Mother's brows arched. "Does she?"

My stomach twisted. I should have kept my mouth shut. I didn't want to get Master Betrys in trouble.

"I believe she will soon find it impossible to remain neutral," my mother said. "A most distressing rumor has come to the attention of the council. It seems the rebels are seeking to reclaim the lost Medasian crown. The one that grants its bearer control of the Black Drake."

I thought of the painting that hung in Master Betrys's library, showing Queen Meda taming the giant sea serpent. His glossy ebon coils churning the sea to pale froth. A massive head, rippling with a mane of sharp spines, split to show a snarling maw of jagged teeth. All that power had once belonged to Meda and her heirs.

"But the crown was destroyed," I protested.

It had happened a hundred years ago, after the death of King Goros, the last of the Medasian bloodline. When Goros died, the Black Drake had gone wild, ravaging the coast, destroying everything in its path. All Medasia might have fallen to ruin had it not been for Terwyn Drakesbane—Master Betrys's great-grandfather—who managed to use the crown long enough to banish the Black Drake to the bottom of the sea, then destroyed the artifact so no one else could ever wield it. After that, Medasia had become a province of the empire, and all had been peaceful. Until now. Until the so-called Liberation began calling for rebellion and the restoration of an independent Medasia, free from imperial control.

"Perhaps not," said Mother. "We have reason to believe that Terwyn Drakesbane only *claimed* to have destroyed the crown. That in truth, he kept it. Hid it. And passed the secret on to his own heirs."

My lips parted, but it took me a moment to find the words. "Master Betrys? You think Master Betrys has the crown? That she's going to give it to the Liberation?"

"Not necessarily," said Mother. "But they may seek to take it from her."

The cool blue gaze of the Furtive stared back at me from my memory. It had been sent to find one of Master Betrys's secrets. Was that secret the location of the crown?

"It would be a powerful tool," continued Mother. "With the crown, the rebels could summon the Black Drake. Could send it against the Imperial Navy. We must all do everything in our power to stop that. You understand that, don't you? You've seen what the rebels are capable of."

My throat squeezed tight. I blinked hard, knowing how Mother hated tears. I had never seen her weep, ever. Not even when the soldiers came to tell us that my brother was dead, killed by Liberationists who had attacked his ship and claimed it for their rebellion.

It was all so *senseless*. Life on the island of Medasia was pleasant, comfortable, and secure. As a province of Regia

Terra, we had the protection of the Imperial Navy, and a market for our fish and oil and our famous Medasian purple dye. What would independence gain us? And was it really worth killing my brother and those other sailors?

"So why don't you just ask Master Betrys about it?" I asked.

"I have. She denies all knowledge of the crown's location. Thus I am forced to consider alternate means of gathering information."

"What do you—oh." The truth hit me hard as a cannon, stealing my breath for a long moment. "You want me to *spy* on her."

I felt cold, as if someone had suddenly shoved me out into a frigid winter night. Of course.

"I want you to be a loyal subject of the emperor. And a dutiful daughter, who understands that everything comes with a price. Including your position here as an apprentice."

"That's why I'm here," I said dully. "That's why you agreed to let me apprentice with Master Betrys. You don't care about me becoming a wizard."

I'd actually let myself believe she—not cared, not anything that soft and sentimental—but at least *respected* my dreams. That she was giving me a chance to prove myself.

But the truth was, I was just another playing piece in her games. I gulped down the tightness in my throat. "I'm not spying on Master Betrys. I won't betray her like that."

For a brief moment, I almost thought Mother looked . . .

hurt. Then her gaze narrowed. "This is the way of the world, Antonia. Everything has a price. If you want to continue your magical studies, you know what you have to do."

"So that's it? If I don't find the crown, I can't study magic?"

"There are greater things at stake than your studies, Antonia." She set her empty cup down with a decisive clink. "You might also consider that if the crown isn't recovered soon—or worse, falls into the wrong hands—your dear Master Betrys might find herself accused of treason. Surely you want to protect her from such a fate."

A cold fist gripped my insides. "Please, Mother, I'm begging you—"

"Don't beg, darling. Focus on the task at hand. Find me the location of the crown. I'll expect a report on your progress next week, at Lord Buccanyl's gala."

She stood then and made for the door. At the threshold she paused to glance back. "Don't disappoint me."

3

I PEERED FROM THE WINDOW of Master Betrys's carriage as we rattled along the highway north of Port Meda. The scrubby cliff tops were bare, save for a few stunted salt pines, their dark branches twisted like old men hunching down against the wind, and a few tumbled stone foundations. A tiny hamlet had once stood here, but the spotted fever had wiped it out two centuries ago. There were no houses now, no people. Only a few wild goats who watched our carriage pass with slitted gold eyes.

We'd already been driving for an hour, and Master Betrys still hadn't revealed the purpose of our journey. On the seat across from me, Moppe fidgeted, staring out her own window, the basic grimoire Master Betrys had given her to review lying limp in her lap. She'd barely made it through the first chapter.

I watched her covertly for a few moments, until she caught me staring and snatched up the book again. I had a brief glimpse of her cheeks flushing crimson before she hid her face behind the covers.

I should have been reviewing my own grimoire—a fascinating treatise on culinary spells—but all I could think of was Mother's ultimatum. I had no doubt she would whisk me away from my apprenticeship and refuse to let me study magic ever again. But would she really go so far as to have Master Betrys arrested?

I had to find another solution. A way to answer Mother's demand without betraying my teacher or getting her thrown into prison. I cleared my throat, scooting sideways, so I was directly across from Betrys. She glanced up from her own magical notations. "Yes? Do you have a question, Antonia?"

"Er . . ." I hesitated. Telling the truth—even just a part of it—was a risk. Mother would be furious if she knew. She'd say I was compromising my position, wasting the element of surprise.

Betrys closed her notebook, giving me her full attention. Her gaze slipped to the book in my hands, and a slight smile touched her lips. "Have you gotten to the part about the enchanted cream puffs? Isn't it brilliant? And he doesn't even consider the possibility of—"

"Layering charms in different types of custard?" I suggested.

"Exactly!" She gave me a nod of approval that filled me

to the core with warmth, until I remembered what I'd really meant to ask.

I gripped my resolution firmly. I was no good at Mother's political games. I had to do this my way. Master Betrys had always treated me with respect. She deserved no less in return.

"I was just wondering . . . you know how my mother visited me this morning?"

"Indeed. I gather it was more than just a social call?"

"Yes. She's worried about the Liberation."

Betrys arched one brow. "Is she?"

"I guess there are, er, rumors that they might be trying to find the lost crown of Medasia. You know, the one that summons the Black Drake?"

A flicker of something passed over her face, too quickly for me to identify. She adjusted the cuffs of her blue velvet coat. "Mmm. Even though it's commonly understood that the crown was destroyed?"

"Mother said the Liberationists don't believe it. They're looking for it. And they—they think you have it. Because you're Terwyn Drakesbane's great-granddaughter."

"They're going to be disappointed then," said Betrys wryly.

"Please, Master Betrys. They're probably the ones who sent that Furtive to snoop around your study, and who knows what they might try next? The Liberationists aren't a joke. They're murderers and rebels."

A faint noise came from the other end of the seat, but

when I glanced toward Moppe, she had retreated behind her book.

Betrys's brown gaze held me with a heavy weight of deliberation. "I'm certain that if the crown were out there, it would be well guarded. And that it would be found only by someone who had earned it. Someone who understood its power and would use it wisely."

What did she mean by that? "Do you—"

The carriage jerked to a stop, stealing the question from my lips.

"Ah, here we are," said Betrys. "Now, I suggest you focus on the task at hand. Both of you," she added, sweeping her intent stare to include Moppe. "There's much you need to learn to walk this path. And I can't give you all the answers."

She was out the door before I could ask anything more. But maybe I didn't need to. A jog of hope lifted my heart. The crown would be found only by someone who earned it. Master Betrys must have told me that for a reason. Was it only to reassure me that the crown was safe? Or was it a challenge?

"What is this place?" Moppe asked as Master Betrys led us to a narrow trail that ran along the top of the cliffs. Behind us, the horses stamped and shivered. I could hear Mr. Thesp trying to soothe them.

The waves surged and fell below. The air held a wild tang that matched my own dizzy spirits, spinning high as the circling gulls. I knew what I had to do now. Finding the crown would solve all my problems. I'd prove to Betrys I was her magical heir *and* I'd satisfy Mother. I could go back to my magic and never have to think about politics again.

Assuming I could do it, of course. I couldn't even make a turnip dance. How was I supposed to find a long-lost magical artifact? I beat back the doubt squeezing my chest. Anything could be solved with hard work and research. And Betrys had said herself I was here to learn. So I'd best pay attention.

"The Cave of Echoes," Master Betrys was explaining, as she marched vigorously onward, completely ignoring the enormous void only a few feet to our left. "Legend says that this is where the god Rhema came to die—or to sleep, depending on what particular branch of religion you follow."

No one believed in the sleeping gods, except for superstitious shepherds up in the hills, who would come into town every once in a while, claiming to have met one of the gods in their dreams. More likely it was too much spice wine, my mother said. Still, a part of me wished it were true. Imagine what all-knowing beings could teach us!

"But what's in the cave?" I asked, alert for anything that might relate to the crown. "Why are we here?"

"You'll see soon enough. Stay close, girls. It gets a bit steep here," Master Betrys warned, before plunging down along a set of narrow steps carved into the cliff face.

I waited for Moppe to go first—and to gather my own courage for the perilous descent. But she halted beside me.

"Are you really trying to find that crown?"

So she had been listening, back in the carriage. "Maybe," I admitted. "Why?"

"What are you going to do with it if you find it?"

I drew my shoulders back. "Keep it safe, of course. Stop the Liberation from using it to destroy the Imperial Navy." My stomach pinched as I spoke. If only someone had stopped them before this. Before they killed my brother.

"You don't know that's what they would do. Maybe they just want to keep the people of Medasia safe. To stop the Imperials from stealing our dye and tossing anyone who doesn't like it on a prison barge."

"What are you talking about? No one's stealing our dye."

"The Dyers' Guild keeps glomming up more and more harvest territory," said Moppe. "How are regular fisherfolk supposed to make a living?"

Heat flushed my cheeks. The purple dye extracted from the spiny-shell snails was Medasia's most valuable export. Mother said it was the council's job to make certain the supply was stable, for the good of everyone. I wished Moppe would stop staring at me like that, with daggers in her gaze.

"I don't know about any of that," I admitted. "But it's my duty to keep the crown safe."

Moppe crossed her arms. "*Your* duty? Why you?"

I floundered for a moment. In truth, Mother had thrust this upon me. I hadn't chosen it. But that didn't mean I wasn't brutally aware of the danger of the crown falling into the wrong hands. Not to mention Mother's veiled threat against Master Betrys. "Because I care about the future of Medasia."

Moppe lifted her chin. "And you think you're the only one?"

Then she marched past me, trotting down the precarious trail after Master Betrys. I hastened to follow, but Moppe must be half mountain goat. Curse it! What had she meant by that? Was she going to try to find the crown too?

The dizzy spin of the gulls seemed to have caught hold of my belly. Everything was whirling. But I couldn't afford to panic. Mother always said worry only wasted energy. I stood for a moment, counting each breath that swooshed in and out too fast. I could do this. I simply had to forge ahead and do my best.

By the time I caught up, Moppe had rejoined Master Betrys, and the two of them were staring at the path ahead.

Or rather, at the broken, tumbled stone and gaping void where the path should have continued. It was gone now. Fallen away, leaving only the sheer cliff.

"What do we do now?" Moppe asked. "Fly across?"

"That is an excellent question," said Master Betrys. She leaned back against the cliff face. "What do you think, Antonia?"

A jolt of excitement rippled through me, driving back my worries about the crown, at least temporarily. A magical challenge was exactly what I needed. I recognized Master Betrys's casual, cool tone. The thoughtful tilt of her brown chin. She wanted me—well, us, I suppose—to find a solution.

"There aren't any true flying spells," I told Moppe. "There's magespeak to rise and lower—so you can float— but if there was a word for *fly*, no one knows it anymore. So much was lost in the Shattering." The great earthquakes had devastated this part of the world ages ago, bringing about a dark time that ended only with the birth of the Regian Empire.

I took a step closer to the edge. The sight of the crashing water and sharp-edged boulders below made my belly flip and spin, but I needed to see what we were working with. The rockslide hadn't taken the entire trail, which zigzagged down the cliff in a series of switchbacks. I could see the next bit below, marked by a single brave salt pine.

"Is there a word for fix?" asked Moppe.

"Yes, but it only works if you have the pieces of the thing you're trying to repair. All the stone's already crumbled away." I gestured to the crashing waters below. As I did so, my eye caught the salt pine again.

"I've got it!" I cried, the spell already forming in my mind. It was elaborate, tricky, and used a variation on Filroy's Technique that I'd been dying to test out. I went over the long incantation twice, feeling the shivery sense of rightness that sang out from a well-balanced spell. Then I spoke the words, clearly and carefully.

I squinted over the edge. Below, the salt pine shivered, branches nudging out a few inches. I ignored the feeling of Moppe and Master Betrys's eyes on my back and recited the spell again. Another shiver, nothing more.

"What's it supposed to be doing?" asked Moppe.

I stifled a groan. "Growing. And then transfiguring into a sort of staircase. Using Filroy's Technique," I added, hoping Master Betrys would see that at least my theory was sound, even if my execution was . . . less than impressive.

"An excellent idea, Antonia," said Master Betrys. "I can always count on you for innovative solutions. Moppe, why don't you assist?"

I ground my teeth. That wasn't fair! I was the one who'd come up with the spell. And there was no "assisting" in magic. Joint spellwork was theoretically possible but rarely attempted. Fine, then, let Moppe try. Though she didn't look particularly eager about the prospect.

She hesitated, hands clasped around her midsection. Was she . . . nervous?

"Do you remember how it goes?" I asked, taking the opportunity to repeat the long string of magespeak a third time. I glanced down hopefully at the salt pine, but it only shivered again.

"I heard," Moppe answered, dropping her arms to her sides. But still she made no move to approach the edge. She swallowed. "It sounded more like a novel than a spell. Why do you need so many words just to make a tree grow?"

"Because we need to tell the magic what to do," I said. "That's how magic works. The first two words tell the tree to grow, but you need the rest of it to add the transfiguration."

"What if I say it wrong? Will it go all"—she made a chaotic gesture—"berserk, like the turnips?"

"Magical power is a responsibility," said Betrys. "I'm glad you recognize that, Moppe. But you can rest assured I won't let anything get out of hand."

"I could write it down for you," I offered. "If you can't remember."

Her jaw tightened, and she gave a sort of shrug, as if casting off a cloak. "I'm fine. It sounds easy enough." She sauntered forward to the edge of the trail, spread her arms dramatically, then called out the spell.

Or at least, the first two words.

"Tree. Grow."

Then she hesitated, stumbling over the tricky conditional phrase for the transfiguration. "Blast, what was the next bit?"

I was about to tell her, when a branch bristling with needles exploded up directly in front of me, followed by a scaly brown trunk. I stumbled back, falling smack on my backside, staring up at the enormous salt pine that suddenly towered over us, shoving out spiky green branches in every direction.

Moppe gave a cry of pure delight. "It worked!"

I smothered a stab of longing. "It didn't work," I said. "You only did half the spell!"

Moppe lifted her chin. "At least now we have something to climb down."

"Only if we transfigure ourselves into squirrels." I scrambled to my feet and marched back to the edge of the cliff, ducking under several inconveniently placed branches. I took a deep breath, then repeated the rest of my spell.

The salt pine quivered, the branches shifting so that they formed a helpful spiral down the trunk. Several smaller twigs even twisted up into helpful handholds. "See?" I said triumphantly.

"Excellent work, both of you," said Master Betrys. "Joint casting like that is rare. It requires a particular harmony between the casters, something not just anyone can attain."

I gave Moppe a skeptical sidelong glance. More likely it was luck. I barely knew the girl, after all. And if I was a pianoforte, she was a blaring trumpet. We would never be in tune, let alone harmony.

"But come along," Betrys went on. "It's not far now."

She led the way down the steplike branches, heading for the lower trail. Moppe and I both moved to follow, meeting at the cliff's edge. "I could have climbed down," Moppe said archly. "But I guess it's not bad to have steps."

I uncrossed my arms. "Steps wouldn't help if the tree was twenty feet too short," I admitted. "You've really never done magic before?"

She bit her lip, shaking her head. "I didn't expect it to be like this. My grandmother always said it was dangerous. But that"—she gestured to the tree—"was like . . . like when you swim way out to sea and the waves scoop you up. Is it like that for you?"

I hesitated, uncertain how much I wanted to admit to this strange new girl, especially after what she'd said about the crown. But I loved magic too much to stay silent. "I—I feel like I'm singing with a grand chorus."

She grinned. "I've never heard any grand chorus. But I guess it's kind of the same."

For a moment we just stood there. More words crowded my tongue. Stories of magic, all the things I loved about it, the wonders and the splendors. It had been so long since I'd had someone to share that with. I realized I was smiling. Smiling at her. Heat flushed my cheeks, and I set off hastily down the steps.

Friendship is a luxury with a very high price, Mother always said. If Moppe planned to try to find the crown too, then she was my competition, not my friend. That's what Mother would tell me, certainly. But when it came to talking about magic, I just couldn't seem to help myself.

Moppe followed after me. "So you can do *anything*, if you know the right words?"

"In theory," I said. "The words tell the magic what to do. If you don't have the right words, the spell won't work. Or it does the wrong thing."

"There must be . . . a lot of them. A lot of words."

"There are five thousand, six hundred eighty-seven known words in magespeak as of the last accounting, not including proper names. Wait, no!" I gave a little hop as I descended the final branch. "Five thousand, six hundred eighty-eight. I forgot about *hiccup*. They just discovered that one a few years ago."

"That many?" Moppe's brown eyes grew wide. "How do you learn them all?"

"You need to have a good memory," I said. "And you need to study. But if there's a word you don't know, you can usually find it in a book."

"A book?" asked Moppe, with an odd flatness to her voice.

"Master Betrys has dozens of grimoires," I continued, warming to the topic. "And the Schola Magica has even more!

The Grand Library's collection contains over a thousand volumes!"

Moppe's expression turned glassy; doubtless she was as overwhelmed by the possibilities as I was. "It's amazing, isn't it?" I said. "Imagine what it would be like to read them all." A happy vision rose in my mind of myself curled in a reading chair at the end of a long aisle of shelves, surrounded by piles of magical tomes. I *would* get there. I'd make that dream come true.

"Indeed," said Betrys as we caught up to her. "But too many grimoires have been destroyed by time, by hateful hands, by the Shattering. Too many words were never recorded, or simply forgotten. That's why we're here." She descended the last slope of the trail onto a wide ledge, where a dark slash split the stone of the cliff.

It looked no different from countless other caves and crevices I'd seen along the shoreline, and yet my heart skipped faster as I moved to join Betrys before the opening. A chill washed over me. My skin shivered, though I couldn't be sure if it was anticipation or foreboding. "What do you mean?"

"You'll see, soon enough."

Betrys spoke a short incantation. A luminous golden orb blossomed in the empty air above us. It floated after her as she stepped into the cavern. "Come along, girls," she prompted. "You'll be safe enough if you stay in the light."

4

MOPPE HESITATED, staring into the cave after Master Betrys's retreating form. "Safe from *what*? Do you think there's something alive in there?"

"Whatever it is, we have to face it," I said, marching forward. Master Betrys had brought us here for a reason, and I didn't intend to disappoint her. Moppe scurried after me a moment later.

We both hastened to catch up with the circle of golden light. Not that I was scared, of course. I simply didn't want to miss anything Master Betrys might say.

But Betrys remained silent as she led us through the downward-sloping tunnel. With every step, the passage seemed to narrow, until I could have reached out my hands and touched both sides at once. Not that I'd want to touch these walls: slimy and tinged green, tufted here and there with pale, bulbous mushrooms that looked disturbingly like watchful eyes.

I let out a long breath when the narrow tunnel finally opened, spilling out into a vast cavern. The glow of the conjured light gleamed across what looked like a forest of glittering conical trees.

But these were trees of stone, grown by dripping water and time: stalagmites. And above, a mirror-forest of stalactites hanging down from the high cavern ceiling. A thousand colors shimmered: rose, nutmeg, gold, charcoal, even a deep purple as vivid as the dye that had made Medasia famous.

We continued on, our footsteps echoing eerily, as if someone were following us. I couldn't help looking back once or twice, just to be sure, but I saw nothing.

The stone forest closed in around us. There were no markings I could see, no trail to follow, but Master Betrys marched on with heartening purpose. She must have known where she was going. Which was good, because I had already lost all sense of direction in this dim, glittering maze.

"Where are we going?" Moppe asked.

Going. Going. Going. Her words whispered back from the darkness, making my skin prickle even though I knew it was only another echo.

"To the chasm," Master Betrys replied.

Chasm. Chasm. Chasm.

"They say you can hear the echoes of the god Rhema's voice there. The legends say that when it came time for her to die—or sleep—she came here, knowing there would be those who needed her wisdom in the future. So as she faded, she spoke the answers to the questions yet unasked, leaving her divine words to echo here, waiting."

Waiting. Waiting. Waiting.

"Waiting for what?" Moppe asked.

"The right person," said Betrys. "It's believed that if you come to the cavern and speak, you might hear the voice of Rhema herself answering your question."

Question. Question. Question.

A buzz of excitement fizzed through me, wild and sudden and reckless. The answer to *any* question. It was dazzling. Like stepping into a brilliant patch of sunshine, flinging my arms wide, staring up into the sky until my eyes burned with the brightness of it all.

Moppe looked dubious. "Then why are we the only ones here? Shouldn't this place be jammed full of people asking what horse to buy or what the weather will be like next Tuesday?"

"The Cave of Echoes is no place for idle curiosity," said Betrys. "No one has ever received more than a single answer in their lifetime. Most people don't receive any answer at all."

My excitement lurched. Only one question. But which one? I had so many! Were the gods truly dead? What was the magespeak for *fly*? Which enchantment could win me entry to the Schola Magica? I couldn't afford to waste this opportunity on the wrong question.

If I asked how to claim the crown, I might win Mother's blessing, but would it be enough to convince Master Betrys I deserved to go to the Schola? Surely I had demonstrated my knowledge of spells, but did that matter if I couldn't actually make them work?

We continued, following Betrys through the dank, echoing cavern until she halted, one arm slashing out to warn us back. I nearly stumbled into her, lost in the labyrinth of possibilities my single question offered.

A deep chasm loomed ahead. I could see no bottom. Even the glow of the conjured light seemed to grow weak and feeble, as if the chasm was not simply empty air, but something dense and weighty. A hungry darkness that consumed all light.

Betrys turned, staring intently at Moppe and me. "Be wary, girls. This is a place of great danger."

Danger. Danger. Danger.

Moppe shuffled uneasily. "What sort of danger? I mean, if we just stay away from the edge, we're safe, aren't we?"

"It's not only the chasm," said Betrys. "Thousands of people have come here over the ages and asked thousands of questions. Only a few are answered. The rest echo on, growing more powerful and dangerous the longer they remain unanswered."

"How can a question be dangerous?" I asked.

"This cavern is full of hopes and fears and frivolities, all desperate for release. Without answers, the questions have become desperate. Hungry."

Hungry. Hungry. Hungry.

A shiver rippled up my spine. I scanned the darkness beyond our ring of light. It might have been only a trick of my imagination, but I could have sworn I saw something move, deep in the shadows. Then a hiss. I took a step back, closer to the center of the light.

"And you brought us here for a *lesson*?" Moppe squawked.

Betrys's lips quirked. "I brought you here because I need a distraction. Our presence has already begun to draw the unanswered. I need you to calm them, keep them occupied."

The shadows hissed again. A plaintive whisper shivered through the air.

Where will I meet my true love?

I marshaled my courage. Master Betrys believed I could do this, and I wasn't going to let her down. "How?" I asked, running through possible spells in my mind. "Some sort of calming enchantment?"

"No. No spells at all," Betrys said. "You simply need to give them what they want. An answer."

The shadows whispered again, harsher now, flashing a glitter of teeth. *Where will I meet my true love?*

"But we don't know the answer," said Moppe, edging closer to me, jostling for a spot at the center of the light.

"It doesn't need to be the right answer," said Betrys. "It only needs to be convincing."

The shadow seethed along the edge of our light, like a prisoner testing the bars of their cell. A single tendril curled out, crossing into the golden glow, reaching toward me with hungry menace. *Where will I meet my true love?*

"Er, at the fish market," I sputtered as the ribbon of darkness slithered closer.

Instantly the tendril retreated, the whispers quieted. The shadows hid their teeth.

"The fish market?" Moppe snorted. "Oh, *that's* romantic."

I flushed. "It's where my grandmother met my grandfather." She'd been a proper Regian lady from the mainland, and he'd been a dye merchant's son.

"Be vigilant," said Master Betrys, "and you shouldn't have any trouble settling the echoes. Just be sure to deal with them promptly." Her gaze narrowed, searching us both. "And as tempting as it might be, stay well away from the chasm."

"But how will we ask *our* questions, then?" I glanced toward the darkness, where the answer to my dreams awaited. Assuming I could figure out the right question, that is.

"You won't be asking any questions," Betrys said shortly. "You're too young. Better to wait until you're older and have something worth asking."

That wasn't fair! My question could change my life! But I forced my expression into artless acceptance. I couldn't let Betrys suspect my plan. Moppe's grumble made me think she shared my frustration.

Master Betrys gave her a sharp look, but Moppe only asked innocently, "What question are you asking, Master Betrys?"

A strange look flickered across Betrys's face, something like pain or guilt.

"I need to be prepared to face someone. A person I knew once. A person who is . . . dangerous." She spun on her heel, striding off along the left edge of the chasm, summoning a second light spell as she went. "I'll be back soon."

I tracked the bobbing glow as it grew smaller and smaller, then finally winked out, vanishing behind the distant stalagmites.

More whispers were already brewing in the shadows nearby.

Where did Uncle Ajax bury his treasure?

"Ahh . . . Under the old olive tree," said Moppe. The shadows subsided. Moppe grinned. "This isn't so bad."

I hesitated, peering into the darkness. Things seemed quiet, for now. And I couldn't waste any time. I needed to ask my question, and I certainly wasn't doing it in front of Moppe. That meant I needed an excuse to get away.

I spun to face Moppe. "Can you handle the echoes on your own for a little while?"

She crossed her arms. "Why? Where will you be?"

"Er. I need to go. I'm going to head back that way." I waved generally to my left, in the opposite direction from where Master Betrys had gone. "I'll be back soon."

Soon. Soon. Soon.

She stared at me. Was she really going to make me say it?

"I need to *go*," I repeated, emphasizing the word. "You know? In private?"

She crossed her arms, looking skeptical. "You mean you need to piss?"

Piss. Piss. Piss.

I cringed as the coarse word echoed around me. Why was I blushing? It didn't matter what Moppe thought of me. "Yes, yes," I said. "I need to . . . use the powder room."

"No, you don't." Her eyes narrowed. "You want to ask a question."

"That's none of your business," I said, drawing myself as tall as I could manage. "Just . . . stay here."

I stalked away, darting between stalagmites. I'd gone five steps before I realized the flaw in my plan. Or, more precisely, before I slammed my nose into the stalagmite that loomed out at me from the pitch blackness.

I had no light.

A whisper tickled my ear. I jerked my head around, but there was only darkness.

I tried to remember Master Betrys's spell, but it had been tricky, full of conditional clauses to make the light move. Blast it, I should have brought a candle!

Something plucked at my hair. *How will I die?* Gasping, I wrenched away. My feet itched to turn and flee back to the safety of the glow behind me. But I couldn't give up. I needed to be brave.

How will I die? All around me, the shadows had begun to boil, lashing whips of darkness out like the tentacles of some ravenous sea creature.

"F-falling into a chasm," I stammered quickly.

Silence fell. I let out a long, ragged breath and took another few steps, carefully scuffing at the ground, feeling for the edge of the chasm. This was ridiculous. I needed light!

It was easy enough to make something do what came naturally to it. Make a candle burn, or make water evaporate. But you couldn't just command water to burn. So while I knew the magespeak for *ignite*, it was useless without an appropriate combustible target.

But I knew another word that might work.

"Antonia. Glow."

Radiance spilled out around me, like the lights that danced around the actors in the play Florian had once taken me to see. I spun a celebratory pirouette, giddy with success. I might not be able to make a turnip dance or a tree grow, but I wasn't useless!

And not a moment too late, for there was the forbidding darkness of the chasm, yawning open barely five feet away. I marched over, casting my own personal spotlight to light the way.

A cold breeze flowed from below, setting goose bumps along my skin. I cleared my throat. Master Betrys was wrong. I wasn't too young. My dreams were just as important as anyone else's. And if I didn't ask the right question, they were going to be crushed forever.

The silence pressed down ominously. My tongue felt like lead, heavy with the weight of my opportunity. I still hadn't decided on a question. If I asked about the crown, it might allow me to win my mother's approval, and the chance to stay on with Master Betrys—for a little while, at least. But it didn't change the fact that I simply wasn't as powerful a wizard as Moppe. On the other hand, if I asked how I could become a more potent wizard, I might win a place at the Schola but Mother might refuse to send me as punishment for failing to find the crown.

And even if I did ask a question, I might not get any answer. What if my query echoed on, like all those others, turning into something vicious and hopeless and hungry?

I just had to choose, and pray that Rhema answered.

"Hello," I said.

Hello. Hello. Hello.

I coughed again, feeling utterly foolish. "Er, I'm Antonia Durant. I suppose you know that, since you're the god of wisdom. Anyways, I'm here because I, um, have a question."

This was shameful. I was the daughter of Councillor Myra Durant, who had once convinced the queen of Zolomen to lower the tax on chocolate by 25 percent. But now that I was here, teetering at the brink of knowledge, my throat seized with the importance of my next words.

I forced my shoulders back, took a deep breath, and spoke from my heart.

"How can I become a Master Wizard? How do I make my dreams come true?"

I leaned forward, holding my breath, as the echoes of my question died away. The chill air had already turned my toes and fingers to ice. My chest ached from holding my breath, but I was terrified I might miss the answer. There *must* be an answer.

Unless I'd asked the wrong question. Ugh, why had I added that bit about my dreams coming true? That didn't mean anything. I should have been more specific! I should have asked about the crown! That was more important than my own magical destiny. And now I was being punished for my selfishness.

Then I heard it. A whisper. An echo, barely audible.

A single word.

The word was nothing I recognized, but it buzzed through my bones like one of the earthquakes that rocked Port Meda every year or so, cracking windows and setting the temple bells ringing.

Magespeak.

"Wait," I cried. "How do I use it? What does it mean?"

Mean. Mean. Mean.

The echoes died away, leaving me with nothing more. I had my answer, for all the good it did me. I had no idea what the word meant, or how to use it.

I bit my lip. It was dangerous to use magespeak you didn't understand. But it wasn't impossible. The power was in the words themselves, not your understanding of them.

I had to at least try.

"*Antonia,*" I whispered. And then I repeated the unknown word.

Nothing. Only a faint fizzle, like a match failing to catch.

Fine. I could make this work. Clearly, I just needed a more complicated incantation. I stalked back to the glow of the floating orb, my mind spinning with possibilities, spells I could use to try to unlock the secret of the mysterious word. I would figure it out. I still had a week.

As I emerged from between two stalagmites I halted, struck by the sight of Moppe standing at the edge of the chasm, teetering over the deadly darkness, one ear cocked as if listening for something.

"What are you doing?" I cried. "Careful!"

She gave a yelp, jerking back from the edge. "*You* be careful," she snapped. "I was perfectly fine until you tried to scare me out of my skin."

I frowned, eyeing her closely. "Were you asking a question?"

She crossed her arms. "Were you?"

"No," I said.

"Then I wasn't either," she said, giving me an odd, overly bright smile. Then she squinted. "Why do you look like you swallowed a candle?"

Oops. I'd forgotten my light spell. In truth, I wasn't entirely sure how to undo it, but Moppe didn't need to know that part. I lifted my chin. "It's a spell, obviously. I can turn it off whenever I—"

A flicker at the corner of my eye distracted me. I yelped as a lash of darkness reached out, curling round my wrist.

What will cure Mother's cough?

"Chamomile tea!" I sputtered, jerking free of the question as it recoiled into the shadows. But a dozen more flitted and fluttered, preparing to attack. Their desperate voices hammered at my ears.

What color should I wear to make him love me?

Who is stealing my turnips?

How do I stop missing her?

I spun toward Moppe. "What happened? I thought you said you could handle them!"

"I was!" She dodged a lash of darkness. "Your neighbor's goats are eating your turnips!"

"You can't stop missing people!" I shouted at another.

"Purple," cried Moppe.

We carried on, fighting the hungry tide of questions. My brain began to jitter, seizing at any possible reply. Finally, the tumult began to quiet. I even had time to drag in a long, deep breath.

One last query echoed out.

How many chickens should I buy?

"Thirteen!" I gasped.

Then silence. I flopped against one of the chilly stalagmites, not caring anymore if it was slimy. I was exhausted, but at the same time, triumphant. We'd done it.

Moppe snorted. "And Master Betrys says *we're* going to

waste questions. At least I know better than to ask a goddess about chickens."

I giggled. "Or stolen turnips. At least you had a good answer for that one."

"Goats eat anything," she said, smiling.

Suddenly I felt awkward and strange. Moppe was still my rival. But a part of me wished she wasn't. We'd made a good team, in spite of everything. Maybe—

A crunch of footsteps interrupted my thoughts as Master Betrys returned. She looked distracted, her brow furrowed, hat askew.

"Master Betrys?" I asked. "Are you all right?"

She stared into the shadows, her expression bleak. She must not have found her answer. Guilt twinged through me. I might not understand my answer—yet—but at least I'd gotten one.

"Maybe you can find what you're looking for in one of your grimoires," I offered. "I could help you research."

I did truly want to help her, to lift the forbidding weight haunting her brown eyes. Even in the worst of times, on the gloomiest of days, Master Betrys had always carried a vibrant spark with her, like the gleam of the first star pricking out against the night. But that spark was muted now. I might be only her apprentice, but surely there was something I could do to help.

"Hmm?" She glanced toward me, blinking, as if she'd forgotten I was there. "Oh. No, Rhema answered me. I only hope I won't need to— Antonia, are you *glowing*?"

Her distraction melted away as she studied me, lips pursed.

"Er. Yes?"

Master Betrys tilted her head. Her voice was clipped and dangerously calm. "And why, exactly, are you glowing?"

"She had to go piss," Moppe said.

Had I heard that properly? Had Moppe actually covered for me? I shot her a quick glance. She only yawned.

"Oh. Well, I'm glad you had the sense to conjure light. Even if that is a rather . . . unorthodox version of the spell. Did you cast it on yourself?"

"I think so. I, er, I'm not sure how to undo it, though."

"Hmm." Betrys tapped one long finger against her chin. "I suppose you'll have to do some research, then."

"What?" I sputtered. "Can't you just *tell* me?"

"If you insist on casting experimental spells, you'll have to learn to be responsible for undoing them, Antonia." The corner of her mouth quirked up in amusement. "Don't feel bad. When I was your age, I gave myself cat ears. I didn't figure out the counterspell for over a year. It drove my poor dog wild, and even now I sometimes have a strange craving for mice." She winked.

I stared at her. Surely she was joking about the mice. *Surely.*

"But I'm confident you'll find a solution more quickly than that," Betrys went on. "You're a skilled researcher."

A bubble of warmth lifted me. Master Betrys had gotten

into magical jams as a girl too. It was something we shared. Maybe one day my glow would be a funny story I told my own apprentice.

"But now we really should get back home to Port Meda," said Betrys, sweeping a stern look over Moppe and me. "We all have work to do."

5

FIVE DAYS LATER I was no closer to any of the answers I sought. I had tried to use the word from the chasm in a hundred spells, but none of them had worked. I had scoured the house for any clue to the location of the crown and found nothing.

The gala was tomorrow night. If I couldn't convince Mother I was making progress, she would summon me home. My magical education would be over, and the crown would still be in danger. I'd have gained nothing and lost everything. This was my last chance to find answers.

Which was how I found myself breaking into Master Betrys's study in the middle of the night.

Surely if there was any useful clue about the crown's

location, it would be in the study. That was where the Furtive had been hunting, after all. And it was where Master Betrys kept her papers, her private journals, and her magical supplies.

I'd snuck into the study a half-dozen times before in order to look up words in the grimoires Master Betrys said were too advanced for me. This time should have been no different. And yet my voice trembled as I cast the *unlock* spell. I had to say it three times before the great oak door swung open.

Gloomy shadows filled every corner. Fortunately, I still hadn't managed to reverse the light spell I'd cast in the Cave of Echoes, distracted as I was by everything else. It had made sneaking out of my room something of a trial, but at least I didn't have to worry about lighting a candle. The familiar golden glow enveloped me as I took a single careful step onto the well-worn carpet.

Betrys's room looked different than it had during my daytime visit. The bookshelves loomed ominously. A bit of twisted wood perched on the corner of her desk cast an odd shadow across the wall, like some great horned beast, watching me, making me feel small and very, very alone.

Unease twinged in my chest. But Betrys herself had said that she couldn't *give* me all the answers. Once I found the crown, she would understand. She'd see that my cleverness and dedication had earned it. And of course Betrys must see how important it was that the crown be taken somewhere safe, where the Liberationists could never get their murderous hands on it.

I glanced uneasily toward the shelf holding the golden cage. It was still covered by the velvet cloth, and no sound came from within. Hopefully the Furtive was sleeping. I crept another two paces into the room, careful to keep to the right side of the carpet as Master Betrys had warned me during my last visit.

As before, the massive desk was covered in scrolls, books, and bits of loose paper. I scanned them quickly, the scrape of unfurling paper loud in the silence. But none of it seemed remotely connected to the crown. I was about to turn away to continue my search when a bit of writing among the papers caught my eye.

My own name.

I jerked back, averting my eyes. I shouldn't read it. They were Master Betrys's private papers.

But it was *my name*. Didn't I deserve to know what it was about? Before I knew it, I was tugging the page free from the heap of other documents. It looked like the draft of a letter. There was no addressee, only a few lines of painfully sharp script.

It is a difficult decision. Antonia has proven brilliantly adept at theory, and her dedication and memory are exceptional, but even with the very best training, she will never rise above a middling level of potency. Whereas Moppe is an *untrained prodigy with seemingly limitless potential. I've truly never seen someone so naturally gifted at our art. It rather staggers me, to consider what she might be capable of with dedicated training and attention. But you know my time is limited, and I must make a decision as to*

It ended there, midsentence. But I didn't need to read any more.

Couldn't read more through the hazy blur of my stinging eyes. I scrubbed a sleeve across my face. I supposed it was a just punishment for sneaking in here, for reading Master Betrys's private papers. I gulped down to clear the tightness in my throat. The letter said she needed to make a decision. But she hadn't made it yet. There was still hope.

"Find anything interesting?" asked a voice from behind my shoulder.

I shrieked and jumped away.

I had a single brief glimpse of Moppe's grinning face, and then I was sinking into the soft pool that had opened under my feet as soon as I crossed to the left side of the carpet. I wriggled and writhed, but was sunk up to my neck. I couldn't free my arms. The sticky molten carpet held me stiff as tar.

Blast! I *knew* there was a spell there. Master Betrys herself had warned me. And then I'd panicked and jumped right into it!

Moppe inched a few steps closer, cocking her head to look at me. "Did you mean to do that?"

"What sort of person gets stuck in carpet quicksand on purpose?" I spat back. Then I forced myself to breathe. I could get out of this. I was a wizard, after all. *"Antonia. Rise."*

I shifted a single grudging handspan.

The words of Master Betrys's letter taunted me. *She will never rise above a middling level of potency.* I tried again, but this time I lifted only an inch. Frustration roared in my chest as I imagined what Betrys would think if she saw me here now. I blinked rapidly, painfully aware of Moppe watching me, arms crossed in judgment.

"Does Master Betrys know you're snooping around her study in the middle of the night?"

I gritted my teeth. "No! Of course not." I looked her up and down. She was still wearing her normal smock and sandals, and there was a smudge of what looked like flour on her cheek. "What about *you*? Shouldn't you be asleep?"

She lifted her chin. "Cook needed help setting the loaves for tomorrow."

"But you're not the under-cook anymore," I said. "You're an apprentice now."

"That doesn't mean I can give up on my duties. Do you think breakfast just magically appears on the table every morning? That Cook is secretly a wizard who just whips food out of thin air for you?"

"That isn't what I meant," I said. "Never mind, just . . .

go wash the flour off your face and leave me alone."

Moppe scowled, but she didn't leave. "Why *did* you sneak in here?" she asked. "Are you looking for the crown?"

"No!"

From the velvet-covered cage on the nearby bookshelf came a chittering laugh. Moppe whirled toward the sound. "What was that?"

"The Furtive," I told her. "He's a dangerous magical creature Master Betrys has locked away."

"Dangerous?" came the high-pitched voice of the enchanted ferret. "Ooh, I rather like that."

"What does he do?" Moppe asked, pacing closer to the cage. She pulled the cloth free, revealing the sinuous velvety shape within. "He doesn't look dangerous."

The Furtive's pale fur fluffed out in annoyance. "I am the Keeper of Untold Mysteries! I am the Seneschal of Secrets! Tremble before me!"

"Oh yes, so terrifying," said Moppe, leaning closer, looking more amused than alarmed.

He set his paws against the bars of the cage, whiskers quivering. "And you have such a nice, juicy one. I can almost *taste* it."

"Be careful," I said. "He only has to touch you to steal your secrets." It seemed only sporting to warn her, even though she could hardly have any secrets all that interesting.

Moppe jerked back the finger she had started to lift toward the cage. She stared at her hand for a long moment, as if checking for burns, eyes wide with alarm. Then she tucked it behind her and refocused her attention on the Furtive. "Secrets, hmm? Like why Antonia's rooting around in here?"

"That is no secret," said the Furtive. "You already know the answer. She seeks the location of the crown crafted by Lyrica Drakesbane for her beloved queen, Meda."

Moppe turned back to me. "Did you find it?" She looked to the desk, then to the floor. Master Betrys's letter lay pale against the carpet, where I had dropped it when she startled me.

"No!" I cried as she bent to take it. "That has nothing to do with the crown!"

She huffed scornfully. "Of course you'd say that."

"I'm telling the truth," I protested, making one last vain attempt to claw my way out of the sticky pool of carpet. "It's a private letter. Don't read it!"

Moppe was already bent over the paper, squinting furiously at the script. Chill despair gripped me. It was bad enough knowing what Betrys thought of my abilities. I couldn't bear Moppe learning the truth. I didn't want her laughter and I certainly didn't need her pity. I braced myself for her reaction.

But it never came. She looked up at me after a moment, still defiant. Demanding. And a tiny bit . . . nervous?

"My name is in this," she said hoarsely. "Did she find out?"

Find out what? That Moppe was a prodigy? Was she trying to make me say it aloud? I hadn't expected her to be that cruel. "You can read it yourself," I snarled, sagging back into my prison of oozing carpet.

"No," the Furtive squeaked coyly. "She can't."

"What?" I frowned at Moppe. "You can't read?"

Moppe jerked, as if stung. "I can!" Her fingers tightened on the paper. And for the briefest moment I saw something all too familiar in her eyes. *Shame.*

"I *can*," she said again. "Just . . . not very long words. Or the ones that aren't spelled like they sound."

Which described just about every word in magespeak. I felt a pang of sympathy. Florian always had trouble reading. He once told me the letters jumped around the page, like fleas, and he could never keep them all straight. Mother had to hire a special tutor from the mainland to get him through his basic schooling.

"Does Master Betrys know?" I asked.

Another flash of shame. Maybe even fear. "Don't tell her!"

"How do you expect to become a Master Wizard if you don't have any way to learn magespeak?" I said. "Maybe Master Betrys can help you."

An odd, hopeful expression flitted over Moppe's face, but it was gone in a heartbeat. Her voice held a bitter edge. "I can't risk it. This is too important. *Please.*"

"What's too important? Finding the crown? Why do you want it?"

Moppe held her chin high. "The same reason as you. Because I care about the future of Medasia."

"Mmm," hummed the Furtive, whiskers quivering as he slunk closer to the cage door. "Secrets. Lovely, lovely secrets."

"Look, do you want to get out of there or not?" Moppe asked.

I sighed. "Fine. I won't tell her. Just get me out of this. It's a simple enough spell. *Antonia. Rise.*"

She repeated the spell. I zoomed up from the carpet and smacked into the ceiling. "Ouch! Watch it!"

"Sorry!"

She lowered me until I could reach the corner of the desk. I clambered down onto the blessedly solid floor.

Moppe held up the letter. "You swear this really doesn't have anything to do with the crown?"

I snatched it out of her hands and placed it back on the desk. "It's just a letter about us being her apprentices," I said. "That's it."

I glanced at the Furtive. Hopefully I'd spoken close enough to the truth not to tantalize the creature.

"The crown." He made a long chuckling noise. "Now *that* is a secret."

"It's why you came here in the first place, isn't it?" I asked, stepping closer to the cage. "The Liberation sent you to find the crown."

"Did you find it?" Moppe asked urgently. "Where is it?"

The Furtive's hunched body bowed as he stroked a paw over one stubby ear. "Why should I tell you what I know?"

I hesitated, then drew in a long breath. "What if I give you one of my secrets?"

The Furtive gave a hum of pleasure and anticipation. His bright teeth glinted in the shadows.

Moppe gave me a dubious look. "Are you sure?"

"I'm sure this is our best chance to find the crown," I said.

Besides, it wasn't as if I had anything so terrible hidden away. What did it matter if the Furtive found out I'd pilfered a raspberry tart from the kitchen last week? My secrets were all boringly mundane.

Moppe's brows drew together. *"Our?"*

"Well, since you're here. And you got me out of the carpet."

She blinked, looking flummoxed. A flush warmed my cheeks. Honestly, the word had just slipped out. Still, it was . . . nice to have someone with me right now. To not have to deal with the Furtive alone. I turned back to the enchanted ferret. "So is it a deal?"

"Mmm. Come closer," said the Furtive.

I hesitated again. "What sort of secret do you want from me?"

"Oh, I'm certain I can find something interesting." His blue eyes transfixed me, sly and hungry. "Everyone has secrets. Hidden fears. Tasty regrets. Delicious dreams. Or even precious knowledge. You wizards know better than anyone how much power there is in just a single, secret word."

I gulped, feeling very much like a roast chicken set out

on the table for supper. Did I dare trust the creature not to simply snatch his meal and run? "You tell us what you know first."

The ferret gave a whiffling sigh. "Oh, very well. But you must ask me properly."

"Properly?"

He preened. "I *am* the Master of Mysteries, after all. The Hunter of the Hidden. The . . ." He paused, whiskers crinkling thoughtfully.

"Emperor of Enigmas?" I offered.

"Indeed!" He nodded in satisfaction, rearing onto his back legs, snowy hair puffed out with pride.

I cleared my throat. "All right, Master of Mysteries. I humbly ask that you, er, bestow upon us the secret you so valiantly acquired about the crown's location. Please."

"The crown may be found . . ." His squeaky voice dipped lower. I leaned closer, quivering with anticipation of the coming revelation. Moppe moved to join me, both of us close beside the cage.

". . . in a location completely unknown to Master Betrys."

"What?" Moppe sputtered.

"That's not helpful. She has to know *something*!" I gripped the bars of the cage in frustration.

"Oh, well, she does have a clue. And that is"—the Furtive sidled closer, whiskers shivering over my fingers as he pronounced the final words in a low, dramatic squeak—"a secret that will be given only to her most deserving apprentice."

He sat back on his haunches, showing his sharp teeth in what looked very much like a sly grin.

"That's not an answer!" I snarled. "Is that really all you know?"

"Of course not," said the Furtive. "I am the Master of—"

"Oh, stuff it!" snapped Moppe. "You're a blasted nuisance."

"And you're definitely not getting any of my secrets," I said, crossing my arms as I glowered at the cage. "Not for that."

"Oh," said the Furtive, twitching his whiskers so that faint glints of light seemed to spark from them, "I already learned the secret I needed from you. *Unlock.*"

With an ominous click, the door to the golden cage sprang open. First Word preserve me, I was a fool! I'd let the creature trick me close enough, and he'd stolen the magespeak right out of my mind.

The Furtive sprang out like a shimmering ribbon of silver, straight at Moppe. She shrieked, catching his velvety body in both hands. "But you," the creature hissed, writhing in her grip, "you have so many secrets. Give them to me. I promise, it will feel so much better to share them."

"No!" Moppe flung the Furtive, sending him tumbling to the floor several yards away.

He rolled with boneless ease, back on all four feet within a heartbeat. "Very well. Our deal is concluded," he chittered. "And it is time I continued my hunt."

Then he was away, bounding across the carpet toward the windows. A tiny voice repeated the *unlock* spell a second time. A window cracked open onto the dark night. By the time I reached it, the Furtive was gone.

"Why didn't you stop him?" I turned on Moppe. "You had him! You could have put him back in his cage!"

"He—he was going to find out"—her voice cracked—"my secrets!"

"Well, that's just wonderful." I groaned. "How are we going to explain this to Master Betrys?"

"Explain what, exactly?" said a voice from behind us.

Moppe gave a faint squeak. Both of us turned away from the window to find Master Betrys standing on the threshold of the study in her dressing gown. "Explain how the two of you ended up in my locked study? Or explain how you allowed a dangerous magical creature to escape?"

"I—I'm sorry, Master Betrys. I was just . . ." I dragged in a long breath, trying to find the words to convince her. It was worse than when I smashed one of Mother's favorite porcelains when I was five and tried to hide the pieces in a potted palm.

"Searching for Queen Meda's crown?" she suggested.

"Y-yes."

"And what did you learn?" Her voice was cool and level as always, and the glint in her brown eyes was considering. Surely Betrys would understand if I could just explain properly. She was fair. She listened to me.

"That you have a clue to finding the crown. And that you'll

give it to your most deserving apprentice." I straightened my shoulders. It was now or never. "That's—"

"Me!" said Moppe. "I know I haven't been an apprentice long, but look at everything I've done. The turnips. That tree down by the cave. Please, Master Betrys, I'm the only one who can keep the crown safe!"

A thorn of disappointment stabbed me, sharper even than my surprise. But it was foolish of me to think our alliance had been anything but temporary. No matter how nice it was to not feel so alone.

"Just because you can cast a few spells doesn't mean you deserve it," I said. "You can't even—"

I caught myself as Moppe's eyes went wide with alarm. No, I had promised not to tell, and I would keep my word. "I'm the one who knows over two hundred words in magespeak," I finished instead.

"Just because you're a walking grimoire doesn't mean *you* deserve the crown," snapped Moppe. "At least my spells actually work."

"Enough!" Betrys's single word silenced us both. "What you seek is a great and terrible power. To claim it would require more than simply knowledge and strength alone."

Moppe and I exchanged glances, each of us standing straighter.

"I have no time for apprentices who value pride and potency over humility and understanding," she said. "By rights I should expel you both."

"No!" I cried, at the same time as Moppe gave her own agonized protest.

Master Betrys held up one slim hand, cutting us off. "I am, however, prepared to give you one last chance to redeem yourselves."

Desperation pulsed under my skin. I bit the inside of my cheek, waiting for her to speak.

"Tomorrow night at the gala, there will be an exhibition," said Betrys. "Dancing, music, and other entertainments presented by the young folk in attendance. You will join them. If you can cast a spell that demonstrates you understand the true power of wizardry, I will continue your apprenticeship."

"And if not?" I asked, my voice shaking.

"Then you will be expelled."

6

"WELL, ANTONIA?" My mother watched me over the rim of her wineglass as we stood beneath the glittering chandeliers of Lord Buccanyl's banquet hall. He had spared no expense in the decorations for the gala. All around us, men and women in embroidered silks and velvet waistcoats paraded past frost-pale tables gleaming with silver and gold platters. But I had no attention to spare for these delectable sights. I felt as if a hive of bees had swarmed into my belly.

I took a breath, preparing myself. "I haven't found the crown yet. But that's going to change. Tonight." I plunged onward, ignoring her dubious look. "Master Betrys does have a clue to the crown's location. I just need to convince her to give it to me."

Mother tapped one ringed finger against her goblet as I explained the situation. Well, really it was more of an . . . optimistic summary. Master Betrys hadn't actually promised to give me the clue if I proved myself. But at least it would give me a chance, and I would have none at all if she expelled me. All that Mother needed to know was that that I was making progress.

"Very well," she said, when I finished. "And you are prepared for this . . . demonstration?"

"Yes." I had the perfect spell in mind, a variation of my smoke-shaping charm, but better. Grander. Something that would display my skill to an entire ballroom. Only a tiny needle of doubt pricked at me: How did such a public performance demonstrate the humility and understanding that Master Betrys wanted from us? Was I missing something?

"And what of this other girl, Moppe?"

I glanced across the room, finally finding Moppe in one of the palm-shaded alcoves. She looked like a cat in a dog kennel. Some part of me panged with sympathy, as I remembered how overwhelming my first grand gala had been. I wished I could march over and pull her off to Lord Buccanyl's library with me, to ogle his collection of petrified bones and the pair of boots said to have belonged to Queen Meda herself. But that was impossible. I had to remember why I was here.

"She's just . . . a girl," I said. "She was the under-cook, then it turned out she had magic too. But she's only been studying with Master Betrys for a week."

"So you should have no trouble besting her."

My enthusiasm for the smoke-shaping spell fizzled, shifting into something sharper and bleaker. Was that all that really mattered? I supposed Mother was right. It didn't matter how wondrous and tricky and delightful my spell was. It only mattered that I was better than Moppe. But I hated it. It made me feel as if the magic no longer belonged to me. It wasn't a secret to unlock, a mystery to unravel. It was just another tool in my mother's political arsenal.

Mother tilted her head, reaching out to gently cup my cheek. "I understand that this is difficult for you, Antonia. But we all must do difficult things. We must honor your brother's memory. The Liberation took him from us. Now it's our duty to prevent them from stealing away even more lives."

Even in death, it was Florian who held our family together. His loss was something Mother and I shared. Maybe the only thing. I leaned into her palm, to show her I understood, that I felt it too.

"I'll try my best, Mama. I swear," I said.

"Yes," she said. "I know, darling. But I need more than your best. That crown will determine the fate of our homeland. Your brother already gave everything for this cause. You must succeed, no matter the cost."

Then her gaze shifted over my head, focusing on someone else. She pulled her hand away, leaving only a ghost of warmth on my skin.

I turned to see a man approaching us, his flawless black

waistcoat and breeches drawing my eye like an inkblot on fresh paper. There was a purpose to his steps, and he had the air of someone who expected attention.

Mother straightened her shoulders, slipping a polished smile onto her lips as she bowed, extending her hand to the newcomer. "Lord Benedict, we're so honored you could join us tonight."

The man smiled, his teeth glinting. He was my mother's age, I guessed, judging by the fine lines crinkling the corners of his brilliant blue eyes. There were threads of silver at the temples of his sleek black hair, which he wore short, in the mainland style.

"Ah, Councillor Durant, I've been hoping to find you." He bent over her hand, kissing the air above it with a flourish, reminding me of the actors my brother, Florian, had befriended. He had loved parties; loved the color and the conversation and the card games.

"I trust you've enjoyed a warm welcome," my mother said. "I know that here on Medasia we can offer nothing to compare to the delights of the court, but you'll find we are not without some charms to entertain the imperial envoy."

Imperial envoy? That would explain his manners and clothing. And from the sound of it, he'd only recently arrived from the mainland.

"Indeed," said Benedict, his gaze roaming over my mother's rich green gown with a freedom I didn't care for. "It's a blessing to find those such as yourself, who manage to preserve the dignity and refinement of the mainland even here on this desolate rock."

Desolate rock? Was he really talking about Medasia? To be sure, it was nothing compared to the populous mainland, but it was hardly *desolate*. There were dense forests, acres of olive groves, herds of silver-spotted deer. My family had spent the summer on the slopes of Mount Pavos when I was younger, swimming in shimmering blue lakes and dining under arbors dripping with wisteria. Florian used to take me on hikes, telling me ridiculous stories about one of the nearby peaks, a funny bulbous thing he said was enchanted.

Mother must have seen my annoyance, because she spoke up quickly, saying, "You said you were hoping to find me? Are you in need of some assistance?"

"Yes. I'm concerned that Councillor Pharon is going to object to the new imperial shellfish quotas. I may need your help to convince him what's in the best interest of Medasia. And please, if you have any mercy, tell me where I can find a decent Regian red? Buccanyl keeps insisting I sample his cursed local specialties." The corners of his lips turned down, and he held up a goblet filled with a cloudy pale liquid. The scent was so powerful I could smell it even from where I stood: a delicious and enticing ambrosia of honey and licorice.

"That's Milk of the Earth," I told him. "The legends say that it's what the gods themselves drank." I'd never had a full glass myself. It was potent stuff, brought out for weddings, funerals, and holidays. Florian used to secretly let me sneak a single sip from his cup every Feast of the Tides, when we'd go down at dusk to the cliffs and watch the fisherfolk push their great woven idols out into the dark waters, a sacrifice to the old powers of the sea.

The envoy's blue eyes slid over me, faintly amused. "If the gods had only this to drink, it's no wonder they all died."

"Lord Benedict, may I introduce my daughter, Antonia," Mother said. Her tone was smooth and serene as ever, but the faint crease between her eyes warned me to behave.

"Ah yes." Interest sharpened his expression. "The apprentice wizard. You must have some considerable gifts, to be studying with Julien Betrys. Did you transfigure that gown yourself?" he asked, nodding to one of my sleeves.

I drew in a quick breath of dismay. "You can tell?" Was it so amateurish even a non-wizard could see that the pattern of leaping dolphins I'd added wasn't true embroidery?

He gave me a reassuring smile. "Only because I've studied Therenval's facsimile technique. That's what you used, isn't it? It's excellent work," he added. "I daresay even Master Therenval would approve, and he's sour as a lemon grove."

I must have looked like a beached blowfish, mouth open, eyes wide. Then the questions began bubbling out, too fast for me to stop them. "You're a wizard? You know Master Therenval? Did he ever explain his notation on the final directional clause? I still don't see why it's even necessary. It feels off-balance somehow, don't you think?"

Benedict smiled. "It's meant to ensure that the print is spaced properly. But I've had better luck including that phrase just after the conditionals."

I ran the words silently through my head, feeling them snap into place, seeing the spell take shape. My breath hushed out. He was right! Reworking the spell as Benedict suggested brought it into balance, pure and perfect as a symphony. "Thank you, Master Benedict!"

Something flickered behind his blue eyes, and he looked down, briefly. "I'm no Master, Miss Durant. Alas, my talents were not found . . . sufficient . . . to garner such a lofty title. But we all serve the emperor in our own way." He gave a sort of bow, gesturing to the imperial insignia on his chest.

"We are, of course, honored by your presence," said my mother, smiling one of her signature smiles—one I had tried to copy for years before realizing I simply didn't have the grace to look both delighted and disapproving at the same time. "But I am sorry you came all this way for nothing. I assure you that our Council has the Liberation well in hand."

"And yet Captain Porphyra remains free," said Benedict, with his own sharp-edged smile. "And the rumors of rebellion spread like witchfire."

Just then a shimmering gong sounded from the far end of the ballroom. I had been expecting it, but still it sent my heart racing like a panicked mare. Around the room, other young people began moving toward an area that had been cleared to serve as a sort of stage. It was time for the demonstration. My last chance to avoid expulsion and save my dreams. Mother's green eyes found me one last time, and her words echoed in my mind. *You must succeed, no matter the cost.*

I fidgeted, jittering from foot to foot as I waited for Lord Buccanyl's son to finish his performance. The lyre sang under his slim fingers, and the song itself was a beautiful old sailor's lament that reminded me of my grandfather. But it brought me no peace. When he finished, I was next to perform. To convince Master Betrys not to expel me.

I leaned into the cool marble of a large urn, running the spell over and over in my mind. It was the only thing that steadied me. I could not fail. Magic was my life, my breath, the constant heartbeat pulsing through every second of my day. Without it, who would I be?

A burst of applause shattered my small calm. The lyrist danced merrily back into the crowd. I swallowed, glancing toward Moppe as she paced back and forth in the alcove where we waited, lips moving soundlessly. Preparing to display her "seemingly limitless potential," no doubt. When she caught me watching, she lifted her chin, a glint of challenge in her eye.

Fine. I had to accept that the spark of camaraderie we'd shared facing the Furtive was long-since snuffed out. Middling potency or not, I'd show her I wasn't going down without a fight. I marched out onto the stage as Lord Buccanyl announced my name.

Master Betrys sat cool and composed in one of the chairs that had been brought out for the exhibition. As her gaze settled upon me, I caught a flash of something like disappointment. I hadn't even cast my spell, yet somehow I had already let her down. I hesitated, glancing back toward Moppe.

Had I misunderstood? Betrys had told us that knowledge and power were not enough. But what else was there?

My stomach buzzed. I forced myself to concentrate on the cup of steaming tea they'd set out at my request. I cleared my throat. This was it.

I spoke the spell.

Murmurs of expectant delight rose from the guests in the front row as the steam spiraled up, forming exactly the image I had described: a triple-masted frigate, just like the one Florian had meant to serve on. It bobbed on a silvery sea of steam. Every detail was perfect.

Except that it was only five inches tall.

The crowd began to grow restless, as my tiny frigate sailed in minute circles before me. I heard one man in the back ask loudly, "Is something going to happen?"

Then another: "Is that it? What is it? I can't see anything."

Every fiber of me urged the ship to expand, to fill the room with its magnificence. Surely my will, my desire, my hunger was strong enough!

"Isn't it adorable?" one woman murmured.

I stifled a groan, then muttered the words to dispel the charm. The scattered applause was more painful than silence.

I didn't dare even look at Master Betrys, for fear the itch in my eyes would become something worse. The misery of my failure clenched tight around my throat. Why did nothing ever go as it should? I'd tried *so* hard. All I wanted was to do magic, but now I might have lost that chance forever.

Moppe met me as I fled the stage. I forced my shoulders back, blinking hard. I wasn't going to let her see my misery.

"That ship was really—"

"What are you going to cast?" I cut her off, before she could pity or scorn me.

She flinched, then drew in a breath, as if bracing herself. "The grow spell."

I glanced around. "On what?"

"This," she said, brandishing a toothsome-looking cherry cake.

"How?" I asked. "Did someone tell you the magespeak for cake?"

She frowned. "I—I don't need that. I already know the grow spell. I used it on that tree, by the cave."

"Right. On a *tree*," I said. "That's a cake. And besides, cakes don't grow. They're not alive. You need to use *enlarge* if you just want to make something get bigger."

Her mouth fell open, brows lifting in alarm. Then she huffed. "You're just trying to throw me off."

I shrugged. "I guess you'll find out soon enough."

I was about to walk away when she caught my elbow. "Wait. What's the proper spell, then?"

"Why should I tell you?"

"Because I'm—" She hesitated, flushing. "You know how important this is for Medasia. The Furtive said Master Betrys would give her clue to her apprentice."

"And you're so sure it's *you*? You've been an apprentice for a *week*!" A poisonous serpent slithered into my belly. All I could think of were the words of that letter. *She will never rise above a middling level of potency.* My dream was dying, right in front of me.

"This is too important," Moppe said urgently. "I know you're jealous, but—"

"Fine. I'll do it." Mother was right. Moppe was my rival, and it was time I started treating her that way.

"You—you will?" Moppe stared at me.

"Enlarge is *enlarge*," I said, squashing down my second thoughts. The crown was too important. It wasn't just my magical future that was in danger. It was Master Betrys. It was all of Medasia. I couldn't let some half-trained girl who talked like a Liberationist get her hands on it.

Moppe repeated the magespeak slowly. "And cake?"

I told her a word. "Be careful not to cast the spell until you're out there," I added, gesturing to the stage. "Or you'll spoil the surprise."

Moppe blinked uncertainly. "Oh. Well. Thanks, then." She started off but paused to look back, lifting her chin with earnest determination. "You won't regret this, Antonia. I swear."

The crowd had hushed, except for one of my hecklers, who called out, "Let's see some real magic!"

Moppe cleared her throat. She raised the cake before her, like a chalice of benediction. "Get ready to see something amazing!"

Then she spoke the words I'd given her.

At first it wasn't obvious. Everyone except me was watching the cake. Then a little girl in the front row cried, "What's happening to her nose?"

Moppe gave a screech of alarm, dropping the cake as she slapped her hands to her face. Her nose had begun to swell. To *enlarge*.

"It's as big as a bread loaf," said another man. "Look at it!"

The crowd broke into a babble of voices, calling out larger and larger items, giggling and laughing at the spectacle.

"Watermelon!"

"Pig!"

"Armchair!"

But I couldn't laugh. The shame and terror on Moppe's face turned my insides to quicksand. By then she could no longer speak and had been reduced to small, furious mumbles and sputters, muffled by her mighty nose.

The little girl cried again. "It's going to squash us! Run!"

The guests began to flee as Moppe's nose smashed into a nearby dessert table, knocking several fine chocolate tarts onto the floor. Shouts of alarm echoed around the ballroom. I pressed myself back into the hedge of potted palms, horrified by what I had wrought.

Bracing herself against the bulk of her enormous nose, Moppe finally managed to free her lips and speak. Or rather, curse.

Her eyes rolled to the side, finding me. "You!" she snarled.

"I—I didn't mean for it to go this far," I stammered, wanting to look away but unable to tear my gaze from the nasal horror.

"Just tell me how to undo it!" Her cheeks were crimson. She dragged in a long, soggy gulp of air, now collapsed to the floor by the weight of her enormous nose. *"Please."*

"Nose. Shrink," I told her, my voice hoarse.

Moppe repeated it. Instantly, her nose began to contract. By the time it had returned to bread-loaf size she was able to stand again, supporting her nose with both hands as it shrank to the size of a grapefruit, a lemon, then finally back to normal.

She pressed one hand to her face for a long moment. Her entire body was trembling. So was mine. Everything had gone horribly wrong.

Master Betrys marched toward us, sending the few remaining onlookers scattering with the sharp sweep of her long robes. There was a stormy darkness in her eyes. "I thought I made myself clear last night." Both of us started to speak, but she cut us off with a raised hand. "No. It's obvious to me now who deserves to remain as my apprentice."

Moppe and I both fell utterly silent, waiting.

Betrys looked us both over, considering. I quivered, every nerve bent toward her next words, desperate to hear my own name.

Finally she spoke, cool and clipped and inexorable. "Neither of you."

7

WE'RE LEAVING," SAID BETRYS. "Now." Then she swept away, heading for the nearest doors.

"You—you're taking us back home?" I asked, a tiny ember of hope flaring.

"I am taking you back to my house," she answered, not looking back. "To pack your things. You can return to your own homes tomorrow morning."

Surely I hadn't heard that. This couldn't be happening.

But Moppe's expression told me I had not misheard. Master Betrys had expelled us both. A dull beat throbbed in my skull. I wanted to throw up. It didn't matter what I did now. I'd tried to follow Mother's orders, to save my magic, to save my dreams, and in the end I'd lost it all. And what would happen if the Liberation found the crown? They would use it against Regia Terra and start a war that would only cost more lives. Betrys might even be named a traitor. My entire world would be flung into chaos. More than just my magical studies were at stake.

"You're going to regret this," Moppe hissed, her voice low and venomous as we trotted after Betrys. "Just you wait."

I already regretted it. I felt small and loathsome, as if someone had cast a shrinking spell on my soul. And all that bitterness wanted to burst out of me.

"Oh?" I bit back. "What are you going to do? You can't even cast a spell without my help."

My eyes stung, and I scrubbed at them, hastening to keep up with Master Betrys's long strides. We exited onto a terrace overlooking a garden. Braziers burned along the crushed-shell walkways that ran between tall hedges out to the street. The lights swam in my blurry eyes.

I was so lost in my own misery, I didn't even notice the man who stepped out of the shrubbery until I nearly trod on his shiny, silver-buckled shoes.

He was an older man, with bronze skin, graying hair, and the smile of a grandfather about to chastise his favorite grand-child. He looked vaguely familiar, which probably meant I had met him once at one of Mother's parties.

"Master Betrys," he crooned, "I'm so glad I caught you before you left."

I glanced at Betrys, catching the pinched lines around her mouth.

"Councillor Pharon," said Betrys, dipping her head.

I frowned at the man. That was why he was familiar. He was on the Council of Seven, along with my mother and five others who administered the provincial government of Medasia. I'd heard my mother call him a rudderless ship, because his votes were so unpredictable, never holding to either loyalist or Liberationist sympathies.

"I'm sorry," Betrys went on, "but it has been a very trying evening. I really must be going." She started forward again, but Pharon blocked her path.

Tall hedges walled us in, but a small alcove opened to one side, containing a sundial surrounded by banks of roses. Pharon must have been lurking there, waiting for us.

"Please, Julien," said Pharon, his voice lowering, now husky and intense. "You know what's at stake. You can't hide in your study and expect this to all go away. We need to find a peaceful solution, before it's too late. If you know where the crown is, you must tell us."

Betrys merely crossed her arms and stared back at Pharon. "I've already told the council I don't have access to the crown. No one does. And I see little chance of that changing anytime soon," she added, with a sharp look toward Moppe and me. I cringed.

"Please let me be on my way, Councillor," said Betrys. "I have nothing more to say to you or any of the others."

"We can't wait, Julien," Pharon protested. "Someone is spreading rumors that you're in league with the Liberation. And the new imperial envoy wants to—"

Pharon's words cut off in a gasp, as the hedge beside us suddenly shuddered. With a snap and crackle of breaking branches, a figure pushed through the leaves.

He stood nearly seven feet tall and appeared to be wearing old-fashioned armor, like the soldiers in the frescoes of Meda's first landing. There was something strange about his skin. It was unnaturally pale, like marble. No, it truly *was* marble. The creature was a moving statue! Bumpy ridges—barnacles?—crusted his shoulders and arms. Strips of dark green hung from his head. I wrinkled my nose, catching a strong fishy stench.

The pale, stony face cast about. "Is it part of the gala exhibition?" I asked uncertainly, as its blank, unseeing eyes skimmed over us.

With a grinding of stone, the warrior lifted massive marble arms and began to advance toward us, lips wide in a soundless bellow.

"I don't think so, girls," said Betrys, already whipping a scarf from her waist and snapping it out at the statue. The length of gold silk coiled around the thing's legs, binding them together. It held, just barely, sending the creature tumbling to the ground.

Then Betrys was shoving Moppe and me into the alcove, muttering words in magespeak too fast for me to recognize beyond our names and the word *protect*. "Stay down, girls!" she ordered. "Don't come out until it's safe."

With that, two more scarves flew from her hands to wrap around each of us. I fought back instinctively, batting at the gauzy stuff. It did no good. The muffling bands of silk swathed my arms, my mouth, even my eyes. Only the barest slit was left for me to squint through. By covering us so completely, Betrys had protected us from all harm. But unfortunately it also meant I could barely move, save for a sort of ungainly hopping. A squint to my side showed me Moppe in a similar predicament.

Meanwhile, the statue had already clambered back to its feet. With a silent roar, it whipped one massive marble hand at Pharon, catching him by the throat. He gave a horrible, strangled scream as the creature lifted him up into the air.

Then the scream stopped. Cut off, like a slammed door. His body went stiff. The statue tossed him aside, and Pharon hit the ground with a loud *thunk*.

I stared in horror at the councillor. His arms remained contorted in the act of freeing himself. His legs had frozen mid-kick. And his bronze skin had turned a sickly, pale gray. I'd never seen magic like this before, but I'd read chilling accounts of such a spell.

He'd been petrified.

Until that point, I'd been more frustrated than afraid. Master Betrys could handle anything. She was the best wizard on the island. But this wasn't ordinary magic. *Petrify* was a solitaire, a word in magespeak that had no counterword. Solitaires were forbidden to all but the highest-ranked wizards of the Schola Magica because they could never be undone.

Pharon wasn't truly dead, but he would never walk, breathe, speak, or feel anything, ever again. And Master Betrys could be next. *We* could be next. With that *petrify* spell bound to its stone fingers, the statue only needed to touch our flesh to turn us to stone forever.

Helpless in horror, I watched the statue swipe at Betrys. She zoomed into the air, out of its reach, muttering a spell. The statue sank abruptly into the earth, the ground under its feet transfigured into mud.

But it wasn't enough. Stone fingers clung to the solid rim of the ground; within moments, it would be free.

In the brief lull, Master Betrys called out another, longer phrase in magespeak, including the word *deanimate*. The statue froze. I started to sigh in relief. Then a sparkling glimmer raced over its body and it was free again.

The wizard who'd created the creature had given it a counterspell. Master Betrys jumped back, crashing into one of the hedges as the statue made another grab for her, snagging the sleeve of her coat. It was going to petrify her! I gave a gargle of outrage and did the only thing I could think to do: I hopped out from the alcove and threw myself at the statue's knees.

The protection spell did its job, encasing me in a hard shell of magical power. The force of the impact rattled my teeth, nothing more. Above me, stone arms pinwheeled as the statue struggled in vain to stay upright. With a great crash it fell to the ground.

Master Betrys knelt beside me. "My thanks," she said. "But you need to leave this to me." She squeezed my shoulder, murmuring a counterspell I didn't recognize.

The statue regained its feet. It cocked its carved head from side to side, as if searching for something. Me, I realized a heartbeat later. The protections Master Betrys had put on the scarves must be shielding me from the statue's sight. But it knew I was here.

It raked one great stone hand along the ground, barely missing my toes. I tried to roll out of the way, but the next swipe caught one end of the scarf that enveloped me. The silk muffled my scream. I braced myself, certain I was about to be petrified.

"Leave her be!" cried Master Betrys. "Your business is with me." She called out a few quick, sharp words in magespeak.

Suddenly I was flying. Silk tore, and a faint spark of magic fizzed along my arm.

A jolt of fear clutched my chest as I slammed down into the ground, but whatever the enchantment was, Master Betrys's counterspell had thwarted it. I was lucky it hadn't been *petrify*, or things might have ended very differently. Instead I merely rolled to a stop beneath the hedges, unable to do anything but watch as the battle played out its final scene.

As the statue advanced upon her, Master Betrys stood cool and defiant. Calmly, carefully, she intoned a final spell. I couldn't make out the last word, but whatever it was, it must have been terrible. It tore out of her, as if she were spitting a sword at the creature, leaving her staggering with whatever great power she'd invoked.

The statue shattered in a cloud of dust.

A patter of grit fell to the trampled earth. Nothing bigger than a single pea was left. A long, ragged gasp filled the sudden stillness as Betrys sighed.

Then came the shouts and thudding boots. A dozen soldiers in gold coats, muskets and sabers at the ready, converged on the scene. Two of them leaped at Master Betrys, seizing her arms.

"What's the meaning of this?" she demanded. "I've done no wrong. Release me!"

A soldier in a tricorn hat with a single gold star—marking her as a captain—spoke. "Master Julien Betrys, in the name of the emperor I hereby place you under arrest for this assault on the honorable Councillor Pharon, and for suspected involvement in the despicable and traitorous rebellion against lawful imperial rule. You will be taken into custody, questioned, and then held until proof of innocence or guilt for these transgressions is determined."

I heard a muffled yelp and turned to see another shrouded, wormlike figure beside me. Moppe. She tried to hop forward, only to stumble and crash sideways into the shrubbery.

None of the soldiers noticed. But Master Betrys's eyes went to us, sudden and sharp. "Prove me wrong. All our fates depend on the crown. But it will take both knowledge and power to succeed. *Turnip*—"

"Gag her!" snapped the captain. One of the goldcoats dove at Master Betrys, stuffing a cloth into her mouth before she could finish the incantation.

"Make certain she's secure," ordered the captain. "Triple-check that gag every five minutes. We can't risk her escaping."

I twisted and writhed, but the silk binding my arms and feet held tight. Master Betrys had enchanted the scarves to protect us. To keep us invisible.

Now that meant we were powerless to interfere.

Guests from the party had begun to drift over, forming a babbling crowd. Someone arrived with a wheelbarrow, into which several of the soldiers began to load the petrified Councillor Pharon. There were gasps and sobs and cries of fear from the onlookers, until one of the men cast his great-coat over the stone body.

I didn't see my mother among the crowd. Only strangers, all of them staring at Master Betrys as she stood silent and stiff-backed between her captors.

"Everything is under control," said the captain, her voice smooth and sure. "Please return to your party and know that the Imperial Guard is here to ensure safety and order."

A jumble of shouted questions met this proclamation.

The captain nodded. "Yes, I'm afraid a terrible injustice has occurred. It appears Master Julien Betrys is a traitor and has turned her magic against a loyal citizen in service to her despicable cause."

I opened my mouth, trying to scream the truth at her. Master Betrys wanted nothing to do with any of this! She was brilliant and absolutely devoted to her art. She *loved* magic. She would *never* use it to do evil. But the muffling silk scarf ate my words, turning them into barely a whisper. There was nothing I could do. Fury and frustration roiled my gut as I wriggled myself upright.

The captain gestured to her soldiers, and they began to drag Master Betrys away toward the front gates. She paused to confront the crowd. "You may trust that the guard will see that this matter is fully investigated. If anyone has information regarding the activities of Julien Betrys, please report it. We also have reason to suspect two others are likely involved."

Two others? The sick feeling in my stomach turned into a heavy weight. Oh no. Surely she didn't mean—

"Betrys's apprentices, Moppe Cler and Antonia Durant, are wanted on suspicion of treason."

8

ALL I COULD THINK OF was getting as far away from the garden as possible. That was something of a challenge, as I was still swathed in magical silk and unable to do more than hop. I glanced toward Moppe and found she'd managed to regain her footing as well. Her wide eyes met mine, reflecting fear and desperation. It made me feel a little better. At least I wasn't the only one who was absolutely terrified.

The scarves, infuriating as they were, were our only hope. Right now, we needed to be invisible if we were going to escape. I jerked my chin toward the twisted iron gates that led from Lord Buccanyl's garden out onto the street, hoping Moppe would understand.

She started hopping toward the gates. I followed. A few agonizing moments later and we were in the streets, mincing across bumpy cobblestones. I spotted an alley across the way, tucked between a tea shop and a bookseller, and made for it.

Once out of sight of the garden, I sagged against the wall, my breath rasping hot and quick through the silk that still swaddled my face. It smelled faintly of carnations, Master Betrys's favorite perfume oil.

Moppe tottered into the alley a moment later, wheezing. Out in the street, the clatter of boots and carriages rattled past. Probably the guard, taking Master Betrys away to the courthouse prison.

The thought jabbed a hot needle through my chest. I was alone. I didn't even have a grimoire. All I had was my magic, and Master Betrys's last words. *Prove me wrong. All our fates depend on the crown. But it will take both knowledge and power to succeed. Turnip.*

I must have misheard that last word. Maybe there was another bit of magespeak that sounded like the word for turnip but actually meant *freedom* or *escape* or *Toss all these soldiers into a heap over there while I run away.*

I would have to figure it out later. Right now, I needed to get free of the scarf. A simple *deanimate* would probably work. The only problem was that I had a wad of silk muffling my mouth.

I tried anyway, holding the word carefully in my mind as I spoke. A muffled sputter came out. Nothing else happened, except that Moppe stopped her own struggles for a brief moment to stare at me.

There were rare mages who could cast spells silently, simply by thinking the words, but obviously I wasn't one of them. I tried again, twisting my head to free my lips a fraction more. Thankfully the scuffle had loosened it just enough.

"Scarf. Deanimate."

The scarf fell away so suddenly I nearly toppled to the ground, no longer gripped by the silk embrace.

Across the alley, Moppe stood straighter. Her black curls had fallen free from their braids, clouding about her head. The scarf still muffled her mouth, but above it her eyes were sharp and demanding and shadowed with fear. She mumbled something that sounded like a plea for help. Or possibly a curse.

There had been times in the past week when I'd wished I'd never met the girl. How different might this have all turned out, if not for that fateful night in the kitchen with the dancing turnips? Our rivalry had cost me tears and shame and despair. But we'd also managed some triumphs. Together, we'd bested the voices of the Cave of Echoes. Without her, I might still be stuck in the carpet in Master Betrys's study. Moppe was part of this now, and I wasn't going to abandon her.

"Scarf. Deanimate."

The blue silk slipped down to puddle at Moppe's feet. She glowered at me. "Took you long enough."

She turned and started off down the alley, away from the main street.

I jogged after her. "Wait! Where are you going?"

She halted, crossing her arms. "You heard what Master Betrys said. I need to find the crown."

"All by yourself?"

"I've had enough of your so-called help. You made me the laughingstock of the gala. You got us both *expelled*."

The bitterness of her words sent a guilty flush to my cheeks. "I got you out of that scarf, too," I said. "In case you forgot."

"You also turned yourself into a human lantern. In case you forgot."

I hadn't. It was hard to forget, given the soft glow that was so clearly oozing from my skin now that we were deep in the darkness of the narrow alley. "But you don't even know where to start looking!" I sputtered.

She lifted her chin high. "Master Betrys told me where to look."

"What do you mean? All she said was *turnip*."

"Exactly." She spun, marching away. There was no way she knew what she was doing. *Turnip* didn't mean anything. Unless Moppe thought Master Betrys had hidden the most powerful magical artifact in Medasia at the bottom of a green-grocer's root bin.

I jogged after her. "The longer we stay on the run, the guiltier we look. We should turn ourselves in."

"And be executed for treason?" Moppe asked sourly.

"They aren't going to execute us."

"They shot two boys last month for writing something

rude about the emperor on the wall of the customs house."

I sucked in a breath. Surely that couldn't be true. There must be more to it. Probably it was just some wild rumor spun into sensationalism by the Liberationists.

"We aren't rebels, and neither is Master Betrys! It's all a mistake. If we go to my mother, I'm sure she can sort it out."

Moppe snorted. "Right. Because she's some high mucky-muck on the council? Maybe she'll save her precious, perfect daughter, but she won't care a toss about some mountain girl. And that's fine with me. I'm going to save myself." She jabbed her thumb at her chest as she spoke.

Precious, perfect daughter? If Moppe knew what my mother really thought of me, she'd never stop laughing.

Moppe quickened her steps, leaving me behind as she crossed out into a wider street, turning south, toward the shore. An evening fog had settled over Port Meda, furling out a thick, gray blanket over the cobblestones, cloaking the dark storefronts in veils of mist.

I ground my teeth, watching her go. It was pure foolishness. And yet . . .

Prove me wrong.

Hope quivered in my chest. Did she mean prove her wrong to have expelled us? By finding the crown? By showing that I had the wisdom to ensure it wasn't misused? There were greater and grander things at stake here than my magical future. Betrys's very life hung in the balance. The safety of all Medasia. If there was even the smallest chance that I could do something about it, I had to try.

My footsteps rang hollow in the mist as I hurried after Moppe.

"Are you sure you're not lost?" I asked as I followed Moppe along the rocky trail south of Port Meda. We'd left the city hours ago. The sky was starting to look suspiciously silvery along the east, and every bone in my body seemed to have transfigured itself into lead, dragging me down with an overwhelming weariness.

"I didn't ask you to come," snarled Moppe.

"No. Master Betrys did."

The girl spun around, confronting me with crossed arms. "She did not."

"She said it would take *both* knowledge and power to succeed. You don't need to do this by yourself. You can't. You're not ready."

"I know." The words wrenched out of her, deep and fierce and edged with unhappiness. "But I *have* to."

"Why?" I repeated. "You're just a girl. No one said you have to save Medasia all by yourself."

Moppe stared at me. A wistful look softened her sharp-cut features. I pressed my advantage. "We just need to find the crown and show the council that we have it and it's safe," I said. "And then they'll let Master Betrys go. The adults will figure out what to do with it and we can go back to being apprentices. She'll take us back, if we prove her wrong. Maybe . . . maybe she'll even recommend us to the Schola Magica."

And like that, the hopeful expression vanished. "That's all this is to you? A way to get to that frilly-necked school?"

"That's not what I meant," I called, but she was already marching onward, up the slope to an open ridge crowned by a stand of young lemon trees.

Leaning against one of them, she paused to tug something from the pocket of her skirt. It was the cherry cake. The one she had been trying to enchant when I gave her the wrong spell. The confection was slightly squashed and sticky with marzipan, but still looked absolutely delicious. Especially after an hour or more of tromping along a dark, rocky trail having just been accused of treason. My stomach rumbled.

Moppe arched an amused brow at me. "Hungry?" she asked, before taking an enormous bite from the cake. She chewed lustily and loudly.

"No," I said, wrapping my arms around my stomach.

"Too bad you didn't tell me how to actually enlarge it," she said, around another bite of jewel-red cherries and flaky crust. "There might be enough to share."

"Cake. Enlarge," I said.

The pastry shivered, growing an inch or two larger. Moppe smirked. "Thanks. It's really good." She took another bite, making no move to share.

I swallowed as my stomach gave another rumble. I was in serious danger of drooling. "Well? Are you just going to stand there and eat cake?"

"Yes," she said, waggling the half-eaten pastry at me.

"I'm going to stand here and eat cake until you go away. Why should I let you tag along? If you think you're going to swoop in and steal my—"

"What was that?" I twisted left and right, searching the hillside. "Did you hear something?"

Moppe gave a hollow laugh. "Oh, and now you're trying to scare me into letting you come with me? Do you really think that's going to work?"

But it wasn't a trick. There had been something, a scuttling and scraping higher on the hill. Maybe it was only a goat, out for a morning stroll, kicking loose a bit of the rubble cluttering the hillside. The odd predawn light turned the world into a gray ghost land, lumpy with boulders, haunted by twisted olive trees. We had wandered inland, away from the coast, but the air still held the salty tang of the sea. I was probably panicking for no reason.

Except . . . "Was that boulder there a moment ago?" I asked, pointing to a craggy lump hunched in the shadow of the hillside above.

"Which boulder?" Moppe asked.

"The one that's MOVING!" I shrieked, as the stone shifted, uncoiling abruptly into a lean, feline form.

"Another statue!" cried Moppe. "Did it follow us?"

It definitely looked like it had been sent by the same unknown wizard. Like the warrior from the garden, the stone lion was carved from fine marble, with a greenish bloom and a crust of barnacles, as if it had emerged from under the sea.

Fine cracks marred the surface as well; it was old. Part of one ear had broken off. Somehow that only made it look fiercer.

It hunched down, giving a low rumble like grating boulders as its blank eyes fixed on us. Those terrible marble jaws opened, showing a mouthful of carved teeth. If it didn't petrify us first, the creature could clearly tear us to bits.

Unless I stopped it.

"Lion. Rise."

A glimmer of light slid over the stone lion, almost too quick to follow. A sharp tingle ran through me, as if I'd touched metal on a dry, cold day. The lion stayed firmly planted on the rocky earth.

"I'll take care of it," Moppe said.

"Wait!" I cried, but she was already repeating my words.

Another flare of light fizzed across the lion's haunches, brighter this time, before sparking back at Moppe. She yelped. "What was that?"

There was no time to answer. The lion leapt. "Move!" I shouted, diving out of the way. Moppe tumbled after me onto a patch of wild thyme as the lion smashed into the lemon tree where we'd been standing a moment before.

"It's counterspelled," I told her, as we staggered back to our feet. "It turns magical energy back against the caster. You saw Master Betrys fighting the statue in the garden. She only beat it because she used a solitaire." At least, that was what I assumed that final, perilous spell had been.

"A what?"

"A spell with no known counterspell. Like the spell that petrified Councillor Pharon. Only the most highly trained wizards are ever taught solitaires."

"Do you know any?" Moppe asked hopefully.

"No."

"Then what do we do?"

"Run!" I shouted, as the lion bounded toward us.

We tore along the trail, winding down the other side of the ridge into a narrow gorge, then up a steep twist of dusty stones onto a grassy hillside dotted with small white flowers. It might have been beautiful, if it weren't for the rampaging stone lion charging after us.

"Will it ever stop?" huffed Moppe.

"No. And it won't get tired. We need to do something," I panted. "We can't attack it directly. We need to use something else."

"Great," Moppe said, holding up a handful of smashed marzipan and cherries. "All I've got is a cake."

"That's it!" I snatched the pastry from her hand.

Glancing over my shoulder, I saw that the lion was only a few yards behind us. Jaws wide, it boomed a roar. This was my chance!

I flung the cake straight into the lion's mouth. "Moppe!" I called. "Enlarge!"

She gave me one incredulous look, before understanding flooded her face.

"Cake," she said, in magespeak. *"Enlarge."*

Instantly the cake began to swell. The lion staggered to a halt, jaw working, but it was too late. Its fierce jaws were sunk deep in the marzipan. It shook its stone head from side to side, trying to dislodge what was now an enormous lump of cherries and pastry. Larger and larger the cake grew, forcing the lion's jaws apart.

And then . . .

Crack!

The statue's head splintered, the ancient battered stone unable to resist the might of the pastry. The creature froze abruptly, one paw slashing in an act of final, headless defiance.

"It worked!" Moppe crowed, swatting me on the shoulder. "You're a real corker!"

I grinned, flushed with success and pleased to have someone to share it with. Master Betrys had complimented me before, but she'd never swatted my shoulder and called me a corker.

"It wouldn't have worked if you hadn't cast the spell," I admitted. "Look at that. That's . . . amazing."

The cake was *still* growing. In fact, it had already started to bump up against my toes. I took a few steps back, just to be safe. There was plenty to eat, but between the churning fear and the exploding lion statue, my hunger had vanished, at least for now.

Moppe smiled. She had a nice smile when she wasn't being a complete pain. It made a dimple in her left cheek.

But the smile didn't last long. She frowned at the ruin of the statue, letting out a long sigh. "I suppose there's going to be more of that, isn't there?"

I nodded. "Whoever it is, they're a powerful wizard. As powerful as Master Betrys. And they want the crown. Probably a Liberationist."

Moppe tensed. "Why do you think that?"

I gestured to the broken lion. "That's an old Medasian statue, from the looks of it. Probably from the ruins of one of the old temples. Besides, who else would it be?"

Moppe dug the toe of one shoe into the dirt. "Right. Well, I guess then . . . it makes sense for us to . . . work together. For a little while. Just to be safe."

"Er. Right," I said. "Good. So." I fumbled in the awkward space between rivalry and alliance. Everything had changed. Maybe that meant that things between Moppe and me could change, too. A part of me desperately hoped so. I didn't want to face this alone. "Where are we going? And what does any of this have to do with turnips?"

In answer, Moppe spun on her heel, leading me onward up the grassy slope. "The Furtive told us that the key was a place we needed to go. And Master Betrys was trying to tell us something about turnips. So, look there," she said, pointing through the predawn haze to the outline of the mountain above.

I cocked my head, staring at the peak. The mountain was familiar: oddly round, with a sudden sharp summit. It was the same peak from Florian's stories.

"What does it remind you of?" she asked.

"A fat carrot," I said, "Or . . . *oh*."

"Its proper name is Mount Zalon," said Moppe. "But most folks call it Mount Turnip."

9

"HE LEGENDS SAY it's where Queen Meda came after she was exiled from the mainland, to seek guidance from the old powers," Moppe said, as she led the way up the slopes of Mount Turnip.

The night was slipping away, the eastern sky warming behind the domed peak, showing streaks of gold and pink. Around us, birds chirruped in the dew-streaked brush. It was beautiful, but I still didn't see what any of it had to do with finding the lost crown.

"How do you know all that?" I asked. "My brother used to tell me stories, but those were just fairy tales. My history tutor certainly never said anything about any magic turnip mountain."

Moppe huffed. "Probably didn't say much about our real history at all, did they? Just some nonsense about a bunch of stuffed shirts on the other side of the ocean who think we should scrape and bow to them because of some promise Meda supposedly made centuries ago."

"It's not nonsense," I protested. "By the terms Meda negotiated when she established Medasia, the island would revert to imperial rule if her bloodline ever failed. And it did!"

"You sound like one of them," said Moppe. "As if we should be happy to be under the thumb of some gold-plated nincompoop who only cares about his purple robes."

"I'm just as Medasian as you are!" I protested. I'd seen my own family tree, inscribed on a thick sheaf of parchment kept safe in Mother's study. Our only recent connection to the mainland was my maternal grandmother, who came to Medasia to negotiate a trade deal with the local dyehouses and ended up marrying the dye merchant's son. My father had been from the south of the island, though he'd died before I was even born.

Moppe didn't look convinced.

"Besides, we need Regia Terra," I went on. "We wouldn't last a year on our own without the Imperial Navy to drive off pirates." I'd heard my mother say so at least a dozen times.

"Queen Meda didn't need cannons and frigates," said Moppe darkly. "She had the Black Drake. The drake kept Medasia safe for centuries."

"Right," I said. "Until King Goros died without an heir and it went wild and tore down the old palace and half of Port Meda."

"Until he was *murdered*, you mean. Along with his daughters."

"Murdered?" I shook my head. "No, they died of the spotted fever."

"Is that what your tutor told you? And where did they learn their history?"

"At the Imperial Collegium," I admitted. Mother had insisted on a "proper Regian education" for both Florian and myself. "Anyway," I said, "who told you they were murdered?"

"My grandmother," said Moppe. "She knows all the old stories. She grew up in these mountains. If anyone knows where to look for the lost crown, it's her. We're nearly there now," she added, quickening her steps.

I peered doubtfully through the brush ahead. "Are you sure she won't mind us just bursting in like this?"

"Of course not. Just be careful of Uncle Goat. He's the grouchy one."

"What?" I must have misheard. "Uncle Goat?"

But Moppe was already yards ahead of me, heading for a small cottage perched along the slope of the mountainside. Bright pink bougainvillea spilled over the whitewashed walls, almost enveloping the tiny house. The door and shutters were vivid blue, the stoop freshly swept and decorated with pots of herbs. More greenery rioted in the garden nearby: a frenzy of dill and thyme and silvery-speared artichokes.

A grizzled black goat stood just outside the door, blinking uncanny yellow eyes as it watched us approach. It looked harmless, but after Moppe's warning I was careful to edge around the far side of the path, keeping well away from the creature as it casually munched mouthfuls of greens.

Suddenly the blue door swung open. Two little girls tumbled out, calling Moppe's name. One of them looked about nine, the other barely six. Both had long manes of curly black hair and sun-bronzed skin, just like Moppe.

"You're here! Aya said you weren't coming to visit until the new moon," said the younger girl, flinging herself into Moppe's arms. "Did you bring me sweets? You said you'd bring back sweets!"

"Don't be a greedy gut, Delia," said the older girl. She eyed Moppe suspiciously. "What happened to your job? Did they sack you?"

"No, they didn't sack me, Lyssa," said Moppe, ruffling the girl's hair. "These are my sisters," she told me. "And this is Antonia. She's my . . ." She trailed off, frowning at me, as if I were a tomato popping up in her cabbage patch.

"We're both Master Betrys's apprentices," I explained. It wasn't *exactly* a lie. We still had a chance to prove her wrong and regain our positions.

"And we're here on important business," said Moppe.

"Best be *very* important business to drag us all from our beds before dawn, Agamopa," said a voice from the doorway.

"Agamopa?" I repeated. "Is that your real name?"

Moppe rolled her eyes. "No. It's just what my mother and Aya insist on calling me."

The woman who had spoken was quite possibly the oldest

person I'd ever seen. Her wind-tanned skin held a thousand wrinkles and her hair was a fog of pure white curls. She—like the two girls, I realized belatedly—wore a thin nightshift that came down to her knees, showing off two sturdy but knobbly feet.

Moppe hunched her shoulders under the old woman's fierce gaze. It was the most humbled I'd ever seen her. "I'm sorry, Aya. I didn't mean to wake you. But—" She glanced at me. I nodded. "Well, we need to find the lost crown Lyrica Drakesbane crafted for Queen Meda and we think there's a clue on Mount Turnip. And there's some wizard sending magical statues after us to turn us to stone."

"And we're wanted for treason," I added. It only seemed polite to warn her, given the circumstances.

"Hmph. Is that all?"

I couldn't tell if the old woman was serious, or amused, or both. Her craggy expression told me nothing.

"Er, yes, ma'am."

"Call me Aya," she said. "And I suppose you'd best come in and tell us all about it."

"So," Moppe said, as she finished the tale of our night's adventures, "that's why we came here."

We were seated around a sturdy oak table spread with a blue-and-white-striped cloth. Aya had listened to the tale silently, all the while dishing up bowls of thick, creamy yogurt with stewed cherries and slices of warm oat bread spread with honey and butter. Now she filled small blue-glazed cups from a pot of tea, setting one before each of us.

Well, each of us except the goat.

The creature had followed us inside, to no one's dismay but my own. He'd curled himself on a pillow propped in one corner, like a pet dog, and watched Moppe tell our story as intently as the rest of them. But now he rose and trotted over, bleating plaintively. His yellow eyes were fixed hungrily on the nearest teacup.

"You know it just gives you a gassy belly, Tragos," said the old woman.

The goat stamped one cloven hoof and tossed his craggy horned head.

"Oh fine. But don't come to me for sympathy when you're rumbling like a thundercloud." Aya rummaged on a shelf behind her, taking down another blue cup, then setting it on the floor and filling it with the minty brew.

"Uncle Goat loves tea," Moppe told me, over a sudden, loud slurping. "And teacups," she added, as the slurping turned to crunching and the snap of pottery. "It's a good thing my cousin Mikos is a potter."

I stared at the goat. I wasn't sure what flummoxed me most. That the creature had just eaten a teacup, or that Moppe was calling it . . . Uncle?

"He's not *really* your uncle, is he?"

"Oh, no," said Moppe.

"Hah." I started to smile. "You almost had me—"

"He's my great-uncle," said Moppe. "Aya's younger brother."

"Seriously?"

The goat gave a resentful snort. Aya chortled. "Just because the fool turned himself into a goat doesn't mean he's not still family."

I shook my head, trying to make sense of this explanation. "Turned himself into a goat? You mean transfiguration? He's a *wizard*?"

"He's a stubborn ninny is what he is." Aya snatched her own cup from the table just as the goat began to nibble at it.

I considered the goat. He returned my stare calmly. It was possible, of course. A wizard who transfigured themselves into an animal—anything that couldn't speak to undo the spell—ran the risk of getting stuck that way.

"Isn't there someone who could change him back?" I asked.

"Didn't work," said Aya. "I figure he always was an old goat, right from the start. Guess the magic knows that. Magic's clever. Too clever for its own good. Remember that, Agamopa." She bopped Moppe lightly on the head.

"I will, Aya."

"Mmph. I suppose I ought to have expected it to crop up in the line again," the old woman went on. "Magic's thick in these mountains." She swished a bony finger through the steam that coiled from her cup. "Especially up near the peak, where the old powers linger."

"On Mount Turnip?" I asked. "That's where Master Betrys

told us to look for the crown. Do you have any idea where we should start?"

A flicker of something ghosted across Aya's face, too fast for me to catch. "No," she said, in a voice like a shutting door. "There's nothing fit for you on that mountain."

"But there is *something* there," I said doggedly.

Aya's lips tightened, her eyes hooded as she looked away. "There is a place. But it's too dangerous."

"Please, Aya," said Moppe. "We're not frightened."

"You should be," said the old woman.

"We've already nearly been crushed, petrified, and arrested on charges of treason," I protested. "We know it's dangerous. But it's also important. It's a matter of life and death, Aya. What if that other wizard gets his hands on it first? He could destroy everything. Moppe and I may only be apprentices, but we know magic. Moppe's more powerful than a dozen other wizards put together. We can do this. We're the only ones who can." I leaned forward, meeting her intent gaze with as much certainty and bravery as I could muster. Master Betrys was counting on us. I couldn't let her down now.

"She's right," said Moppe. "We can do this. Antonia's memorized practically every grimoire there is. If anyone can beat that petrifying pustule to the crown, it's us. It has to be us." She drew in a long breath, lifting her chin as she met Aya's gaze. "I need to prove I can do this."

The old woman studied us for a long moment, before finally giving a sigh and a shrug. "Very well. But don't say I didn't warn you. Now off to bed," she added, as Moppe tried to stifle an enormous yawn. "You've been up all night, and everyone knows it's best to be fully rested when plotting perilous adventures."

When I woke it was late afternoon and the cottage was empty, except for the goat, who stared at me in such an unnerving manner I quickly made my escape outside. The sun had begun its slow fall into the western sea. The cottage stoop had a breathtaking view of the azure waters. I could even see the Arch of Fate, the odd rock formation just off the southern tip of Medasia, where ancient stones formed a natural arch that supposedly granted good fortune to anyone who could sail through it.

From this perch high on the mountainside, the scattered fishing boats were like children's toys bobbing across the blue. Far away but ever-present, the sea filled my vision, wrapping half the horizon in turquoise and azure. I'd never seen my home like this. It made something catch in my throat. Awe. Or maybe thankfulness. It was so *beautiful*.

Florian used to talk about how lucky we were to be Medasian, but I'd never really understood. It made me wish, all the more fiercely, that he was here. He'd always helped me out of scrapes when I was younger. Smoothed things over with Mother. Slipped me extra coins for books when she refused to indulge my "foolish fancies." Believed in me when I didn't even believe in myself. But now I was on my own. I didn't even have Master Betrys to advise me. All I had was . . .

"Delia. Rise," Moppe called out from the grassy slope

below. Her little sister zoomed up into the air, shrieking with delight.

"Higher! Higher!"

The girl swooshed down again, to hover just above a clump of frothy yellow wildflowers. Moppe continued her spells, sending the girl up and down until she was breathless with giggles.

She was getting better at control. That was a good thing, given how much raw power she had. I forced myself to look away. I had other things to focus on. Like my gown. The silk was beautiful, but impractical for the journey ahead.

"Silk. Transfigure. Linen."

The spell snapped neatly into place, sparkling from my collar to my knees, transforming the crumpled silk into a more practical blue linen. I added a few more touches, getting rid of the ruffles and lace, loosening the waist and sleeves. I even managed to transform the skirt into a pair of flowy trousers. As usual, it was the sort of magic I was best at: complicated, finicky, and practical. Not showy, not powerful. Not fireballs and lightning bolts and turning back the seas like the great wizards of old.

The words of the imperial envoy, Benedict, echoed back to me like a warning. *I'm no Master,* he'd said. *My talents were not found . . . sufficient.*

"That was *amazing*," said a voice behind me.

Lyssa watched me wide-eyed from the stoop. Behind her stood Uncle Goat, calmly chomping on something that looked distressingly like the handle of an iron skillet. "What else can you do? Can you change my peas into gold?" She thrust out a wooden bowl full of fat green peapods.

"No," I said. "Transfiguring can't change the deep nature of something. You could turn a spoon into a dagger, but metal stays metal. Food stays food. Besides, the magespeak for *gold* is a state secret. Only a few wizards in the Imperial Treasury are ever taught it."

Her face fell.

"I could do this, though," I said. *"Peas. Transfigure. Cake."*

The peapods shimmered, re-forming into my favorite type of cake: a soft pillow of cardamom-scented dough filled with almond cream. I'd even managed to get the fancy pink icing just the way it was from the bakery.

"Ooh," said Lyssa, gazing with longing and adoration at the plump pastry. "Do you think . . ." Her voice fell to a whisper, her cheeks flushing. "Can you teach me how to do it?"

"Maybe," I said cautiously. "Could you hear me, when I was casting the spell? Can you hear this? *Cake.*"

"Sort of," she said. "I mean, not really. It's all fuzzy, like you're whispering."

My heart twinged. "Can you repeat it?"

Her brow furrowed, making her look even more like her older sister, as she sputtered a few syllables. They sounded nothing like magespeak.

I regretted casting my spells now. She still looked so hopeful. But if she couldn't hear magespeak now, she was no wizard.

"I'm sorry," I said quickly, to get the hard part over with. "I don't think you're a wizard, Lyssa. It's something you're born with," I added. "Not something you can change. It's like being really tall or really short. It doesn't mean you can't do all sorts of other amazing things."

I braced myself, afraid she was going to burst into tears. But instead she looked thoughtful.

"I want to be a sea captain," she admitted, glancing out across the vast blue horizon. "Like Mama."

"There you go," I said, relieved she'd taken it so well. "I bet you'll be amazing. Me, I'm terrible on boats. I get horribly seasick. I turn green, and I don't even need magic to do it."

Lyssa giggled, lifting some of the weight of guilt from my chest. I knew how it felt to be born without all the gifts you hoped for, but at least I was still a wizard. What if I'd been born without even that?

"Is that where your mother is now?" I asked. "Out sailing? Is that why you're here with your grandmother?"

The girl stammered. "Er, w-well . . ."

"Yes," said Moppe, making me startle. How long had she been standing at my shoulder, listening? "Go on, Lyss. We still need peas for dinner. And Antonia and I have wizard-work to do."

Lyssa nodded, trotting off to the garden, munching her cake as she went.

"Thanks," said Moppe, watching the younger girl disappear behind the artichokes.

"For what?"

"That," said Moppe, jerking her chin in the direction of the garden. "Not making her feel bad. She's always been that way. Always wanting to prove she can do anything I can. She nearly drowned trying to follow me out to the Caphos Lighthouse last year."

I shrugged, trying to smile. "I know what it's like being a little sister. Florian was everything to my mother. I could be Grand High Wizard and I'd still never get her to smile at me like she did when he got his commission."

Moppe's brow furrowed. She wasn't a fool. She'd heard the *was*.

"What happened to him?" she asked, after a moment.

"He was murdered," I said, looking out over the distant waters. There was a frigate in the distance. Just like the one Florian might be on now, if things had been different. "He'd just been posted on the *Victory*, as third mate. They said he must have gone on board early, maybe to settle his gear. So he was there when Captain Porphyra and the Liberation stole it from the harbor. They never even found his body. The Liberationists just tossed him into the sea."

I heard Moppe's breath catch, but I didn't dare look at her.

Maybe I shouldn't have said anything. I felt exposed, like an oyster cracked open, soft and pink and raw. But Moppe didn't try to tell me he was brave, or that it was a noble sacrifice, or any of the other things people told me at the funeral. She didn't try to hug me, or stammer over apologies and lamentations.

She sat beside me, on the stoop, not close enough to touch, but close enough that I could feel the faint warmth of her shoulder beside me. We sat and looked out over the sea. The sun had slid down, sinking into the pink-streaked clouds above the western horizon.

Moppe's grandmother found us there, as the world turned to dusk. "All right, girls," she said. "It's time."

"Time for what, exactly, Aya?" asked Moppe.

"Time to be brave."

10

WE CLIMBED THE MOUNTAIN by starlight. Aya led the way, striding swiftly along the dusty track that wound up past groves of lemons and rocky ledges tufted with wild thyme. The goat trotted behind us, yellow eyes mirroring the waxing moon above.

Frogs fluted from the darkness. And other, less familiar creatures too. Every so often I heard the rustle of something larger, a deep huff, a slow heavy tread. Once, I even caught a glimpse of gleaming silver antlers above a long, solemn face set with ghostly pale eyes. I shuddered, feeling as if the creature could look straight into my soul.

"Silver deer," said Aya. "Don't worry, they're the least of your concerns."

She smiled, as if that was supposed to make me feel better.

"Where are we going?" I asked. "And do we really need to go there in the dark?"

"Not so dark with you around," said Moppe.

Indeed, as the night deepened, my cursed glow became more obvious, emanating from my exposed hands and face.

"Could be worse," said Aya. "At least you didn't turn yourself into a goat." She gave what I could only describe as a cackle. In return, the goat made a particularly rude bleat. "It's not far now," the old woman went on, jabbing a gnarled finger toward the denser forest ahead. "Behold, the Forest of Silent Fears."

I peered into the shadows, which suddenly seemed full of the dim hulks of nameless terrors and the faint glitter of a thousand watchful eyes. "Is that just a scary name people call it because it's so dark and mysterious?" I asked hopefully.

"No," said Aya. "They call it that because anyone who dares enter must face their greatest fears if they wish to survive."

"What happens if you don't face them?" asked Moppe.

"Then you become part of the forest forever."

"And we're going in there?" I asked. "On purpose?"

"Not *we*," she said, halting before the thick dark wood. "*You*."

"You're not going with us?" squeaked Moppe.

Aya cocked a dubious brow. "I thought you two were the only ones who could do this. That you were ready to face any challenge to claim the crown. Did you change your minds?"

A part of me wished desperately that I could. But everything I'd said earlier was still true. We had a duty. And I could see the same defiant answer on Moppe's fierce face.

"No," we answered, in unison.

"There you have it, then. This is your quest, not mine. Besides, if my nightmares came out to play, I doubt any of us would survive. But don't worry. I'm sure Tragos will take good care of you."

"The goat?" I sputtered. "You think a *goat* is going to keep us safe from a magic nightmare forest?"

The goat snorted, as if insulted, but Aya seemed not to notice. She was waving us toward a slight gap in the thick brush that bounded the dark wood. "That way," she said. "Head toward the peak. That's where she lives."

"Who?" asked Moppe.

"The Speakthief. A foul creature, but even the gods envied her powers of prophecy. Nothing like a glimpse of the future to lure even the wisest folk into foolishness. If the stories that Terwyn Drakesbane came here are true, no doubt he was seeking her advice."

"Er, and why is she called the Speakthief?" asked Moppe.

The old woman's eyes glinted in the starlight. "Some say she was a mortal woman, once. That she was the first wizard, who stole the language of the gods, so they took her voice as punishment. Now she can only speak in the voices she's stolen from the unwary and the unwise. That's the payment she demands. Words. So take great care what you say in her presence."

A chill rippled through me. My feet seemed to sink into the ground, heavy as boulders. Words were everything. Wizardry was founded on them. If I lost my voice, I would lose my magic. Was it worth the risk?

Maybe Aya was right. Maybe this was too dangerous. What were we doing, traipsing off into an ominous woods called the Forest of Silent Fears in search of a creature that could steal our voices? If only we could let someone else fix this mess!

But there wasn't anyone else. Only Moppe and me. And yes, losing my voice would be horrible. But not as terrible as losing Master Betrys. Or losing our home to war and chaos. We had to take the risk.

I drew in a long breath, then forced my feet onward. "All right. Let's go find the Speakthief."

My golden glow lit our path across the deep green moss that carpeted the Forest of Silent Fears. The soft stuff muffled our footsteps, rendering the utter hush of the forest all the more ominous. No frogs, no silver deer. Nothing but clouds of fluttering pale moths that crowded around my head, soft wings beating at my glowing skin. I tried to wave them away, but they returned moments later.

"What's that?" Moppe whispered, pointing off between the trees. Faint shimmering knots hung from the branches in the distance.

"Some sort of vine, maybe?"

But as we moved closer, I saw it was something far more unsettling. The threads were woven in vast spirals, sweeping in enormous filmy curtains from tree to tree. Spiderwebs. My skin crawled at the sight, and yet I couldn't look away. The woven patterns drew my eyes, shifting with half-formed images I couldn't quite make out. I started to bend closer, to get a better look, when Moppe gave a shriek, pointing ahead to a bundle of twigs caught in one of the webs.

Except it wasn't a bundle of twigs.

The bones poked out knobby and pale from the shimmering strands of webbing. A thighbone, a jaw, one gaping eye socket. And most disturbing of all, a hand that seemed to be pointing back the way we'd come. Like a warning from the dead, telling us to retreat before it was too late.

I coughed, trying to clear the quiver from my throat. "Do you want to go back?" I asked.

Moppe swallowed, her eyes enormous. "Do you?"

Part of me did, desperately. But I wasn't going to be the first one to admit it. "No. Of course not."

"Good. Then let's keep going."

There was a bit of a clearing ahead where the path split. One trail rambled away to the left, the other to the right. I considered the two options. "Which way now?"

Moppe crossed her arms, looking uncomfortable. "You go left and I'll go right," she said. She'd already started along her path before I registered what she was proposing.

"Wait! No, we should stick together." The goat gave a bleat, as if he agreed with me.

Moppe halted, half turning. "There're two paths. There're two of us."

"But what about the nightmares?" I said. "What if you run into yours? I should be with you."

She waved a hand. "I'll be fine."

But she didn't look fine. She looked nervous.

"Are you sure—"

"Yes! I don't need your help."

The words stung like the pinching bites of a swarm of beach flies. "Oh," I said, my throat going tight with disappointment. I'd actually started to think we were a team.

Uncle Goat gave another bleat, nearly tripping me as I started to pace away. "You heard her," I told him. "She doesn't need me. I guess we'll just see who gets to the Speakthief first."

I strode off along the lonely left trail. There were more spiderwebs veiling the trees on either side, some of them bulging with gruesome bundles, but I kept my gaze straight ahead. I could make out a faint prick of starlight. I must be near the peak.

A branch snapped behind me.

I froze, praying I'd only imagined it. Was this my nightmare? My pulse pounded. My mouth felt dry as chalk as I waited for the forest to test me. What would it be? Reliving Florian's death? My childhood phobia of ants, thousands of them crawling over me?

Another crack, loud as cannon fire against the strange silence of the forest. My nightmare was right behind me.

"You're not real," I said, fighting the urge to turn. "I'm going to ignore you and keep going, so you might as well just give up."

Something hard butted my legs. I looked down to find a pair of slitted gold eyes glowering up at me.

My nightmare was a goat.

He butted me again, harder. All right, so maybe this wasn't my nightmare.

"Ouch!" I danced out of the way before he could bump me again. "What is it?" I asked. "Where's Moppe?"

The goat bleated, giving me a look of severe disapproval. "What?" I demanded. "What am I supposed to do? She's the one who insisted we go different ways!"

Then I heard it. A thin sob, from somewhere in the distance. I didn't think. I just ran, pelting toward the sound. "Moppe?"

I raced back down the trail, lungs gasping, searching the dim shadows to find her. Back to the clearing, then up the right-hand trail, with Uncle Goat galloping beside me.

There!

She was standing just ahead of us. A few silver strands of webs tangled in her hair and plucked at her arms, which she raised trembling above her head. Her eyes were wide, not seeing me. Sweat and tears ran down her cheeks, and her breath came in quick, desperate puffs.

The goat bleated at me.

"I know!" I snapped. "But *how* do I help her?" What sort of spell would free a person from a nightmare?

The goat bounded over to Moppe and began nibbling at one of the threads wound round her left hand. "The web?" I asked. "That's what's causing it?"

That, at least, I could help with. I flew to Moppe's side, brushing away the silvery webs that frosted her dark hair. The world shifted. . . .

Color bloomed around me. The air turned brighter. I could smell the sea. Hear the nearby crash of waves. Shapes ghosted into solidity.

And now I could see why Moppe's arms were trembling. Now I understood the desperation in her face.

She held an enormous boulder, sharp and terrible, above her head. It was impossibly large: a chunk torn from a mountain, craggy and brutal, large as a frigate. Her arms strained, sweat slicked her dark curls, as she struggled to keep it aloft.

"I can't do it," she panted. "I have to put it down."

"No," said a voice. I turned, to see a tall, dark-haired woman with dusky olive skin. She watched Moppe with a fierce certainty, as if the power of her gaze could fill the girl's bones with iron. "You have to do this on your own, Agamopa."

"Help her!" I cried, but neither of them appeared to hear me.

"Mother, please," begged Moppe. "It's too heavy."

I stared again at the tall woman. This was Moppe's mother?

The sea captain? She was dressed like a sailor, with close-fitting breeches and tall boots, and a loose white tunic. But how could she just stand there, watching Moppe struggle?

"You don't have a choice," said the woman, her voice tinged with sorrow. "It's your destiny. They're all counting on you. See?"

She gestured to the sand beneath the great boulder. The dream had shifted. A dozen kittens tumbled and mewled around Moppe's ankles.

"You must remain strong, Agamopa," said the woman. "You know what's at stake. If you give up now, you doom them all. But I believe in you. I always have."

Moppe's ragged gasp tore at my heart. Her arms stiffened, locking tightly into place. She was trapped. She couldn't set the boulder down, not without crushing the kittens. All she could do was stand there, forever, holding up that terrible weight.

"Please, Mama. I need—I need help!"

The woman shook her head. Her voice was heavy with regret. "I'm sorry, Agamopa. No one can help you with this. The burden is yours alone."

"Rot that!" I snarled. "There must be something we can do!"

If I could get the kittens safely out of the way, she could set down the boulder! But when I reached for the tiny squirming bits of fluff, my fingers slid through them as if they were mist. I couldn't affect the dream.

A chunk of the boulder cracked away, slamming down onto the sand, missing one of the kittens by a whisker. Moppe gave a despairing cry. She'd closed her eyes, and her lips were twisted in agony.

All the bones we'd seen along the trail seemed to rattle in my ears, like the drumming of a funeral procession. If Moppe didn't break free, she was going to become just another withered bundle. There had to be some way to break her out of the nightmare. Some way to change it!

"It's just a dream, Moppe," I said. "You're not really here. You're in the Forest of Silent Fears. Please, wake up!"

She only shuddered.

"You're a wizard, Moppe," I told her. "You don't have to accept this. You can change it! Let me help you!"

"I—I have to do it alone," she quavered. "Mama said it's my destiny."

"That's ridiculous!" I snapped. "Listen to me!"

Moppe blinked, opening her eyes. She was listening. Now if only she'd act!

"*Stone,*" I said. "*Shrink.* Like your nose. *Shrink!*"

A flare of hope glimmered in her eyes. She murmured something, too soft for me to hear.

"Louder!" I urged her.

"*Stone! Shrink!*"

The great boulder began to dwindle. Only a few inches at first, but then faster, until it seemed to be melting like ice in warm water. A few more heartbeats, and it was merely a pebble, gray and harmless in the palm of Moppe's hand.

She stared at it, wide-eyed, her breath still ragged, as it faded into nothing.

All around us, the dreamscape began to dim, colors and light fading back into the shadows of the forest. The tall woman melted away with a breathless huff. One last mewling cry shivered through the woods.

Then the nightmare was gone. Moppe drew a long, trembly breath.

"What was that?" I asked.

Moppe dusted her hands together. "A nightmare, obviously."

"I know that," I said. "But what did it mean? You didn't actually get trapped under a giant boulder, did you?"

Her expression froze, her eyes fixed on some distant point. She gave a small shake of her head. "No. I just have a lot of . . . responsibilities."

I frowned. "You mean your sisters."

"Right," she said quickly. "My sisters. I need to take care of them."

"Can't your mother help at all?" I asked hesitantly.

"She's busy. And besides, she knows I can do this. She's counting on me."

"But you said your mother's a sea captain. I don't see why you needed to take the job working for Master Betrys if—"

"That's right," she said sharply. "You don't see. Because you don't know what it's like for people who aren't *you*. People who don't have a mother on the council and coin dripping out of their ears. People who still remember that we're Medasian, not Regian, and are willing to fight for it."

"Fight for it? You mean like the criminals who killed my brother?" I took a step back, crossing my arms.

She hissed through her clenched teeth. "No. I mean people like my father, who was just trying to harvest enough spiny-shells to make a living and ended up tossed onto a prison ship because the dyehouses claimed he stole from their territory. Territory that the council had reallocated without telling any-one! Tell me who the real criminals are, Antonia."

"I . . ."

She looked at me then, eyes bright and fierce. My tongue turned to lead. I shook my head. "I'm sorry."

She turned away. "It doesn't matter. Let's just go."

I stared at my toes, pressing into the green moss. I could apologize a hundred times, but it wouldn't make it right. All I could do was try to be better.

But when I raised my head to tell Moppe that, she was gone. So was Uncle Goat. And the forest.

11

I WAS IN A BALLOON. Or rather, a basket, suspended by strong cords beneath an immense, billowy bubble of crimson cloth. Below, spread out like a grand tapestry, lay the glory of Medasia. Green mountains, blue seas, and a ribbon of pale beach between them.

"Look, there's Mount Zalon!"

The familiar voice jolted my chest, like the slamming of a door when you thought you were all alone in the house. I spun to see a young man perched along the basket wall. A young man with green eyes and a dazzling smile. "Florian?"

"Hullo, Ant," he said, hooking an elbow around one of the cords and leaning out over the dizzying drop. "Isn't this grand?"

"Careful!" I squeaked, dashing over to drag him back into the safety of the basket.

But he was too quick, scrambling away from my grasp to stand atop the basket wall. The wind rumpled his dark hair as he grinned out across the perilous, beautiful expanse so far, far below. I caught my breath, holding it as my heart thudded.

"I'm fine, Ant," said Florian. "Don't worry. It's too nice a day for worries."

Of course he was right. Look at all the birds, swooping and wheeling against the bright blue sky without a care in the world. They looked like crows. Except . . . was there something odd about their beaks? Strange how they flashed silver in the sun. "Florian, come down. *Please.*"

"Don't fuss at your brother, Antonia." My mother sat serenely in a gilt chair against the other side of the basket, watching me over the rim of her steaming teacup.

I glanced back at the strange crows. "But Mama, he—"

With a sharp screech, one of the birds dove at the balloon. A harsh sound tore the air. The basket heaved, listing to one side.

I smashed into the woven wall, all the air shoved out of me. I could only give an aching, wordless cry as Florian fell from his perch.

Panic sent me scrabbling for the edge of the basket, my throat jammed tight with hope. He was there, clinging to one of the ropes! "Hold on!" I called, straining to reach him.

Above us, black wings tore through the air. The crows swirled around the crimson balloon, silver beaks snapping.

No, not beaks. *Shears*. Each bird had a pair of sharp silver blades where its beak should be. And with every swoop, they sliced into our balloon. Bits of crimson silk fluttered down, speckling the air like drops of blood.

Desperate, I shoved myself over the edge of the basket, reaching for Florian's hand. I could save him! Please, let me save him!

But my fingers clasped on open air. He spun away, falling, falling, falling.

The balloon lurched again, tipping me out of the basket too. I clung to the edge, hanging over the perilous void, agony and loss ravaging through me like a wild beast. My brother was gone.

"Antonia!" called a voice.

I dragged in a ragged gasp as a face floated into view. It was a girl with curling dark hair, riding a . . . flying goat? I must be imagining things. That was *ridiculous*.

But the girl didn't go away. She flew closer, reaching out, trying to grab at my hand. Her fingers slid past mine, as if she were a ghost, and she cursed.

"You're not real," I said. "You're riding a flying goat."

"And you're getting attacked by crows with scissor-beaks!" the girl spat back. "I'm trying to help you, Antonia! You need to listen to me. I'm Moppe. Remember? This isn't real!"

But it was. I had never seen anything more real than the look in my mother's eyes as she leaned out from the balloon, looking down at me. The ravaged ruin of her happiness.

"Where is he?" she demanded. "Where's Florian?"

"He's gone, Mama." I barely managed to croak the awful words out. "Please. Help me!"

My grip was getting weaker. I couldn't hold on much longer. And now the crows were diving at my hands. Black wings slashed across my face. Silver shears sliced at my arms, leaving painful crimson lines. "Please, Mama!"

But she only stood there, staring down at me, her eyes sharp with accusation. "Why? Why should I bother saving you? What use are you, if you can't bring him back?"

"I—I can't. I don't know how."

"Then you're useless to me."

"I'm your daughter, Mama!"

Her expression turned remote. "I don't want you, Antonia. I want Florian. And you can never return him to me." She backed away.

A tortured sob wrenched from my throat. One of my hands slipped free of the basket. I dangled over the empty air, alone and abandoned.

"Don't listen to her!" shouted the girl on the flying goat. "You don't need her help. You can save yourself! You're a wizard!"

A tiny flare of warmth kindled in my cold chest.

"Come on, Antonia. I know you've got a thousand words crammed into your skull. Use them! *Antonia. Rise!*"

"*Antonia,*" I said, as my grip slipped free and I began to plummet down, down, down. "*Rise!*" I screamed.

And suddenly, I wasn't falling anymore.

Moppe's warm fingers dug into my shoulders. Her dark

eyes lanced into mine, transfixing me. I dragged in a shuddering breath. What was happening?

The world shifted back to darkest night and looming trees. The scissor-beaked birds, Mother, the balloon, all of it was gone. All of it except for the faint scream of someone falling endlessly. Still, Moppe's eyes held me steady, demanding my focus, until even that soft cry finally dimmed.

"We're trying to find the crown," she said. "Remember?"

The truth fell back into place. The crown. The Forest of Silent Fears. Nightmares come to life. Oh. I gasped, understanding.

Moppe released me. My shoulders felt cold without her grip.

"Sorry," I said. "It just seemed so real."

"I know," she said, leaning back against the trunk of one of the nearby trees. "Did your mother really say those things about your brother? Because if she did, I swear I'll blow her nose up as big as the island."

I stared at the moss, studying the frothy puffs that clouded around my feet.

"No." My voice slipped into a bare whisper. "But I know she thinks them."

Moppe pursed her lips, as if fighting the urge to argue.

"Let's keep moving," I said. "We must be getting close. But this time we stay together. Unless—" I hesitated. "Unless you still hate me."

Moppe rolled her eyes. "I don't hate you."

"My mother sent your father to prison. I mean, practically. And I humiliated you at the gala and got us both expelled. No wonder you didn't want me to see your nightmare."

"That wasn't why I wanted to split up. I mean, I did kind of hate you after the gala," she admitted, with a wry grin. "But really, I was . . . well, who wants other people seeing their worst nightmare?"

I nodded. I understood now. I was glad that Moppe had saved me, but even so, I felt vulnerable. She knew a piece of me now that no one else did—not even Master Betrys.

"I won't tell anyone about your nightmare," I said.

"Me neither. And . . . I'm glad you came. I might have been trapped there forever if you hadn't made me see the way out."

I managed a wavering smile. "And I would have ended up murdered by scissor-birds. I guess we make a pretty good—"

Moppe's eyes went suddenly wide, fixed on something over my shoulder, farther up the mountainside. She slapped a hand across my mouth, silencing my last word.

Behind me, a woman's voice echoed. "No, please, do go on. It's been ages since I've had anyone to talk to."

I turned slowly, keeping my lips clamped tight, remembering Aya's warning. *Take great care what you say in the creature's presence.* We didn't know exactly *how* the Speakthief stole voices. Maybe just speaking in her presence was enough.

Moppe's shoulder pressed against mine so close I could feel her shivering. Or maybe I was the one shivering. The sight before us was very much like something out of a nightmare, only this time we couldn't wake up.

The Speakthief was a woman. Sort of.

She wore a pale, sleeveless tunic that trailed down to the forest floor. Long, moon-white hair flowed past her shoulders, reaching nearly to her waist. Her face was a creamy oval, perfectly proportioned.

But she had no eyes. No nose. Instead, she had mouths. Hundreds of them. They rippled across her skin. Down her arms, across her collarbone, large and small. The red-lipped, sharp-toothed mouths covered her body like sores.

One of the mouths on her shoulder spoke, the voice deeper now, with a gravelly edge. "So few survive their nightmares. And then all I have left are their screams. . . ."

Several of the smaller mouths opened, filling the air with a chorus of pitiful wails. The Speakthief smiled then, over her entire body. It was fascinating and horrifying and made my stomach flip.

The creature tilted her head. Two of the larger mouths were set exactly where her eyes should have been. They opened, then closed, in a terrifying mockery of blinking. "Well?" said a high-pitched, childlike voice. "Who are you? Why have you come?"

I glanced sideways at Moppe. Her eyes were huge, her lips tight. She remembered Aya's warnings too.

But I had to say something. We had come here for answers. Maybe if I just said as little as possible, I would be safe.

"The crown," I said.

The words were tugged from my lips, as if a cold breeze had blown over them, tearing them away.

"The crown." My own voice echoed from the Speakthief's lips.

I shuddered. Was it as easy as that? Had I already lost my voice? Or just those words? My lips felt frozen.

She laughed, a booming, hearty rumble, and continued in a man's voice, rich and melodic, with a strange foreign twist. "You aspire to claim it?"

Moppe gave the Speakthief a vigorous nod.

"Oh, my poor dears. So frightened," rasped an old man's crackling tones. "You need not worry. They may call me thief, but I take only what is freely given."

Moppe and I shared a dubious look. She started to open her mouth, but I squeezed her hand hard, giving a small shake of my head. I'd already spoken. I had to find out what it had cost me.

"The crown," I said. Once more the chill breeze snatched at my lips. The words sounded fainter, hollowed out and faded. But they were still mine, for now. "We've come for the crown. We've passed your tests."

"Mmmm." The noise was noncommittal. It might have been agreement, disapproval, or simply an appreciation of how juicy and tasty we looked. The Speakthief's lips curled in another hundredfold smile. "But there are so many more delicious fears to explore. Guilt. Envy. Loss. Custard."

Custard? I looked at Moppe, quirking a brow.

"Don't look at me like that," she whispered. "It's all jiggly and oogly and disgusting. It looks like someone sneezed in a bowl."

The Speakthief drifted closer, licking her many lips. "Jiggly and oogly," she whispered back, in Moppe's voice.

Moppe gave a tiny moan.

"The crown," I said fiercely.

"Are you certain that is all you seek?" the Speakthief asked in a young man's vivid, resonant voice.

A voice that stabbed me through my heart, making me gasp in wonder and fear.

A voice I knew well but had thought I'd never hear again.

"That's my brother's voice!"

"Ahhh," said the Speakthief.

"He came here?" I demanded. "When? Why?"

"I don't recall." Her voice turned childlike again, lisping faintly. "Perhaps if you gave me his name?"

"Florian," I said instantly, just as Moppe cried, "No, don't!"

"Florian," said the Speakthief, in my own voice. "What a lovely name."

It was as if I'd plunged into the icy waters of a mountain lake. I gasped, then clapped a hand to my lips. I removed my fingers, forming his name in my mouth, pushing the air past my tongue and teeth.

It came out as a hush. A breath. No word. No name.

I'd lost my brother's name.

"Thank you," said the Speakthief, her voice scratchy,

high-pitched and sour. "I haven't had a new word in ever so long. Florian," she sang, off-key and ear-twisting, "Florian, Florian, Florian."

"Stop," I croaked. I should have been happy to find I still had other words, but how could I be, when that horrid thing was speaking my brother's name? Taunting me with what she had stolen?

"I tried to learn his name," she went on, "when he came to ask me about—"

I leaned forward. "What? Why did he come here?"

She blinked her hungry-lipped eyes. Her voice smoothed into a soft tenor. "But I thought you wanted to know about the crown?"

"Yes," said Moppe, giving me a hard look. "We do."

The Speakthief sighed, her voice turning weary and monotone, like a bored shopgirl. "Seeing as you've given me a gift, it's only fair I give you one in return. But only one. So, which will it be? The crown? Or *Florian*?"

Again, my own voice echoed out, repeating the stolen word, a word I couldn't even hold in my mind, couldn't even speak silently in the quiet of my own thoughts. A savage yearning tore through me. Why had he come here? Aya said the Speakthief was a prophet. Had he come to learn his future?

Moppe pressed close against my side. She leaned in, her breath tickling my ear.

"I could give it something else," she said. "Another word in exchange for the crown, so you can still ask about Florian.

I could give her custard. Or sardines." She wrinkled her nose.

I managed a wan smile. "I don't think it works that way. She wants words that mean something. Whatever she takes, it'll be . . . important."

"Fine," Moppe said. "Then I'll give her something important."

A lump lodged in my throat. "No," I said. "Thanks. But it's too dangerous. Besides, F—" Air huffed out, and I had to try again. "My brother is dead. Whatever he came here for, it doesn't really matter now."

I took a step forward. The Speakthief tensed, hundreds of small tongues darting out, licking hundreds of lips in anticipation.

"The crown," I said, forcing determination into the word. "Give us the crown."

"Are you certain?" Her voice crackled with age, like an old smoky fire.

"Yes," I said. Moppe reached for my hand, pressing it tight. I squeezed back.

"Oh," said the Speakthief, sounding disappointed. Her voice developed a drawl, mellowing into a baritone. "I cannot *give* you the crown. I don't have it. But I can tell you what I told Terwyn when he came to me."

"What?" Moppe said. "What did you tell him?"

"Terwyn asked me where the crown would be safest. A place it could await the day the true heir came to claim it. And I told him."

"Where?"

"In the keeping of the daughters who dwell between the head of the bear and the tail of the lizard."

Moppe and I stared at each other. "Some sort of chimera?" Moppe whispered.

The Speakthief snickered. In the wispy voice of a young child, she said, "And here I thought you wizards were clever with words."

"It must be some sort of riddle," I said, frowning as I turned the strange phrase over in my mind. There must be some trick to it. I just had to look at it the right way.

Moppe groaned. "Haven't we done enough?" She scowled at the Speakthief. "Just tell us where to go!"

"Where to go." Hundreds of mouths whispered the words back in a ghost of Moppe's own voice, then smiled.

Moppe growled in frustration. "What else do you want, you disgusting creature? Do I need to give you a word too? Fine, how about—"

I tugged Moppe's hand. "Wait! I've got it! It's the letters. The head of 'bear' is *B*. And the tail of 'lizard' is *D*."

"Then we're looking for the daughters who dwell between *B* and *D*?" Moppe frowned furiously. "In the . . . *C*?"

"Exactly! The sea. Mermaids!" But my triumph poofed away like a blown-out candle flame as I realized what that meant. My stomach tightened. "We have to go into the water?"

"Perhaps. Does that frighten you?" The Speakthief's eye-mouths smiled at me knowingly.

"No," I lied.

"Can we go, then?" Moppe asked, eyeing the Speakthief with loathing.

"So soon?" lamented a chorus of voices. "Without even a last word? Perhaps one you might someday wish you'd given away?"

Moppe frowned at the creature. "What does that mean? No, wait, don't answer that. You're just trying to trick us again!"

Several of the Speakthief's mouths pursed horribly, almost as if blowing us kisses.

"Ugh. Let's go." Moppe started backing away down the trail, tugging my hand.

I hastened to follow, stumbling only when my brother's voice floated after us one last time. "Farewell."

12

WE LEFT THE MOUNTAIN the next morning. As we made our goodbyes outside the cottage, I stole quick glances at Moppe, wondering if she'd slept as miserably as I had. My dreams had been full of birds with sharp silver beaks and my brother's voice calling to me from some far place I could never reach. Even though we'd left the Forest of Silent Fears behind, my nightmares traveled with me.

Had I made the right decision? Now I might never learn the truth about what my brother was doing in the Forest of Silent Fears. And I'd never speak his name again, not even in the quiet of my own thoughts.

But he would have wanted me to choose the crown. He loved Medasia. He used to beg our grandfather—the dye merchant's son who had charmed my Regian grandmother at that fish market long ago—to tell him stories about Queen Meda and her heirs. I only remembered them dimly. Tales of moonlit hunts, magical pools that reflected only truth, wise kings who sent their daughters on perilous quests to prove their bravery and strength. Mother, of course, would shush him at once, the moment she caught him "prattling on" about fairy tales.

My brother had even performed with some of his actor friends at the old amphitheater in the hills above Port Meda. They'd put on a set of short plays in the old style, using the same grotesquely beautiful masks the first Medasians had worn in their sacred theater.

It only made the broken-glass feeling in my chest more piercingly sharp, knowing that someone who loved Medasia had been murdered by the Liberationists who claimed to be setting it free. No, I had made the right choice. My brother wouldn't want the crown falling into the hands of Captain Porphyra or any of her vicious band. I had to make sure I got it first. Then we could set everything back to rights and prevent any further bloodshed.

"Best go straight down the south road," said Aya, as she and the two little girls prepared to wave us off. "That will take you to Mermaid Rock."

"I always thought the merfolk were just a story," I said.

"You mean like voice-stealing monsters and enchanted echoes?" said Moppe.

She had a point. I certainly hoped the merfolk were real,

considering they were our only lead on finding the crown. But the thought of having to go into the water . . .

There was no sense worrying about it until we were there. Right now, I needed to focus on getting down the mountain again in one piece, and without being petrified by another of those cursed statues. Whoever had sent the others would not have given up. They'd still be hunting us. They might even follow us here, to Moppe's family. We had to get moving, and soon.

"Stay strong, Agamopa," said Moppe's grandmother. She pressed her thumb lightly to her granddaughter's forehead, tracing a line along her bare brow. She folded Moppe into her arms for a long hug, whispering something in her ear I couldn't make out, then finally released her and turned to me.

"Thank you for everything—" I began, only to falter, my breath huffing out as she hugged me just as tightly.

I tensed, startled by the unexpected embrace. I wasn't used to being hugged. Master Betrys certainly wasn't the hugging type. And Mother . . . The last time I'd tried to hug my mother, she twitted me for mussing her ruffles. She'd been on her way out to a Council meeting, a month after my brother died.

But this was . . . nice. Moppe's grandmother might be old, but her arms were as strong as bands of iron, and for one brief moment I let myself be soft within their strength. It must be nice to have someone to keep you safe. To love you no matter what.

Enough. I had work to do. I pulled away. Moppe had just

finished hugging her little sisters. She tossed a spiny artichoke to the goat. "Try not to eat the whole house," she told him. "And keep an eye on the girls."

The goat bleated, and all four of them watched us as we set off down the mountainside, heading back to the sea.

It started out as a way to distract myself from boredom and fear and the endless downhill trudge. It seemed like a perfect time to give Moppe an impromptu lesson in magical theory, maybe teach her a few more practical spells. But by the time we reached the marker stone for the south road, it had become something far less practical but much more fun.

"Here, watch this," I said. *"Hair. Color. Blue."*

The brown braids hanging down my shoulders shimmered, turning the same shade as the waters crashing and rolling over the sandy cove below.

"Ooh!" Moppe ogled my azure locks approvingly.

"Wait, there's more," I said, and spoke a more complex enchantment that spun a constellation of small pink dots over the blue.

"Polka dots! You made polka dots in your hair!" Moppe actually halted, bouncing up on her toes. "Oh, teach me how. Please!"

"It's not too complicated," I told her, even though it was actually a tricky bit of wordplay to get the polka dots to come out properly. "Just be careful to put the emphasis on the right syllables or you'll end up looking like you've got the spotted fever." The magespeak words for *skin* and *hair* were distressingly similar. I repeated all the words for her until she had them.

"And then it's easy to undo," I said. "You just reverse it. *Hair. Color. Brown.*"

The magic unspun itself as my spotted blue braids reverted to their normal color.

"I don't know why Master Betrys doesn't have a new hair color every day," said Moppe.

"Master Betrys doesn't like using magic for frivolous things," I said with a twinge of guilt. Here I was, giggling over Moppe's crimson-dotted green curls, when Master Betrys was a prisoner. When some mysterious villain was sending murderous statues after us. When the Liberation might even now be beating us to recovering a magical artifact of unspeakable power.

But it was such a relief to laugh. Just to walk in the sun and share something I loved with someone who understood. Because Moppe *did* love magic too. I could see it in her eyes when we finally worked out a way to do stripes instead of polka dots. That familiar spark of triumph. Like the whole world suddenly shifted into something more true, more certain.

It was different from talking magical theory with Master Betrys. I loved learning from her, of course, and it was thrilling to hear her conjectures on this or that recent experiment. But right now, with Moppe, I wasn't trying to learn, I wasn't trying to impress. I was just . . . having fun. And so was she.

"Can we try purple next?" Moppe asked, admiring a tuft of her currently bright-orange-striped green curls.

"No one knows the magespeak for *purple*. That's why our Medasian dye is so valuable on the mainland. They can't make things purple any other way."

"But there must be a word for *purple*," Moppe protested. "Otherwise how did the gods make grapes? Or mussels? Or irises and violets?"

"There is," I said. "But no one knows it. It's forgotten. Like the word to undo *petrify*, or any of the other solitaires."

"So maybe someone could rediscover it," she mused, twirling a green-and-orange curl around her finger.

"Maybe," I said. "There are wizards who dedicate their entire lives to tracking down lost words, discovering long-lost grimoires, or going to places like the Cave of Echoes."

I thought of the word the cavern had whispered to me. The word that would make me a Master Wizard. I still had no idea how to use it. I had experimented as much as I dared, using it on turnips, rocks, even myself. I had combined it with *animate* and *transfigure* and all the standard magic I knew. But it had done nothing.

"But it's really rare to actually find one," I said. "The last I've heard of was *hiccup*, and that was five years ago. They had a gala to celebrate that lasted a full week."

Moppe chortled. "*Hiccup*? And they threw a weeklong party for *that*?"

"The Master who discovered it saved the Zolomeni peace

accords. The Prince of Zolomen had a terrible case of the hiccups, and she cured them."

Moppe had been leading the way along the track, as it zigged and zagged down the final slope to the curve of white sand below. She paused, pointing past a fringe of storm-tattered palms out across the blue. "There it is. Mermaid Rock."

I followed her gesture, squinting out at the distant nub of stone. It looked small. And far, far away. I swallowed uneasily. "Do you think we can find a boat?"

Moppe gave a wave of disregard. "We don't need a boat. It's an easy swim."

There was no such thing as an easy swim, not for me. I bit my lip, wondering just how ridiculous Moppe would think I was if I told her the truth.

But I didn't have the chance. As I opened my mouth, Moppe gave a screech of alarm, pointing to the heights above. "Another statue!"

The marble warrior posed on the overlook, its blank gaze fixed on us. As I watched, it began striding down the trail, heading straight for us.

We scrambled down onto the beach, a narrow band of pebbles and sand clasped between sharp stones. Looking out across the frothing waves, I could just make out the peak of Mermaid Rock. A few gulls swooped above, screeching as if in warning.

"Come on!" Moppe cried as she raced to the waves, her orange-and-green hair streaming behind her. "We need to get to the island!"

I followed her to the very edge of the water, where cold froth streamed through my sandals, chilling my toes. "I can't!"

She turned, incredulous. "What?"

I crossed my arms, hugging myself. "I don't know how."

"You live on an island and you don't know how to swim?"

Heat flooded my face. "Mother didn't think it was a good use of my time. My brother was going to teach me, but . . . Never mind. The point is, I can't swim." I glanced back up the road. The statue was still coming.

There was only one thing I could do. "Get to the island," I told her. "Find the crown. I'll try to lead it away."

"What?" Moppe exploded. "That's ridiculous! You expect me to just leave you here? What if it petrifies you, like it did that councillor fellow?"

"We can't let it get the crown first. And there's no way for me to get to the island."

Moppe flung her hands up in dismay. "You're a wizard, Antonia! There must be a way."

A great wave crashed down just then, sending a shower of salty water over us both. "There isn't time!" I jabbed a finger at the statue thundering down the trail toward the cove. "You have to go!"

"What about *transfigure*? Turn yourself into a fish?"

"That wouldn't work. It needs to be something warm-blooded, something close to the same size. Like a dolphin."

"Go on, then! That thing could be here any moment."

"But dolphins can't speak magespeak. I couldn't turn

myself back. Remember what happened to your uncle?"

"Then change me. I'll swim you across and you can change me back. You can hold my fin." She marched several paces out into the water, stumbling as another powerful wave smashed down. "Hurry!"

I ran the words through my mind, praying they were correct. *"Moppe. Transfigure. Dolphin."*

Nothing happened.

"It's not working!" A storm of sharp shards pierced my chest. Why couldn't I manage this? It wasn't fair!

"We're running out of time!" Moppe cried. The statue had reached the sand now.

I looked to Moppe, ready to order her to leave me, but her lips were already parting to call out three words. *"Antonia. Transfigure. Dolphin."*

What? No! That wasn't the plan! I opened my mouth to protest, but the magic was already prickling over me.

13

I PLUNGED INTO THE WAVES, my body shifting, melting, legs merging, neck shortening, nose sliding back to somewhere behind my head. The water that had been painfully cold was suddenly warm and soft and welcoming.

I flexed my tail experimentally and found myself zooming forward into deeper water. The ocean beat against my skin, a drumbeat calling me to dance. I thrummed out an answering shiver of sound that pulsed through the water.

"Antonia!"

Someone was calling in a strange, frail voice. A two-legged creature on the shore waved her arms at me. *Moppe*, I told myself. The word echoed oddly in my mind, as if it didn't belong.

I had to focus. Even with something clever, like a dolphin, it was easy to forget yourself, to let natural instincts take over. I had to remember who I was and what I was doing.

Moppe fought her way out into the waves. But the statue was nearly upon her, stone hands thrust out, promising the cold eternity of petrification.

I angled my long gray body back toward the shore, swimming as close as I could. Warm hands clutched my dorsal fin. "Go!" she cried. "Go!"

Moppe shrieked as I beat my tail, sending us slicing out into the open water. The booming footsteps of the statue receded to a dim tread. I didn't look back.

The water billowed around me, soft as feather down. My heart matched a deeper pulse of wave and tide. I was part of something grand and glorious, dizzy with delight. I would have swum away into the sun-streaked horizon if it weren't for the thump of a fist against my head, a tinny voice shouting, "Left. Left! Or you can see how fast you swim after I *enlarge* your nose."

I gave a plaintive whistle. There was the most delicious-looking school of herring drifting past only a few hundred yards out.

"No," the voice snapped. "Mermaid Rock! We need to get to Mermaid Rock. Remember the crown? Master Betrys? Magic?"

Magic. A shiver went through me. I couldn't forget magic. I was a girl, not a dolphin. I didn't even *like* fish!

Suddenly all I wanted was my voice back. My legs, my tongue. My *magic*.

"Yes, there," Moppe said. She tapped the left side of my head, and I veered toward a curve of paleness along the base of some rocks.

I swam up to the shallows until the sand brushed my belly and Moppe could scramble free. She staggered onto the beach and collapsed, digging her fingers into the sand.

A wave shoved me against the shore, then tugged me back. I beat my tail desperately, flinging myself up onto the sand. I was done with the sea.

Turn me back! I shouted, but it only came out as more squeaks and clicks. Moppe blinked, then shook her head, a look of dawning horror coming over her face.

"I don't know how to turn you back," she said, in a hollow, helpless voice. "I didn't think—I just—Oh, rot me. What do I do?"

She must be joking. I let off another string of squeaks. She covered her ears, squinting her eyes shut. "What do I do?" she said again. "I don't know how to turn you back!"

But she did! She had all the words she needed. It was so *obvious*!

I rolled back into the shallows, slapping my tail. A wave sluiced over Moppe. She sputtered. "That doesn't help!"

No, it didn't. The fire of frustration burning in my chest only flamed more fiercely. I hadn't asked her to transfigure me. She'd just done it. Because she could. Because she was so naturally talented and powerful.

Well, so much for natural talent. I'd have to find help somewhere else.

I twisted my sleek body, preparing to swim away, but Moppe's desperate cry echoed through the water after me. "Wait! Antonia! Please! Don't leave me!"

The painful desperation pierced my fury. I twisted around to stare at her. She was panicking. That was the problem. Her hands fluttered, twisting together. Her cheeks burned red.

I had a choice. I could leave, give up on Moppe and our quest. Or I could believe in her.

I swam back slowly. She waded out to meet me, her face crumpled with misery as she knelt in the shallows. "I'm sorry. I guess I really am just a useless scullery maid."

I gave a sharp whistle of disapproval, then butted my snout against her shoulder. Catching a mouthful of her orange-and-green hair, I gave a tug.

"Ow!" She scowled at me. "You don't need to bite me," she said. "I know I messed up."

I tugged again, as softly as I could manage. Moppe's expression shifted to sudden realization. "Wait. Are you trying to tell me something? A clue? About my hair?"

I clicked excitedly.

"Oh!" Hope shifted to excitement. "Reverse it! Is it really that easy?"

Nothing about this was easy. But my stream of whistles seemed to give her confidence. She rubbed one hand across her eyes, then stood, shoulders pushing back in determination. She dragged in a soggy breath, then said the words in reverse. *"Dolphin. Transfigure. Antonia."*

My body melted, re-forming and splitting into legs and

arms and soft skin. Nose between the eyes, no more odd echoing sense of space around me. I let out a gusty sigh.

Moppe flung her arms around me. "It worked!"

"Of course it worked," I said, returning the hug awkwardly, still not quite used to having arms instead of flippers. I was back in my tunic and trousers, but they were sopping wet. There was sand in my shoes, in my ears, and a half-dozen other places sand had no right to be.

Moppe blinked, rocking back on her heels slightly. I shimmied and twisted, trying to shake the grit from my underthings. Finally I lifted my gaze, meeting her eyes. "You're not useless," I said. "You're brave and smart and you're a *wizard*, Moppe. You saved me."

Her cheeks were still flushed. She gave a little shrug. "What are friends for?"

Friends. That made my own cheeks go hot. Was that what we were now? Not rivals, not merely allies, but friends?

A week ago I would have laughed even to consider it. But now . . .

"Moppe," I said, "Master Betrys won't care that you have trouble reading. All she cares about is magic, and you've got that in spades."

Moppe had started to cringe away at my words, but now she halted, frozen, staring at me.

"Remember that letter I was reading when you caught me in the study? She said you were a prodigy. She said you had unlimited potential." I forced the words out. Even though I knew it was right, I couldn't help thinking of the rest of that letter. The part about me, and my "middling" abilities.

Moppe shook her head. "But I can't do it. I can't remember the words like you, and I can't look them up, either. It doesn't matter how hard I try. The letters just keep jumping around."

She turned away, hunching her shoulders. A lump fell into my throat.

"It's not your fault," I croaked. "It's just the way you are."

"You mean broken? Useless?"

"Stop calling yourself that! My brother had a terrible time reading too. It was something about his eyes, or the way his mind worked. Mama brought a special tutor over from the mainland to help him. Maybe we can find one for you, too."

"Oh, well, why didn't I think of that?" She gave a bitter half laugh.

"You can learn. I swear, Master Betrys won't care."

"Right, because she expelled us. Or did you forget that?"

I waved a dismissive hand. "She also said to prove her wrong, and we will. Once we find the crown, she'll take us both back. She'll pay for a dozen special tutors. Whatever it takes. You've got more magic in your little pinky than I have in my whole body. I wish—" My voice went froggy. "If I could trade my magic for yours, I'd do it in a heartbeat."

She was very quiet. The waves rolled and rolled, matching my pounding heartbeat. "You really think so?" she asked. "I could be a wizard? Go off to that fancy school across the ocean? Come back with everyone calling me Master Cler, like I'm some la-di-da?" She gave me a smile, but it faded quickly. "I don't think they'd want some island girl mucking around their fine halls and putting her fingers all over their fancy grimoires."

"I'm an island girl too. Remember?" I said. "And if anyone says anything about that, they'll answer to me. I bet none of them have memorized the entire *History of Curses and Imprecations*. There's a really good one for bubbling warts."

Her lips twitched into a grin. "Sounds like . . . fun."

My old dream seemed to suddenly split open, like a rosebud bursting into sudden bloom. Every treasured image I'd clutched tight to comfort me through sorrow and loneliness shifted, expanding. Now, when I pictured myself tucked into some cozy turret, poring over grimoires, Moppe was there too, our heads bent together over the tome. I saw us racing along golden halls, evading the stern regard of some grouchy Master.

But even as my dreams unfolded, Moppe's smile fell away. She dropped her gaze to the sand. "No point thinking about that now," she said, with an odd twist in her voice. "Better focus on finding the crown. It's going to get dark soon."

The sun had already slid low, dimming the sky to dusky pink and gold. Moppe began scrambling along the rocks, heading for the seaward side of Mermaid Rock. "The tales say the mermaids live in what's left of the old palace," she said. "This way."

"The old palace?" I jogged after her, past clods of seaweed and over knots of pale driftwood. "I thought the Black Drake destroyed it after Goros and his daughters died."

"The palace used to cover all of Mermaid Rock. There was a causeway that ran out from the shore. The drake broke the causeway and tore down most of the palace, but there's still some left."

She pointed to a line of broken columns poking up from the rocks ahead, like jagged teeth catching the fading sunset. I began to notice other bits of rubble that had clearly been worked by human hands. Carved arches. Drifts of colored glass that might once have been mosaics. Even a graceful winged torso, poised for flight but armless and headless.

"How do you know all this?" I asked.

We clambered up onto the ruin of an old marble walkway, spanning a crystal-blue inlet. "My father used to take me here when I was little." She pointed out into the deeper waters. "He's the one who showed me this."

The water was a clear blue-green. Peering into the depths, I could make out pale shapes. Arches, pillars, porticoes. Statues arrayed in a line like warriors on parade. And everywhere I looked, the same motif of fringed vegetation, bundles of what looked suspiciously like turnips.

"It's all been sunk!" I said, leaning out to get a better look. Below, a bewitching glimmer of color beckoned. Part of an ancient mosaicked floor showed what looked like a crowned figure standing before a giant, black-coiled serpent.

I crossed the bridge, then scrambled down into the shallow water to get a better look. The mosaic crown itself was pale and glossy—not silver or gold, but mother-of-pearl. Fitting, I supposed, for an island nation like Medasia.

I shivered. Even in this tiled mosaic, the drake was terrifying. The black rings of his massive body throttled a warship. Another of the vessels floated broken, with small figures cast helpless upon the waves. All the more reason to find the crown quickly, so that no one could release such a danger ever again.

"So where should we look for the merfolk?" I asked. "Moppe?" I added when she failed to answer. I turned.

A female creature, her torso shimmering with scales, bobbed in the water behind me. Pearlescent armor covered her shoulders and chest. Her long hair fanned out like strands of seaweed. Dark eyes as remote and merciless as a shark's watched me with cool precision as she swept the tip of a long spear to rest lightly against my collar.

More of the creatures drifted beyond. Two of them flanked Moppe. One held a glittering crescent dagger to her throat.

There was no need to find the merfolk. They had found us.

14

THE DOOR ON OUR CAGE slammed shut with the ominous clatter of rattling bones. Which was probably because it was, in fact, built from the skeleton of some massive sea creature. A vaulted arch of enormous ribs rose over us, bound with braided strips of seaweed. More bones had been woven along the sides, forming a sort of overturned basket, trapping us in one of the pools along the shore of Mermaid Rock. Cool water lapped at my ankles as I regarded our half dozen captors in the dimming light.

"We don't mean any harm," I said.

Moppe was less tactful. "Let us out of here, you sea-witches! Or you'll regret it!"

I elbowed her. "We're here to negotiate, not to insult them."

"How is it negotiating when we're in a cage and they're about to carve us into fish food?" Moppe gestured to the array of spears still pointed in our general direction. "Why don't I just magic them all?"

"How? I don't know the word for mermaid, and we don't know their proper names," I told her. "Besides, if we make them angry, they're hardly going to tell us where the crown is."

I turned back to the nearest of the mermaids, who sat propped on the rocks beside us. "Please, we're not your enemies."

The mermaid girl tilted her head thoughtfully. She was beautiful—they all were, though it was an eerie beauty. Her scaly torso and tail were a deep blue-green, flecked with silver. Small fins edged her elbows, and her skin was a shimmery turquoise. Like the others, she wore armor that looked as if it had been carved from the inside of a giant mussel shell, pearly with hidden rainbows. Her bottomless black shark-eyes watched me, unblinking. Then her blue-tinged lips curved, revealing a mouthful of pointed teeth.

It was terrifying. My mind filled instantly with images of needle-sharp teeth ripping into flesh. All the stories I'd heard of mermaids involved foolish sailors being lured to their doom.

A mermaid with green-tinged skin advanced upon our cage. The others drew back in deference to her. Her coppery hair flowed like molten caramel. A large tooth hung from a golden chain around her neck, sharp as despair. And on her brow, gleaming pale, sat a delicate mother-of-pearl crown.

It looked exactly like the one I'd seen in the mosaic. I gasped, nudging Moppe. "She has the crown!" I whispered.

"Why have you trespassed in my domain, drylanders?" she demanded. "I am Thalassa, Queen of the Sea. Answer, or be judged by the waves."

I tried to remember anything Mother had told me about politics and diplomacy. Unfortunately, the only thing I could recall was that I shouldn't wear yellow to a Zolomeni oath-binding ceremony.

"Our most sincere apologies," I said. "We didn't mean to trespass in your glorious domain. But we come on a great quest, and you are our only hope of fulfilling it to save our people."

"Why should we care about drylanders?" Thalassa demanded. "You are a pestilence to our waters. Our mothers have told us the stories. Before the great ships came, the cove was rich with spiny-shells. Now you come and sweep them away before they are even full-grown."

"See?" said Moppe, in a low whisper. "I told you the Dyers' Guild was taking too much!"

She might be right. I was beginning to realize that the situation was more complicated than Mother had led me to believe. But I had to find some common ground—or water, as it were—with the merfolk.

"The danger I speak of threatens both land and sea," I

said. "An evil wizard seeks to claim the lost Medasian crown, and through it, control of the Black Drake."

A dissonant thrum filled the air, as the merfolk hummed their disapproval.

"The drylander who made the statues move," one of them whispered. "The one we chased away on the half-moon."

"He was here?" I asked. It made sense. That would have been two weeks ago. Around the same time the Furtive came sniffing around Betrys's study. Whoever had sent the magic ferret after her secrets must have also come here, looking for answers.

Queen Thalassa lifted her chin proudly. "One of your kind came poking about the old ruins. The fool tried to use the god-speak upon us. He did not realize that we have magic of our own. He will not trouble us again. Nor will you."

She jabbed her crescent dagger toward the sky. "Tonight, we go to war! Tonight, we take back our waters from the greedy drylanders who steal our fish and snails."

The merfolk hooted and trilled, a chorus of hungry fury that made me want to cower and hide. But there was nowhere to run. The sky had begun to deepen to dark blue in the east. The water in our cage was up to my waist now, and small fish had begun to nibble at my ankles and fingers, possibly mistaking me for a giant glowing worm.

"Wait," I protested. "Please, we can find another way."

"We cannot wait," said Thalassa. "Every day you drylanders take more and more of the ocean's bounty and will not be satisfied."

What had that Imperial Envoy Benedict said to my mother, at the gala? Something about new shellfish quotas? "We can stop that!" I said. "My mother is on the council. I'm sure once she understands what's going on, she'll find a way to fix it. Just give us a little more time."

Thalassa pointed to the great golden moon waxing full in the sky above. "There is no more time. Tonight the moon is with us. The sea is strong and hungry, and ready to strike back against those who would plunder it."

"Please!" Moppe shouted. "You have to listen to us. We can help you. If you give me the crown, I'll make sure they stop taking all the snails. I swear!"

Queen Thalassa ran one coppery finger along the crown, looking thoughtful. "Our people were entrusted with this crown, to keep it safe until the day it was claimed by one who deserved it. But you drylanders have proven you do not deserve it. You have flaunted the gifts of the sea. You have no claim to this crown. It is mine now. I will unleash the Devastation to cleanse the drylanders from Medasia, and then *I* will rule both land and sea!"

The other merfolk trilled and roared, except for the turquoise girl nearest our cage. She glanced at us, then along the shore, in the direction of Port Meda. Distant lamps had begun to spark out along the coastline, glittering in the twilight.

"My queen, it is a great risk," she began. "The drylanders are strong. The Devastation will strike a mighty blow, but it will also enrage them. They come with weapons of smoke and iron. The seas will run red, but the blood will not be theirs alone."

"Silence, Nerine," said Thalassa. "You forget your place. You are not queen. You are barely even a daughter of the sea."

The turquoise mermaid snapped her lips tight, ducking her head.

I slid a quick look at Moppe. "Have you ever heard of the Devastation?"

"No. But with a name like that, I'm guessing we want to avoid it."

"We go now, to prepare," cried Thalassa. "When the tide is high, when the moon rises full, I will invoke the ancient rites!"

"Wait," I cried. "What are you going to do? What's the Devastation?"

Thalassa considered my question. "You will see soon enough. If you survive that long." She swept a grand gesture to the waves, which continued to roll inward with the rising tide.

"Come, Melite, Amara, Ashera, Halia," the queen called to the other mermaids near her. She glanced at the turquoise mermaid, her dark eyes narrow with scorn. "Nerine can guard the drylanders. She's no use for anything better."

The girl made a choked sound. One of her hands curled into a fist. Not that Thalassa even noticed. She was already swimming away with the other four mermaids. Their laughter echoed back across the waves, wild with delight. As one, they dove, flipping graceful tails in a shimmer of blue and green and silver, before plunging down into the deeps.

I glanced cautiously at our captor. She gripped her spear with fierce determination, but her shoulders bowed slightly. I even thought I saw a tear slip down from one black eye. It might have been only a splash of seawater.

"She doesn't look that tough," Moppe whispered to me. "Those other merfolk don't think much of her. I bet I can take her."

"And then what?" I whispered back. "We'd still be stuck in this cage, getting eaten alive." I swatted at a few of the fish that continued to nibble at my fingers.

"Eaten alive?" Moppe looked dubiously at the empty water around her.

I groaned. "Never mind, it doesn't matter." The water was up to my chest now. Before long, our cage would be fully submerged. A thrum of panic beat inside me, but I had to fight it. I hadn't come this far to give up. I had to be cool and collected, like Mother during one of her trade negotiations. *The trick is figuring out what other people want,* she had once told me. *And then convincing them you can give it to them.*

"Let's try to talk to her first," I said. "And this time, please don't try to help."

Moppe rolled her eyes but didn't stop me as I bobbed past her, pressing myself against the cage beside the rock where Nerine sat. The girl stared out over the sea toward where the other mermaids had vanished. I cleared my throat.

"So," I said, "what exactly is the Devastation?"

Nerine gave me a suspicious look, then shrugged. "I suppose there is little you can do to stop it. It is a great wave. Thalassa plans to send it against your city."

"Port Meda?" Moppe said, her voice cracking.

A chill flooded my limbs. "The breakwater will help protect the docks."

"It won't protect the fishing villages," protested Moppe. "The shore-folk will be helpless! It'll be worse than the winter storms!"

I turned to Nerine. "You're right," I told her. "A war between our people would spill blood on both sides. Isn't there some way we can stop it?"

Nerine twiddled a long strand of her shimmering violet-black hair. "Thalassa has commanded it."

"Why do you have to listen to what she says?" Moppe said scornfully. "She treats you like mud."

"Because she is the queen."

"And how did she become queen? Is she the old queen's daughter?"

"No. Our queens are chosen by brave deeds, not bloodline. Thalassa became queen because she endured the Trial." Nerine snorted. "Or so she claims."

There was an answer here somewhere. I just had to find it.

"Then . . . you don't think she deserves to be queen?" I asked.

"No. She is an arrogant, egotistical blowfish."

"And what's the Trial?"

Nerine perked up slightly, showing her fangs. "You must face the Ravager, the greatest hunter of the sea, and survive."

"Ow!" A sharp pain lanced up my leg, and I kicked instinctively.

"What's wrong with you?" Moppe asked.

"The blasted fish think I'm bait, that's what," I grumbled. "Aren't they bothering you?"

"No," she said.

Of course they weren't. I must be the tasty one. I tried to focus back on the more important issue of Thalassa. "So the Ravager is some sort of monster?"

"Oh, it is a marvelous creature!" said Nerine excitedly. "With eyes black as the abyss, and skin that bites, and endless teeth. Its fin slices the water like a sword, and it can taste blood a hundred miles away. It is as cold and merciless as death."

"Sounds like a duskshark to me," said Moppe. "My father used to tell me stories about them. He saw one once, when he was shell-diving late one night. He said it ate his lantern and nearly him along with it."

"So how exactly does the Trial work?" I pressed on.

"You have to bring back a token," said Nerine. "Thalassa wears the Ravager's tooth around her neck. Did you see it?"

I shuddered, remembering the fang hanging across her pearly armor. It had been as large as my palm. The creature itself must be enormous.

But Nerine looked unimpressed. She blew out a huff of air. "It was an adequate attempt. But the legends say the queens of old actually tamed the Ravager and harnessed it to carry them into battle. Thalassa is not so brave."

"What about you?" I asked. "Could *you* harness the Ravager? Are you brave enough?"

Nerine lifted her chin, looking offended. "I have a heart of ice and bones of iron. But that matters little. The Ravager dwells in the everdark, far below." She gave her tail a sad swish. "I cannot swim so deep."

Now that I was closer, I could see that there was something . . . different about Nerine's tail. One of the flukes was withered, barely a ruffle.

"Were you injured?" asked Moppe.

"No," she said. "I was born like this."

"What if we helped you?" I said, already running possible enchantments through my mind. "There must be a spell. Maybe I could make you heavy, or—"

"I have a better idea," said Moppe. "What if we bring the Ravager up here to the surface, to you?"

Nerine and I both looked at her. "How?" we asked in unison.

Moppe gave me an evil and decidedly significant grin. "With *bait*."

15

"I DON'T KNOW ABOUT THIS," I said, peering into the dark waters around my feet. We were at least a mile offshore, drifting just above one of the deep crevasses where the Ravager hunted, according to Nerine. I'd swum out in dolphin form carrying Moppe, and then she had transfigured me back.

Now, I dangled over the water, clasped by the power of Moppe's *rise* spell like a great, glowing worm.

"It will be fine," Moppe said from where she floated above the water several yards away.

"Easy for you to say," I muttered. "You're not the bait. Can't we just get a lantern?"

"There isn't time," she told me, glancing toward the great

golden disk of the full moon as it ascended the night sky. "It's going to be high tide in an hour. We need to stop Thalassa before she summons the Devastation. Which means we need a new mermaid queen *now*." She looked to Nerine. "Are you ready?"

The mermaid girl was fiddling with a length of woven seaweed she'd brought with her, tugging and testing it as she swam nearby. "Yes." She tossed the length over her shoulder. "I am prepared to face the Ravager."

"*Antonia. Lower,*" Moppe said.

"You didn't ask *me* if I was ready!" I cried as her magic lowered me into the dark waters. Icy salt water sloshed against my bare feet, my knees, my waist, my chest, and finally my shoulders.

A wave crashed into my face, turning my protest into a gargle. I beat my arms against the water, kicking uselessly, caught in the grip of the spell.

"Oh, excellent idea," Moppe called out. "Thrashing around like that should get the Ravager's attention."

I finally managed to spit out my mouthful of brine. "You're enjoying this, aren't you?"

Her grin flashed from where she floated in the shadows. "Not at all."

She did, however, lift me a few more inches. I peered up, trying to make out her expression. "You know I'm trusting you to keep me from ending up a Ravager's midnight snack, right?"

"I know," she said, her voice suddenly serious. "I swear I won't let you get eaten, Antonia. By the First Word."

And I believed her. If you'd asked me a week ago if I would be putting my life in the hands of a half-trained prodigy who had humiliated me—and, to be fair, whom I had humiliated in turn—I would have thought it a joke. Yet here we were.

It was nothing I'd expected.

And yet, it filled me with a strange fluttering.

Or maybe that was just my stomach turning over with the knowledge that a giant duskshark might even now be preparing to chomp me in two.

As we waited, I distracted myself by running through possible incantations to counteract a giant wave, just in case. It had occurred to me that I might be able to use a variation of Therenval's Technique to replicate a hundred small calming spells across the waters, to defuse the worst of the deluge. Or perhaps—

"She comes!" cried Nerine, sounding almost gleeful as she held her rope of seaweed ready.

A swirling current tugged at me. A swell of chilly water spun past, just under my toes. All around me, the water heaved and shifted as something massive circled closer. I shrieked.

"Antonia. Rise!"

An invisible hand yanked me skyward, just as an enormous fishlike creature surged from below. I had a terrifying glimpse of bleak black eyes and a gaping maw ridged with teeth. Then it crashed back into the sea.

Nerine dove after it, trilling a fierce cry, only to pop back up a few moments later. "I was too slow. We need to lure her closer."

"Closer?" I sputtered, from above. "Any closer and I'm going to end up shark food!"

"I nearly had her," Nerine said, with an angry swish of her tail. "If you wish to challenge Thalassa, we must do this properly."

"Antonia?" asked Moppe. "We don't need—"

"Yes," I said. "We do. Go on. Cut it as close as you can." I grimaced. Maybe *cut* wasn't the best choice of words.

"All right," said Moppe, lowering me back into the water.

This would be the perfect time for a protection spell. Why had I spent so long memorizing plumbing enchantments instead of charms to prevent myself from being chomped by a giant shark? Assuming I survived, I definitely had some studying to do.

But for now, I could only kick my glowing feet temptingly and try not to imagine how it would feel to have them snapped off by those terrible jaws. Small fish clustered around me, drawn to the light. I held my breath, wincing and trembling at every eddy, every brush of small bodies against my legs. The fear pressed my chest tight, making it hard to breathe. I forced myself to look up instead, to Moppe, who gave me a reassuring grin.

"At least the fish don't have scissors for mouths, right?"

I gave a hollow laugh. She was trying to distract me.

"There!" cried Nerine. I curled myself into a ball, tensed for the rip of teeth, the taste of my own blood. The water surged around me. Something huge pressed close, bumped against me. Nerine tossed a loop of seaweed at the creature.

The harness snapped tight. Nerine gripped the rope, trilling in triumph, heaving back against the Ravager's weight as it snapped and gnashed barely inches from my toes. Moppe had raised me just in time.

The giant shark twisted and heaved like a bucking horse trying to throw its rider. But Nerine clung tight, one hand wrapped around the harness, the other gripping the shark's dorsal fin. The water boiled, foam and spray whipping into the air as the Ravager fought to free itself.

Dread filled me as I watched from above. The shark was enormous! Nerine was a tiny blue speck against its rough gray skin. How could she possibly subdue it?

"Hold on, Nerine!" I called. "Maybe we can cast—"

"No!" she snarled, as bleak and black-eyed as the shark. "I can do this! I just need to convince her to listen!"

"Listen to what?" Moppe asked.

Nerine began to sing. Or at least, that was the closest word I had for the sounds that came from her lips. It was certainly nothing like any singing I'd heard before. It sounded like several voices speaking at once, layered together in a shivering tapestry of sound. The words were strange too, though some of them sounded bewitchingly like magespeak.

Whatever they were, the Ravager seemed to understand them. As the mournful, haunting song spiraled over us, the boiling waters calmed. The great shark slowed, no longer thrashing or trying to throw Nerine from its back. As the mermaid finished her song, the creature bobbed its great head from the waves.

Nerine held herself very still. She gave a faint questioning hum. The shark beat its tail, sending them slicing through the water, together. The mermaid stroked a hand across the Ravager's gray flank, her intense concentration melting into confusion and wonder. She looked like a girl who had just discovered the sun after a lifetime in the shadows. Like I had felt the first time I spoke magespeak. As if a new world had just cracked open out of the old.

"Aha!" Nerine's smile blazed. "Isn't she gorgeous!"

"Gorgeous isn't the word I'd use," said Moppe, peering down at the rows of teeth edging the creature's mouth. I agreed. The shark circled lazily below, but I could still feel her black eyes tracking me with a distressing intensity.

"Look at these marks," said Nerine, patting the Ravager's head, where the dark gray skin was marred by calluses. "She's worn a harness before. She must be very old. Perhaps she is even the Ravager first tamed by Queen Meris!"

"Tamed?" I repeated uneasily.

I could have sworn the Ravager leered at me.

"Come," said Nerine, gesturing to the great dark fin along the shark's back. "I have explained everything. She will take us to face Thalassa. We must hurry," she added, glancing up at the great pale moon. "It is nearly time."

I kept my eyes fixed on the horizon. The full moon turned the rolling waters into fields of rippling black and silver. Thin clouds striped the stars. It might have been peaceful if I weren't riding a giant shark toward a vicious mermaid queen who was about to unleash a murderous wave against my people. You'd think venturing into the Cave of Echoes, narrowly avoiding petrification, and traipsing into the Forest of Silent Fears was enough danger for one lifetime, let alone one week. But apparently Moppe and I were overachievers when it came to embroiling ourselves in deadly peril.

"There," called Nerine, pointing ahead.

I could see them now. Hundreds of merfolk, bobbing in the glimmering waters. They floated in a sort of half circle, all attention turned toward a single figure at their center.

Queen Thalassa's voice rang out across the water, singing into my ear. Some of it was magespeak, mixed with a wordless melody. Thalassa didn't have the same range or depth as Nerine, but it was likely that wouldn't make a difference if she completed the spell.

I leaned closer to Nerine as she guided the Ravager toward the gathering. "She's already begun the ritual! We have to stop her!"

Nerine rapped the side of the great shark's head lightly, and the creature surged forward. The flash of its teeth still made me flinch, tame or not, but I had bigger worries now. I angled my head, trying to make out the words of the ritual.

"What's she saying?" Moppe called from her perch on the other side of the Ravager's fin.

I frowned, recognizing some of the magespeak interspersed into Thalassa's song. *Power. Wave. Imbue.*

"I think she's almost done," I said. "We need to stop her before—"

"Thalassa!" shouted Nerine, as the Ravager's enormous body knifed into the crowd, sending merfolk scattering and screaming. "I challenge you! I have endured the Trial of the Sea and conquered the Ravager!"

The screams became a buzz of interest, even a few whoops of excitement. Singsong voices called out. *Nerine. The withertail has tamed the Ravager!*

Nerine tugged on the reins of her shark, holding it back even as it snapped and snarled. "People of the Sea," she called out. "I come before you to lead. I come to offer another path. Unleashing the Devastation will only lead to ruin. It will bring war and bloody seas. But there is a better way."

Thalassa scoffed, "There is no better way. The drylanders are our enemies, and we must crush them once and for all."

Nerine didn't bother addressing Thalassa. Instead she turned to the crowd of other merfolk drifting in the dark waters. "You know better than this, my people. You see the proof here before you." She gestured to the Ravager. "This terrible beast might also be called our enemy. And yet she has consented to join me, to carry me, to become my partner. Not everything that we fear must be our enemy. But if we send the Devastation against the drylanders, we will turn them into a beast more dangerous than any duskshark. We will kill many, but more will come, with their weapons of smoke and metal."

A murmur of agreement went through the merfolk.

"Then we will fight them!" snarled Thalassa. "We will tear them to bloody pieces. The ocean will boil crimson, if it must!"

"Is that the future you wish?" Nerine called to the merfolk. "Do you wish to raise your children in seas choked with blood? Do you wish them to learn to carry a trident before they learn to laugh and sport in the waves? Because that is the future Thalassa will give you."

The murmurs and mutterings grew angrier. "She's good at this," whispered Moppe, who had been following the debate with an intense expression, almost as if she were memorizing the words.

"I just hope it's enough," I whispered back, my own attention fixed on Thalassa. Even if Nerine swayed the crowd, I didn't trust the vicious queen to simply give up.

Nerine went on, her powerful voice flung out across the dark sea, brave and bold as a festival pennant. "As your queen, I will make common cause with the drylanders. We will work with them to restore balance to the seas. It will not be easy. But it will be better than war and ruin. Are you with me?"

The cheers were ragged at first. Then louder, as a chant began to spread of "Queen Nerine! Queen Nerine!"

Even the mermaids I'd seen with Thalassa earlier had begun to drift away from their former queen.

"Do you think they're cheering because they don't want war?" I whispered to Moppe. "Or because they don't want to get eaten by the Ravager?"

Moppe snorted. "Probably a little of both. But it's the right choice. Once we have the crown, I'll stop the overharvesting of the spiny-snails. We'll set things to rights."

I hoped she was right. But surely Mother would listen to us, if I brought her the crown. I would *make* her listen. I had faced my nightmare. I could face her, especially if it was for the good of all Medasia.

"The people have decided," said Nerine, giving her new subjects a fang-fringed smile. "Thalassa, give me the dry-lander crown. It is time for the promise to be fulfilled."

Thalassa beat her tail slowly in the dark waters. She did not look like a woman defeated. She looked . . . dangerous.

I could feel a buzz of magic in the air, a hum of power waiting to snap into place. The ritual to call the Devastation was nearly complete. I didn't know the word for silence. But there must be some way to stop her!

"Thalassa," I called, as the former queen opened her mouth. *"Hiccup!"*

"Tail!" she sang.

Magic snapped like a jolt of lightning. I couldn't tell if it was her spell or mine. Or both.

"What happened?" Moppe demanded. "What did she do?"

"Too—*hic*—late!" Thalassa tore the crown from her brow and held it high. "You will never—*hic*—have the crown," she cried, "and you cannot stop the Devastation!"

With that, she flung the crown away, out across the waves.

Then she slapped her tail down, cracking her flukes against the water with a crash like thunder.

I yelped, my body tensing even as the pearly crown slipped under the roll of the sea. "Quick, Moppe! Transfigure me! I can still get it!"

But her gaze was elsewhere. "Look!" She jabbed a finger out into the open ocean, to the north. Far off in the distance, a great mountain was rising. The sea swayed and pulsed, swelling higher and higher. "We have to stop it!"

"But the crown—"

Moppe cut me off. "It's going to destroy the shore villages!"

I blinked at the empty, frothing waters where the crown had vanished. Our chance to free Master Betrys. For me to prove myself. With every second that hope slid down, down, down into darkness. We might never find the crown if we didn't go after it now. *Right* now.

But I couldn't do it. Not with the terrible crushing fury of the Devastation swelling and building, preparing to thunder down upon the shores of Port Meda. If there was even a chance we could stop the wave, we had to try.

"I have an idea," I said, then recited the long string of

magespeak I'd been working out while serving as human bait earlier. Unsurprisingly, it had barely any effect when I spoke it.

Moppe's mouth hung open. "What was that?"

"A spell."

"More like an entire grimoire."

"You try it," I said, and repeated the spell again. The great wave had begun to curl toward the shore. It spread as fast as breath, growing wide as a frigate, then five frigates, then a dozen. The merfolk murmured and wailed from the sea around us, captivated by the unfolding horror. But there would be nothing to see, surely. Moppe could do this. She had to!

She started off well enough—the basic calming incantation—but she completely flubbed the facsimile clause.

"No, you need to emphasize the third and seventh syllables of *replicate*," I told her. "Try again."

But she was starting to panic now. I could see the fear in her eyes, how she kept looking past me to the wave. "This isn't working! You have to do it, Antonia!"

"I can't!" I grabbed her shoulders, giving her a tiny shake. "I don't have enough power."

Her expression crumpled. "I can't hold that many words in my head. I'm not like you!"

If only I could give Moppe my knowledge. Or if she could give me her power. Or if we could combine them, somehow . . .

Wait! Maybe that was it. We'd done it before, to grow

and shape the salt pine along the broken path to the Cave of Echoes. Moppe had made the tree grow, and I had shaped it. Master Betrys had even complimented us on it. *Joint casting like that is rare. It requires a particular harmony between the casters, something not just anyone can attain.*

I'd thought it was only luck, back then. But maybe it wasn't. And maybe we could do it again.

"We need to work together!" I shouted over the thunder of the wave. "I'll say the first part of the spell, and you finish it with me. You can do that, right?" I repeated the last three words.

Moppe's brows drew together, but she nodded. Nerine's dark eyes watched us, wide and expectant. In the rippling sea around us, the other merfolk pointed and cried out as the wave thundered toward shore.

I had no idea if it would work, but I had to try something. Port Meda was depending on us. People would die if we couldn't stop the Devastation. I took a long breath, then spoke the first part of the spell. With each syllable I felt a buzzing pressure building inside me. As I prepared to speak the final triggering phrase, I reached out to Moppe, linking my hand with hers. A shiver shot through me.

Moppe's fingers spasmed, clenching so tight I thought my bones might break as she spoke the final words of the spell along with me. The magic rang through us, pure and powerful as the tolling of a mighty bell.

Dozens of small furrows whipped across the water from

where we floated. Merfolk shouted, diving out of the way of the tiny, swift waves carrying our calming spell toward the Devastation. I held my breath, my eyes stinging as I fought not to blink so that I could follow the movements. *Please, let it work!*

My heartbeat thudded loud in my ears, as the terrible thunder swept away. Silence gripped us, broken only by the slosh of waves, as we waited to see what we had wrought. The great tower of water plunged onward toward the shore. Implacable. Unstoppable.

And then, the slightest wobble.

I blinked, squinting. Had I only imagined it?

No! The great surge had begun to waver. Just as the Devastation reached the breakwater, the watery peak crumpled, collapsing. The enormous mountain of water broke apart into dozens of smaller waves. Another heartbeat, and even those subsided. Moon-silvered foam spread in a tattered veil across the sea as it returned to lulling rolls.

I let out my breath in a long sigh of relief.

"You did it," Nerine said, sounding impressed. "You stopped the Devastation."

I slid a sidelong look at Moppe and found her casting her own cheeky grin in return. She squeezed my hand, her fingers warm. I could still feel the shiver of our magic. Because that's what it was. *Our* magic. We'd cast the spell together. It wasn't just luck. In spite of all that we'd been through together—or maybe because of it—Moppe and I had created a harmony between us more powerful than the might of the sea. A connection that still hummed deep in my heart.

"We make a good team," she said.

I squeezed back and matched her grin. "Yes," I said. "I guess we do."

It was dawn when Nerine and the Ravager towed Moppe and me—in a coracle that appeared to have been carved out of an enormous clamshell—south to a rocky spit where we could find a road back to Port Meda, according to Moppe. We had managed to catch a few hours of sleep in the shell-boat, lulled by the waves, while Nerine sent her scouts to search for the lost crown. But they had not found it.

As our coracle scraped up against the sand, I turned to look out across the sea. The crown was out there, somewhere, but there was little chance we could find it now.

"Do you regret it?"

I turned to find Moppe watching me warily.

"No," I said. "I'm glad we stopped the wave. And maybe it's for the best. I'm not sure anyone should have that sort of power."

"I thought you wanted the crown for the glory of the empire," said Moppe, her voice strangely flat. "So they could use the Black Drake to wipe out the Liberation once and for all. Isn't that what your mother wants?"

"Probably. But that doesn't mean I want it. I think"—I hesitated, still trying to shape my fragile new thoughts into words—"I think maybe Medasia is more complicated than I thought. I mean, the Liberation did murder my brother. But it's not as if the council has been fair either if they send people to prison ships just for trying to feed their families."

Moppe chewed her lip. She leapt up lightly onto the shore, feet digging into the sand. I had the impression she was avoiding my gaze.

"I just wish we'd found something to clear Master Betrys's name," I said, as I followed. "Maybe we can track down the wizard who sent those statues. He's the real villain."

"Yes," called Nerine, from her perch along the Ravager's back. "Beware the drylander. Doubtless he will seek to steal it from you."

"Steal what?" I asked.

"The crown," she answered, tossing an object through the air toward us. I lifted my hands instinctively as something round and gleaming and cool smacked into them.

It was the crown. The crown of Medasia. Not lost at the bottom of the sea. But here. *In my hands.*

"But . . . how did you find it?" Moppe demanded even as she gaped at the pearly circlet in my hands. "You said none of the scouts could find it!"

"None of the scouts can track like Rava," said Nerine, patting the skull of her enormous shark.

The creature nosed up out of the water to give me a toothy grimace, as if to demonstrate she was more than willing to take the crown back, along with my arm and maybe a bit of my shoulder as well. I backed up the sandy shore a few steps.

"I can visit the everdark now," the mermaid went on with a fangy smile. "If she carries me down. It was a simple enough matter to find the trinket."

"Thank you!" I sputtered, still not quite believing the silky weight of the circlet in my hands. "Thank you, Nerine!"

The mermaid tossed back her shimmering black hair, giving us a fierce smile. "Be well, drylanders. I am in your debt. If you ever have need of me, speak my name to the sea, and I will come."

Then she gave a sharp trill, and the Ravager sliced off into the sea, carrying her away.

I should have been achingly tired, but the buzz of triumph ran through my bones, making me feel as if I could run all the way to the peak of Mount Turnip and back. I spun around to face Moppe, bouncing up on the balls of my feet. "We did it! *We did it!*"

I don't know which of us moved first. All I know is that suddenly her arms were tight around me, and my arms were hugging her, as we nearly danced with the delight of our victory.

"I can't believe it's almost over," I said, my words muffled by Moppe's curly hair. The possibilities danced before my eyes, bright and beckoning. "Now that we have the crown, we can *make* the council listen to us. Fix the laws, free your father, make proper peace with Nerine's people. We can change everything!"

But I felt Moppe jerk slightly at my words. Her hands suddenly went loose around my shoulders. She backed away from me, clasping her hands across her chest.

There was a strange, terrible look in her eyes.

It was the look of someone about to say something horrible. I knew that look. It had been in my mother's eyes when she came to tell me about my brother.

"Don't," I whispered, though I had no idea what I was protesting. I just knew I didn't want to hear it.

"I'm sorry, Antonia," said Moppe. She took a step back from me, then another. Her gaze slipped over to someone behind me. I started to turn, just as heavy hands gripped my shoulders. I caught only a fragmented shattering of images. A tall, sturdy man with a wind-tanned face. A rowboat, drawn up into one of the farther coves. Then an enveloping mass of cloth, falling over my head and blocking my view entirely. I breathed in a sharp, sweet smell, and darkness took me.

16

THIS TIME, MY PRISON WAS wood and iron. I woke in a dim chamber that creaked softly and smelled of salt and fish. There was no lamp, but my ever-present glow provided enough light to make sense of my surroundings. Wooden floors and wooden walls that sloped just slightly outward. An iron cage of the sort used to transport animals. And a gently rocking floor that was already giving my poor stomach the heaves.

I was on a boat.

I dragged myself upright using the iron bars. There was nothing in my cage except for a single flask of water and what looked like a chamber pot. Lovely.

But it was easier to think of chamber pots and seasickness

than of Moppe. The look in her eyes just before everything went black. The strange mix of sorrow and guilt and triumph.

Behind me, someone coughed. I spun around. It was a mistake, setting my belly heaving. Instead of confronting my captor, I had to scramble for the chamber pot.

When there was nothing left in my stomach, I stood. My legs trembled, but I forced my back straight.

"I could bring you some ginger tea," said Moppe softly. "Sometimes that helps."

"What, you mean it makes betrayal hurt less? So instead of feeling like you stabbed a dagger through my chest, it will feel more like you just chopped off a finger or two?"

She was wearing different clothes: black breeches and a white shirt, and a vest dyed rich Medasian purple. "I'm sorry," she said. "I didn't want it to happen like this. But we had to make sure the crown didn't fall into Regian hands. We need it to free Medasia."

"You sound like a Liberationist," I said.

"That's because I am."

The air thumped out of my chest as if I'd been punched. I gripped the bars of my prison. I'd suspected her of favoring the Liberation. But I hadn't thought she was actually one of them. One of the villains who murdered my brother!

I opened my mouth to speak the most terrible curse I could think of, but Moppe was quicker. *"Antonia. Hiccup."*

A spasm caught me before I could even pronounce the second word, spoiling my spell. I glared at Moppe. "So that's—*hic*—how it is. You—*hic*—lied to me. Tricked me into—*hic*—teaching you magic just to—*hic*—use it against me. Were you—*hic*—planning this all along?"

"No," she said. "I didn't know I was a wizard. I was only at Master Betrys's house to spy. I didn't plan on becoming her apprentice. Or your"—she hesitated—"friend."

"Well, no—*hic*—worries on that count," I said. "You're not—*hic*—my friend. You've never—*hic*—been my friend. You can go—*hic*—rot for all I care." At least that was one good thing about the hiccup curse. It hid the terrible soggy edge in my voice, the tears that were desperate to come pouring out.

Hinges creaked. A trapdoor opened, and two booted feet appeared on the ladder leading down into the hold. I'd slept the morning away in the cage, judging by the dusty shaft of afternoon sunlight filtering down around the newcomer.

She was a woman around my mother's age. She strode toward my cage with quick, purposeful steps, her dark, curling hair bound by a purple scarf, her eyes sharp and watchful. Something about her was strangely familiar. Had I seen her before?

"I told you to fetch me when she woke, Agamopa," said the woman.

"She only just woke up, Mama," said Moppe.

That was it. It was the woman from Moppe's nightmare. The one who had stood there, relentless and demanding, expecting her daughter to shoulder the weight of a mountain.

Moppe's mother arched a brow. "And what else did I tell you?"

"Oh. Sorry, Captain Porphyra."

Captain Porphyra? I blinked at the black-haired woman. "She's—*hic*—your mother? The leader of the—*hic*—Liberation *is your mother*?"

"Captain Porphyra," said Moppe, "this is Antonia Durant."

"Indeed she is," said Porphyra, looking at me as if I were a pastry in a shop window. "You've done well, Moppe, bringing me not only the crown, but also a very useful bargaining chip. Councillor Durant won't dare interfere once she knows we have her precious daughter."

I snorted. "You don't know—*hic*—my mother very well, then."

Moppe frowned. "Bargaining chip? You didn't say anything about that. Antonia's smart. She'll understand, once we explain everything. She can help us."

"I'll help you—*hic*—jump off a cliff, murdering scum!" I snarled. "You killed my brother!"

"You don't understand," Moppe began. "It wasn't like that. He was working with the Liberation."

The words exploded over me, staggering me so that I had to grip the bars of my cage to keep from toppling over. I shook my head. "F—my brother was no—*hic*—rebel. You're lying."

That must be it. I couldn't believe anything she said. She'd pretended to be my friend all this time, knowing she was going to steal the crown for her mother. And now she was trying to trick me again. But I wasn't going to fall for it this time.

"It doesn't matter," said Porphyra. "We don't need the girl."

"She's Medasian," Moppe said, crossing her arms. "I thought we were freeing all Medasians from the empire. That includes Antonia."

"We can only save the ones who want to be saved," said Porphyra. "The ones who still remember who they are." She stalked closer to my cage, peering down at me. The tilt of her head was skeptical. "What are you, girl? Medasian or Regian?"

Both. I was both. In my blood and in my heart, I was both. But obviously that didn't fit into Porphyra's world. And I knew one thing for certain: I wanted no part of the Liberation. They had killed my brother.

I lifted my chin. "Regian," I said. "I'm—*hic*—Regian."

Moppe made a small, sad sound. Porphyra merely nodded, as if she'd expected that answer. "Very well," she said. "Then you will return to Regia Terra, along with your mother and every other loyalist. The Imperial Navy will no longer hold sway over our waters. Those who have been sent to work their lives away on prison ships"—her resonant voice faltered—"will be returned to their families."

She stepped away from my cage, sliding one arm around Moppe's shoulders. "We will restore Medasia to her rightful place as sovereign of the seas, under the rule of their rightful queen."

Wait. What? I stared at Porphyra. "But they all—*hic*—died of the fever. King Goros and his three daughters."

I avoided Moppe's gaze, remembering her ridiculous suggestion that Regia Terra had somehow been behind that.

"They were murdered by a Regian sympathizer," said Porphyra, "a man promised power in the new colony. Fortunately, his betrayal was discovered in time to save the youngest of Goros's daughters. She was smuggled away in secret, to be raised among the fisherfolk, while the rest of the world believed her dead. So that one day one of her descendants could reclaim the throne and punish those who'd betrayed Medasia."

I shook my head. "How do you—*hic*—know that?"

Porphyra hugged Moppe tight against her. "Because my husband heard the story from his grandmother. How the young princess had to flee the palace in secret, disguised as the huntmaster's daughter. How she had to grieve in silence and hide her tears. How she learned to hunt and fish and run free across the sands."

"How did his—*hic*—grandmother know all that?" I asked.

"Because it was her own story. Her own life."

"Then . . ." My brain was stumbling to catch up, to make sense of the fantastic tale. "Moppe's great-grandmother was—*hic*—the only surviving princess of the royal line. Which means Moppe . . ."

I faltered, finally turning to look at my former friend. Her cheeks were flushed, her eyes fixed on the floor as if she wished it would turn to quicksand and swallow her.

Porphyra gave her a small shake. "Chin up, Agamopa. This is your destiny."

Finally, Moppe lifted her head and looked at me, haunted but defiant.

"Moppe," I said, my voice hoarse. I wasn't sure if it was a question, a plea, or a consolation.

"Her name is Agamopa," said Porphyra triumphantly. "And she is the rightful queen of Medasia."

They brought me up onto the deck later, as the sun began to dip low, casting a dazzling net across the waters. From what I could see, Captain Porphyra's ship was somewhere south of Port Meda, a few miles offshore.

I'd managed to undo the hiccup curse by then. It had taken several dozen attempts to get the incantation out between spasms. I still gave the occasional *hic*, though, as I stood beside Moppe along the railing. The fact that she thought my magic was stifled by the hiccup curse was the only advantage I had.

Not that I'd come up with any useful spell to get myself out of the mess.

There were Liberationists everywhere. The deck was a flurry of activity as men and women tended the three enormous sails and moved briskly, carrying supplies. Captain

Porphyra stood at the helm beside a great boulder of a woman who had the wheel in her large and capable hands.

All of them were armed. I saw sabers, wickedly curved daggers, pistols. A handful of the rebels hunkered down along the railing, cleaning out muskets and measuring powder.

And then there were the three rebels who stood a few paces away from Moppe and me, their expressions watchful and intent. Royal bodyguards, I supposed. The youngest of them, a brown-skinned boy only a few years older than me, watched me like a hawk after a mouse. I resisted the urge to curse him. It would do no good to attack the rebels when I had no way off the ship. I had to wait for the right moment.

As I looked out along the prow of the ship, my heart clenched when I saw the name painted there. It was worn, the paint scraped and faded, but I could still make it out.

Victory.

This was my brother's ship! This was where he'd died. I clutched the railing behind me, fingers biting into the wood. My stomach churned, imagining what had happened. The smell of gun smoke. Screams and shouts. When I stared down at the smooth wooden deck, all I could see was the scarlet pool of his blood.

"Antonia—" Moppe began.

"Don't speak to me," I snapped. "You can use me as your bargaining chip, but don't expect me to be happy about it. I have nothing to say to you. *Hic,*" I added belatedly.

She frowned. "Your brother—"

"If you say one more word about my brother, I swear I will curse you with the boiling hives and never, ever give you the counterspell."

The hawkish bodyguard set a hand on the pistol at his hip, but Moppe waved him back.

"You undid the hiccups," she said. "I guess it doesn't matter. Florian *was* a Liberationist. You know I'm right!"

I stared harder at the deck.

"I never met him," said Moppe, "but Mama told me he was very brave. It was his idea to steal the *Victory*. He had it all planned so no one would be hurt. But someone raised the alarm, and the watch started shooting. He was helping tack the mainsail when he got hit. He fell into the sea. They tried to save him, but . . ."

I swallowed, fighting the claws squeezing my breath. I didn't want to believe her. It would be easier to just hate Moppe, to hate the entire Liberation for taking my brother away from me.

But I also knew my brother. He had never been particularly loyal to the empire. He'd loved the stories of Medasia and her old kings and queens. It had been Mother's idea for him to join the Imperial Navy. They'd had terrible fights over it for the better part of a year before he finally agreed to let her buy him a commission.

I remember going to his room that night and finding him sitting on his bed, holding one of the old Medasian theater masks in his hands, staring into its empty eyes. It was the mask of the fox, a trickster character who had rescued Queen Meda from a pack of wolves when she first landed on the island. It was my brother's favorite part to play in the old epics. He was wonderful, prancing and slouching and lurking in the corners of the stage, every gesture rippling with playful menace, every smile a tease and a promise.

I asked if he was sad about enlisting, because there was something broken in his eyes as he stared into the mask.

No. This is important, Ant. He looked up, tweaking my nose. *You'll see. Sometimes our dreams don't turn out exactly as we expect. I always wanted to be a dashing hero,* he said, lifting the fox's mask to his face, grinning at me beneath it. *And now I have my chance. Don't worry. I'm going to help make Medasia a better place for everyone. Including you.*

I gave a sharp shake of my head, banishing the memory.

"Antonia—" Moppe began, but I cut her off.

"Even if he was a Liberationist, he'd never approve of summoning some horrible sea monster that could murder hundreds of people. That isn't brave. That isn't heroic!"

"I don't want to murder anyone," Moppe said, her voice softening. "You remember the Cave of Echoes? When you went off and left me at the chasm, I did ask a question."

I crossed my arms. "What question?"

"I asked how to free Medasia without a war. And Rhema answered."

"What did she say?"

Moppe shrugged. "Some magespeak. But it didn't work.

Or I didn't remember it right. *You're* the one who can memorize entire grimoires, remember? I'm the one who can barely read. The only thing I have going for me is the crown, so that's what I'm going to use."

"You've got a lot more than that," I snapped. "You're amazing."

Moppe almost smiled. My heart twisted, not understanding how someone who was my friend could also be my enemy.

"What about you?" Moppe asked.

I scuffed the deck with one sandaled toe. "What about me?"

"You asked a question too. Don't try to deny it."

"Fine, yes," I admitted. "I asked a question, and I got an answer. But for your information, mine didn't work either." Probably because I was too middling of a wizard. Because this most *certainly* wasn't my dream come true. It was the exact opposite. I was a traitor, my home was about to collapse into civil war, and I was trapped on a boat with my enemy. The Schola Magica had never felt so impossibly far away.

"Then you see why I have to do this," she said. "It's the only way to free Medasia. The Regians will have to leave once they recognize that I'm Meda's heir. It's part of the original treaty."

"So why all this?" I sputtered, gesturing at the ship, the muskets, the promise of bloody war. "Just announce you're queen."

"Because they murdered King Goros and two of his

daughters. We can't trust the Regians. They'd probably call me a fake. I need to prove to the entire island—to the entire world—that I'm Meda's heir. And Mama says the only way to do that is with a show of force."

"And you're just going to go along with that?" I demanded.

"I—I have to," she said. "Everyone's counting on me."

"Do you *want* to be queen?" I asked.

Her gaze slid toward where Captain Porphyra stood at the helm. "What I want doesn't matter. I'm the queen. It's my destiny."

"What about your father?" I asked. "Isn't he the rightful king?"

"He's on a prison ship on the other side of the Windwash Sea. If he's even still alive," she added, her voice cracking. "I'm the one who has to do this, Antonia. It's my responsibility."

I remembered Moppe's nightmare then. How she'd fought so hard to hold that great boulder aloft. The fierce determination in her mother's eyes. What must it have been like for Moppe, growing up knowing she might one day be queen? "How long have you known?" I asked.

She swallowed, looking out across the sea. "Papa told me stories when I was a little girl, about the princess escaping. But I didn't know the truth until after he got sent away last year. That's when Mama told me. She said that since the Regians had taken him away, it was my job now, to be queen."

I could almost see the boulder looming over her, the crushing weight bearing down on her thin shoulders. "There must be another way. Just because your mother says—"

"I'm not doing this because of her. I'm doing it for Medasia," said Moppe. "I'm not going to hurt anyone. I know my mother wants vengeance, but I swear, I won't let the Black Drake hurt anyone. All I need to do is show everyone that I have the crown. That Medasia has a queen again."

"You think you can summon up one of the most ancient and powerful monsters in the world and no one is going to get hurt?"

Moppe said nothing. Boots cracked against the deck as Captain Porphyra stalked over to join us. "It's time," she said.

I watched Moppe and her mother as they stood together near the helm. "You can do this, Agamopa," she said. "You are a daughter of Meda. I know you're brave and strong. Now it's time for the whole world to find out."

For a brief moment, I thought the captain's eyes looked sad, but it might have been only the shadow of one of the gulls spinning overhead. Watching them together, I felt a keen sense of longing. My own mother had never hugged me so fiercely, had never looked at me like that, like I could change the world, like I held stars in my hands. Then again, that love was its own sort of burden. I'd seen that clear enough in the Forest of Silent Fears.

They broke apart, and Porphyra gestured to one of the waiting rebels, who marched forward briskly, holding out a bundle wrapped in silky purple cloth.

The rest of the rebels had gathered on the deck below,

arrayed in silent, expectant lines. One young woman clung to the highest mast, keeping watch over the seas from beneath the snapping purple flag of the Liberation. I stood to one side, guarded by the suspicious boy. My heart rattled against my ribs, but I tried my best to remain calm. If I was going to act, it had to be soon. But first, I needed a plan. How was I, with my middling magic, going to stop a ship full of rebel pirates and an enormous sea monster?

Porphyra lifted the cloth-wrapped bundle, gently tugging free the silk to display the gleaming, mother-of-pearl wonder of the crown.

There were sighs. Cheers. Oohs and aahs. Joyful sobs.

"This is a great day for all true children of Medasia," called Porphyra, her voice ringing bright as the noon sun across the sea. "On this day we reclaim our land. Our crown! Our *queen*!"

Now only cheers, as Porphyra placed the crown onto Moppe's curly head of hair. As it settled onto her brow, her eyes caught mine, and for one moment she looked as panicked and uncertain as she had on Mermaid Rock, trying to transfigure me from a dolphin back into my human form. I wanted to run forward and tear the crown from her head, to cast it back into the waves, to save her from the weight of all these expectations. She was just a girl!

But this was no nightmare to be broken by a spell. This was real.

I must have made some movement, because the hawk-boy

snapped briskly to attention, giving me a warning look and taking a step to block my route to the helm. I glowered at him, but by the time I could see Moppe again, her expression had turned resolute. Porphyra was leading her to the prow of the ship.

The *Victory* bobbed in open waters, just at the mouth of the bay that held Port Meda. "Three ships coming from the port," called the lookout. "Two sloops and a heavy frigate. Looks like the *Thorn*. They're signaling us to surrender."

"Send back our refusal," called Porphyra. "And a demand that they retreat."

One of the rebels who had been standing ready with a half-dozen different-colored flags began sweeping them through the air in precise patterns, signaling the response. Porphyra returned her attention to Moppe.

"Go on," she said. "Call the drake. Let them see what they'll face if they don't heed our warning."

"Moppe," I called, unable to help myself. "Don't do it! You're going to start a war!"

"We didn't start this," snapped Porphyra. "They did."

Moppe met my gaze for a heartbeat, one hand raised to the crown. Hope fluttered in my throat, making it hard to breathe. But her fingers tightened, gripping the crown to keep it firmly in place as she spun round to face the sea.

I had no other choice. I had to stop her!

"*Moppe.* Mmmmph!"

A hand slapped over my mouth, stifling the spell. It was

the hawk-eyed boy. I writhed and twisted, but his grip was too strong. There was nothing I could do except watch and listen as Moppe called out across the water.

"BLACK DRAKE! I, AGAMOPA, QUEEN OF MEDASIA, SUMMON YOU TO RETURN!"

17

AT FIRST THERE WAS only the crash of waves, the creak of rope and wood. Everyone on the ship had gone utterly silent. Then a hum came from below, like a voice so deep you felt the words more than heard them.

Bubbles frothed up suddenly, a dozen yards off the starboard side. The water sloshed and swelled, bulging up in a great dark bubble that split to reveal the beast himself.

He was even more terrifying than the painting in Master Betrys's study: an enormous black-scaled serpent, as big as a naval galleon. Spines as long as spears rippled along his sinuous neck. Slitted golden eyes rose like crescent moons above his wedge-shaped snout. He made the *Victory* look like a rowboat. My stomach heaved along with the deck in the wake of the monster's surfacing.

The Liberationists seemed struck with awe and fear. Even the iron arms of the hawk-boy fell slack around me, his hand slipping slightly from my mouth. But I had no spell for this.

Slowly, the great dark head wove through the air. Gleaming eyes came to rest on the prow of the *Victory*. Cords of muscle slid beneath shimmering twilight scales as the creature arched his neck, peering down at Moppe.

By the First Word, that thing could have snapped her up in a single mouthful! And yet she faced him square-shouldered and resolute. She had always been too brave for her own good.

Desperately, I searched my mind for any spell that could help. The drake was going to eat her! I had to do something!

But the creature made no move to attack. Instead he made an odd, keening noise. His shivering voice was full of secret echoes: *"Long have I slumbered, deep in the abyss. Eagerly have I awaited the command of my liege. And now a queen has returned! Oh, glorious day!"*

He bobbed with delight. It might almost have been endearing if he weren't the size of a small mountain, which meant his motion sent an enormous wave crashing over the *Victory*. My captor cursed, tugging us both back against the ship's railing and clinging to it one-armed as a torrent of water poured over us.

The icy sea dashed my eyes, burning. I sputtered, spitting salty brine. The bodyguard released me and did the same. All the Liberationists had managed to stay upright, clinging to rigging or mast or railing.

Moppe straightened from the prow, her purple vest drenched, the pearly crown tilted rakishly on her head. She scowled up at the monster. "If you're so glad to see me, try not to drown me next time."

The drake blinked at her. *"I am sorry, magnificent one."*

The creature loomed over the ship, his great muzzle opened to expose a terrifying maw of jagged teeth. But Moppe seemed somewhat mollified. "That's all right. I suppose it was an honest mistake."

"What is your will, splendid queen?"

The drake's breath was a stormy gust, filling my mouth and nose with a strong fishy stench. And something else, rank and metallic. I squinted up at the clots of seaweed trailing from the drake's mouth. There were pale splinters caught between his teeth. Lumpy splinters with knobby ends.

I choked back a surge of sickness as I realized they were not wood. This was no time to panic. Besides, he had quite a large vocabulary for a ravenous sea monster. Maybe he wasn't as bad as the legends told.

"Shall I visit destruction upon your enemies?"

Or maybe the legends were entirely accurate.

"Tear the hearts from your foes and let the sea drink their blood?" The creature sounded hopeful as he offered this last suggestion. He even gave what I took to be a smile. It might have been charming, had it not revealed the shattered, yellowed skull caught on one of his rear teeth.

Moppe paled, just slightly. "No, ah, not right now. Thanks." She hesitated, looking to her mother.

Captain Porphyra stepped forward. "We wish you to guard this port and prevent any ship from entering or leaving. If attacked, you will defend yourself. And above all else, you will guard Queen Agamopa and keep her safe from harm."

The drake's enormous golden eyes swung from the older woman back to Moppe. *"I follow the will of the one who wears the crown. Is this your command, most effulgent one?"*

Moppe took a deep breath, then spoke. "Yes. That is my command. Prevent ships from entering and leaving, and keep me safe from harm."

The drake nodded in satisfaction. *"Very good. I have waited long in the dark depths for redemption. I will not fail the crown again."*

"Excellent," said Moppe, sounding relieved.

"Ware the Regians," called the scout in the crow's nest above. "They aren't retreating."

"Neither are we." Porphyra turned to Moppe. "Order the beast to attack."

Moppe frowned. "No, that isn't part of the plan."

"We need a show of strength," Porphyra said. "You're queen now, Agamopa. You have to do what's best for Medasia."

"What, you mean starting a war? How is that best for Medasia?" I cried. If I didn't do something, this standoff was quickly going to become an outright war. But what could I do? The drake was bound to follow Moppe's commands. I had heard the order myself.

I could think of only one thing. It was a long shot, but it was better than the alternative. I knew Moppe didn't want war, but would she be able to stand up to her mother's demands? I couldn't risk it. At least this way I could give her more time to figure out a better solution. Quietly I muttered the spell, praying that the guard beside me would not notice what I'd done.

Then I gave a bloodcurdling scream, pointing dramatically at the boy. "Ahhh! He's got the spotted fever! Look, look, his skin!"

Every eye turned toward us, including the great golden orbs of the drake.

The young guard looked completely befuddled. Then, slowly, he held out one hand, staring at it as if it belonged to a stranger.

Bright crimson polka dots covered his brown skin. He gasped in horror. "What? No!"

All around us, the other Liberationists took a step back, some making warding gestures toward the spotted guard, others giving yelps and gasps of alarm.

"Black Drake!" I called out. "Beware! If you wish to keep Moppe safe from harm, you must take her away from here before she falls ill! Don't waste a single moment!"

The drake gave a perilous bugle of alarm. *"My queen, fear not, I will save you!"*

Moppe waved her arms. "No, you great fool, can't you see it's just a—"

The serpent dove, jaws snapping at the prow. Wood shattered. Moppe shrieked, stumbling back. For one frozen moment, I saw her silhouetted against the open air; then she was gone.

My plan was working a little too well. I'd gotten Moppe away from Porphyra, but only by getting her tossed overboard. And it looked like I might be next. The ship heaved as a great wave sluiced over the deck. I scrabbled for a hold, but the slosh of water was too strong. I lost my grip.

An icy torrent swept me down, down, down. Water closed over my head, beat at my lips as I fought the urge to scream. I clawed through the waves until my fingers found wood. The painted face of a woman floated beside me. It was the *Victory*'s figurehead. I clung to her, gasping for breath.

"Antonia!" cried a voice from somewhere high and distant.

I craned my neck, tracking the sound until I found her.

Moppe hung from the jaws of the Black Drake. She didn't appear to be injured, thankfully. The drake had caught her delicately, the way a cat might hold one of its kittens.

"Do not fear, my queen. I will guard you with my life."

With that, he arced his massive coils, heaving abruptly away from the ship. The motion set off another great wave. I clung to the figurehead as the torrent ripped over me, tearing at my hands, my hair, my clothing.

It was too much. My grip failed. The waves sucked me down, tossed me up, left me gasping. Blinking through the streams of brine, I glimpsed the drake slithering away through the waves.

"After them!" shouted Porphyra, from the *Victory*. The drake might have snapped off the prow, but the vessel was still seaworthy. "Bring her about!"

I gulped and sputtered as the frigate began its turn to chase after the drake.

Relief spilled over me. My gamble had worked.

Except for the part where I was now floundering in the sea. Alone. Unable to swim. I beat the water with my legs and arms, trying to stay afloat. I screamed after the departing ship, but the rebels were already too far away to hear my pitiful cries.

My sodden clothing dragged at me. Lead seeped into my limbs. I tried to scream, but the brine sloshed into my mouth and down my throat. The sea was going to take me; fill me and drown me and make me part of it. I gagged. My head felt strange and dizzy. I tried to focus. *"Antonia,"* I sputtered. *"Rise."*

I jerked up a few inches, enough to catch a breath, before I sagged back down again. Again and again, I repeated the spell, but each time I managed to gain only a single breath. The edges of my vision turned sparkly, then dim.

It was only a matter of time.

I sank down into the waters. They felt warmer now. Almost comforting. I could sleep, pillowed in their soft embrace. I tried to call out again, but my lips were too heavy. Everything was too heavy, and it all fell away.

18

I WOKE IN A SOFT BED, gauzy with gray light filtering in through wide glass windows. A familiar blue coverlet tickled my nose, smelling of lavender. I blinked at the wallpaper before my eyes, a pattern of overblown pink roses I had chosen when I was seven and quickly came to regret when my brother declared they looked more like cabbages.

Home. I was home.

I could almost believe it was all just a terrible nightmare. Except for the constellation of bruises peppering my body and the rough, brine-soaked dryness of my throat. And the deeper bruises on my soul. I felt as if someone had torn out my heart and used it for a game of croquet, thumping it from mallet to mallet.

"You're awake. Good."

I rolled over, wincing at the twinge of my tired muscles, to find my mother sitting beside my bed.

"Mama?" I asked, bewildered.

"If you don't recognize your own mother, Antonia, perhaps I'd best have the doctor back to take another look at you."

Of course I recognized her. Glossy dark braids, green eyes that could find any errant number in an account book, the full lips that curved just so when she knew she'd maneuvered an enemy where she wanted them.

But there were shadows under her eyes, too dark even for her rose-scented powder to cover. One of the buttons along her sleeve was askew. Her fingers plucked at it, as if she was nervous.

Mother was never nervous. Or at least, she never showed it. Something terrible must have happened.

"What's wrong?" I croaked, fearing the worst.

There was a strange, haunted look in her eyes, and when she spoke, each word honed her voice to a sharper edge. "What's wrong is that my daughter was plucked half-drowned from the sea yesterday evening. It's very fortunate the *Thorn* was close at hand, or—" She caught herself. After a moment she went on, her tone calmer. "And thank goodness Lord Benedict owed me a substantial favor. Otherwise you might be sitting in the courthouse prison cells with your Master Betrys right now."

I pushed myself up from my pillow, heedless of the dizziness swirling around the edges of my mind. "I'm no traitor, and neither is Master Betrys!"

"So you didn't help some upstart girl declare herself queen of Medasia?"

"She *is* the queen," I protested. "She's King Goros's great-great-granddaughter. I was . . . I was trying to do the right thing." In spite of myself, I felt tears stinging the corners of my eyes. I squeezed them shut, fighting the swell of misery.

A soft warmth touched my cheek. I opened my eyes in time to see my mother pull her hand away, looking almost guilty. She sighed. "You always were too caught up in books and magic. I should have taught you better."

I had chased after useless magic. I had mussed her dress. I had helped start a rebellion. Nothing I did was ever good enough.

"I—I'm sorry, Mama."

"Apologies don't solve problems," she said, needlessly straightening the coverlet.

"What's the Black Drake done?" I asked, bracing myself for a tale of death and destruction.

"Thankfully very little, as of yet. The beast has retreated to Caphos Lighthouse. It hasn't attacked Port Meda directly, but it's gone after any ship that attempts to enter or exit the bay."

"And Moppe?"

"The upstart queen? We believe the drake has her there, at the Lighthouse. But no one can get close enough to see. Not the Imperial Navy, not even that rebel Porphyra."

Relief swept through me. My plan had worked! Maybe

there was still some way to end this without all-out civil war, if we could just get everyone together to negotiate with words, not muskets and sea monsters. "And the crown?"

Mother gave me a hard look, as if she could see the hope thrumming inside me. "Perhaps we should start at the beginning. There are still many questions. Accusations of treason. I need to know everything that's happened if I'm going to carry our family through this."

And so I told her while I got washed and dressed. Mother helped me herself, something she hadn't done since I was a little girl. Plucking the hairbrush from the bureau, she gestured for me to sit in the slim, velvet-pillowed chair. Her hands moved the brush steadily through my hair, pausing only to take up the comb when she encountered a particularly defiant tangle. I could feel her watching my reflection in the silvered glass as I spoke.

I kept my own gaze on one bit of the gilded frame, where my brother had carved a secret smiling face into the filigree to cheer me when I had the grippe for a whole month when I was little.

I whisked rather lightly over our time visiting with Moppe's family on Mount Turnip. As far as I could tell, they had little to do with the Liberation—though it must have been Moppe's grandmother who sent word to Captain Porphyra so she knew where to find us after our encounter with the mermaids. Even so, I didn't want a troop of gold-coated soldiers marching up the mountain to arrest them.

I also skipped over our nightmares in the Forest of Silent Fears. I couldn't bear to repeat my own to Mother's face, and it seemed unsporting to share Moppe's. Besides, they had nothing to do with recovering the crown and preventing the Black Drake from destroying Medasia.

"And then I woke up here," I finished. Mother was intent on tying a ribbon at the tail of my freshly braided hair. "But there's one more thing. Moppe said F—" Blast it! I still couldn't say his name. "My brother was a Liberationist."

Her hands faltered. A faint crease appeared between her brows.

"It's true," I said. "Isn't it?"

Her lips crimped, as if she were tasting something bitter.

I stared at her. I'd expected shock and denial. But I could see that this was no surprise.

"You knew," I said dully. "You *knew* they didn't really murder him, and you never told me!"

"They might as well have," she snapped harshly, looking away. "He was only a boy. He didn't know what he was doing. Your grandfather filled his head with stories. And of course Florian believed them. He was brave and fearless." Her voice snagged, and she blinked several times. "Brave and fearless and foolish." When she finally met my gaze, her eyes were hard and sharp as cut gems. "They used him. Just as they used you. They killed my son. But they did not kill you."

For the first time ever, it didn't sound like an accusation. She laid her hands lightly on my shoulders. It was barely the ghost of a hug, but it made my breath stop.

I didn't know what to think. Nothing made sense anymore. It was as if someone had taken my life and smashed it to bits and then put them back together, all mismatched, sharp edges. My brother was a Liberationist. And my mother was actually looking at me. Not to criticize, not to correct. Looking at me as if she actually . . . cared.

I caught her hands in mine, clinging to her, searching for the right words to hold the moment fast. "I wish there were a spell to let me take his place. So you could have him back." My voice cracked. I'd thought the words a thousand times, but I'd never said them aloud.

She startled sharply. My mother, a woman who anticipated the turnings and twistings of every conversation five steps ahead, stared at me in what I could only describe as horrified shock.

In the long moment that followed, I could almost hear the cry of the flocking crows, snipping with their silver-shear beaks. Then her grip tightened painfully, as if she were trying to heave me back from the edge of a perilous chasm.

"I don't want that," she said. "I never have. You're my daughter, Antonia."

Deep inside my chest, a crushing band seemed to loosen, freeing my heart to beat again. My throat burned with relief. Things might never be easy and smooth between us, but we belonged to each other. And for now, that was enough.

Finally she squeezed my hands and pulled away. "Goodness, the day will be half spent if we sit here much longer," she said. "I need to start packing a trunk."

"Packing? Why? We need to send word to the Liberation-ists. We need to try to negotiate! And Mama, there's a problem with the snail harvest. The mermaids—"

My mother held up her hand, silencing me. "No. That's no longer your concern, nor mine."

"But you're on the council!"

"Only until I compose a letter of resignation," she said grimly. "It's time to face the truth, Antonia. Our family has no place on Medasia any longer."

"Yes we do!" I exclaimed. "Medasia is our *home*!"

Mother ignored my outburst, continuing as if I hadn't even spoken, "And with the situation this unstable, it's best we consider an alternative."

"You mean you're giving up."

"No. I'm being sensible. And I expect you to do the same." She pinched the bridge of her nose. "We'll leave tomorrow. I've already arranged for a driver to take us to the southern cove. There's a frigate there that will take us back to the main-land. Your great-aunt Eglantine has agreed to take us in while I settle our business affairs. It will be a substantial loss, but better that than losing everything."

"But this is our home!" I protested. "We can't just aban-don it! We need to negotiate with the Liberation, or there's going to be a war. People will die!"

"Which is exactly why we're leaving." She paced over to the wall where I'd hung the Medasian mask my brother had given me just a few days before he died. It was the fox. The trickster who had saved Meda. For a long moment she stared into the brightly painted wooden eyes, then gave a small shake of her head. "This has never been our home. We'll never be . . . It's just not *possible*, Antonia. And it's time we faced that."

She straightened her shoulders, turning away from the mask. "We leave tomorrow at dawn. I expect you to be packed and ready."

I stared out my window, watching a thick fog roll in. It was only midafternoon, but the city was dark, lifeless. I saw a few figures scurry past on the streets, along with a single heavily laden cart. According to Mother, hundreds of the city residents had already fled inland for fear of the drake. Squinting over the rooftops, I could just make out the distant gleam of the Caphos Lighthouse, struggling to pierce the gloom.

There seemed to be a fog in my head as well. It was hard to focus. Memories dragged me back into the events of the past few days. The first time Moppe and I worked together to banish unanswered questions in the dark. Our shared triumph in the Forest of Silent Fears. The dizziness of laughter as we raced back down the mountain, tossing magic between us like a toy. The triumphant spark of our joint spell as it burst forth to tame the Devastation.

The pitiful truth was that I missed her. I missed our adventures, being brave and free and daring to challenge the world together. Moppe had taken a piece of me. She had seen my deepest fears. She knew my greatest dream. We had been rivals, competitors, and maybe in some ways we always would be. But we'd forged something new and powerful out of that rivalry. A way to be stronger together than we were apart.

We'd become friends. True, honest friends.

Until this vast chasm of family and politics and duty cracked open between us. Could we cross it? Could we still find a better way?

I blinked at the distant light. She was out there, imprisoned by the Black Drake's protectiveness and my own trickery. But for how long? What would happen if the drake attacked the Imperial Navy? We stood on the brink of a great and terrible chasm. One more step, and we might never find our way out.

And Mother was giving up.

She wanted to run away to the mainland, to leave all this behind like a torn dress, too tattered for mending. But it wasn't! There had to be another way. Something I could do to fix this.

If Mother wasn't willing to stay and try, fine, but I wasn't going to give up so easily. I pushed myself away from the window, ignoring my half-packed trunk, and began pacing. I needed an ally. I needed someone with the power to stop the Black Drake, to give Moppe and me the chance to set things right. I needed someone I could trust.

I needed Master Betrys.

19

"COUNCILLOR DURANT WANTS THESE right away," I said, brandishing a bundle of papers at the two soldiers guarding the courthouse door. "They're important tax documents. I rushed them straight from the print shop."

The man looked to his partner. "I thought Councillor Durant had left for the day. There's a curfew. Everyone off the streets." He frowned at me. "You shouldn't be here."

"You know Councillor Durant," I said quickly. "She never stops working. And she was very eager to see these reports as soon as possible."

The woman shrugged, then peered at the top page of my bundle. "*A Statistical Analysis of Ten Ways to Improve Your Next*

Garden Fete? She really needs this now, when some giant sea monster's going to destroy the island?"

I tucked the papers to my chest. The "important documents" were actually just a few loose broadsheets I'd managed to collect from the gutter along the way to the courthouse. Obviously my transfiguration spell hadn't been entirely successful. At least my cap and trousers seemed to be working to convince the guards I was a humble print shop girl. "They're extremely sensitive documents. She's very eager to get them. And you know what she's like when she's kept waiting."

The woman grimaced at her partner. "That's true enough. Councillor Durant's got a tongue sharp enough to flay steel."

"Go on, then," said the man. "But then you get home to your master."

A heavy tramp clattered nearby as a troop of goldcoats marched through the street, heading toward the harbor. The guard's worried gaze followed them before sliding back to me. "Or better yet, get out of the city."

I nodded dutifully even as I scampered up the steps and through the great arched doorway into the courthouse.

There were more soldiers inside. Officers in tasseled tricorn hats clustered together, speaking in low voices, their expressions grim. I passed an armory where a dozen goldcoats were cleaning muskets, measuring out powder, and filling their belts of ammunition. Preparing for war. A sick, queasy feeling rippled through me.

I had to find Master Betrys. It had already taken me too

long to sneak out of Mother's town house while she and her staff were busy packing. But I was nearly there. The stairs that led down to the prison cells were through the next door. I just had to wait for the knot of soldiers down at the other end of the hall to move on. In the meantime, I pretended to fish a stone from my boot as I struggled to remember the layout of the dungeon.

I'd been to the prison only once, when my brother snuck me down a few years ago after telling me the story of how the infamous pirate Bloody Jax had died there and still haunted the dungeon. He'd rigged up an old shirt in one of the cells to scare me silly.

The memory cut into my chest. That had been only a few weeks before he died. He must already have been working with the Liberation by then. But he'd said nothing. Why hadn't he told me? And what would he think now, of Porphyra's plans? Was this what he had hoped for? Medasia on the brink of war?

He'd gone to the Speakthief to learn about the future. Had he known he was going to die? Did he know it would come to this?

The soldiers finally moved on, leaving the hallway clear. I darted through the doorway, then down a short flight of steps to a narrow hall flanked by storage niches holding the soldiers' clothing and lunch baskets. Cautiously, I peered around the corner into the next passage: there was the door to the prison cells.

And a soldier guarding it.

I ducked back instantly, my heart pounding. How was I going to get past him? I doubted he would believe my printer-girl story, and besides, that would only work if I could convince him Mother was in the dungeon. I didn't know the words for *invisible* or *silent*.

There must be some other magic I could use. I could try to enlarge his nose, but it might not be enough to render him helpless.

Or maybe I could distract him. . . .

If I could just draw the soldier's attention away for a few moments, I might be able to slip through the door without him noticing. I scanned the hallway around me for anything I could throw. My gaze fell on a lunch basket in one of the niches. A heel of bread poked out from one side, while a bulbous purple-and-white root bumped up from the other.

A turnip!

Before I could doubt myself, I seized the vegetable from the basket, then whispered three words in magespeak: *Turnip. Animate. Dance.*

The thing wriggled in my hands. Not powerfully, not bounding and leaping as it would have if Moppe had been here. But enough, I hoped, to give me the distraction I needed.

Creeping to the corner, I rolled the turnip down the hallway.

The root toppled end over end, rolling several feet beyond

the guard. I held my breath as the turnip spun upright, roots quivering, and began to sashay along the flagstones.

I couldn't hear the man, but I could see the sudden alarm in his abrupt, jerky movements. He ran forward, making a swipe at the turnip, only to have it pirouette out of his grip. The soldier cursed, crouching to make another attempt, his back to the door.

I dashed forward, heaved open the heavy portal, then slipped through and tugged it shut again. My breath rasped loudly, echoing from the stones. Outside, occasional thumps and curses continued. My turnip was doing well, but it wouldn't occupy the guard forever. I had to be quick.

My golden glow created a ring of light upon the chilly stones. There were no lamps lit, only a few dark torches. My footsteps echoed as I made my way deeper, following the tunnel-like passage, peering into each barred chamber I passed.

All were empty.

"Master Betrys?" I whispered.

There was no answer.

But of course there wouldn't be a response. She'd be gagged, of course. I quickened my steps, trying another passage. She must be here somewhere!

Something scuffed in the distance. I couldn't tell if it was ahead of me or behind me. Was it Master Betrys? Or a soldier come to arrest me? I hurried on, rushing from cell to cell, but found nothing.

Nearly galloping, I raced around another corner, seizing the next set of chilly iron bars and peering within. A shape loomed before me, terrified eyes wide and unblinking, arms raised as if to ward off a blow.

I shrieked.

Then I realized what I was looking at. Councillor Pharon! Locked in stone forever. I stared into his eyes, horror seeping into me. Could he see me? Was he trapped there, forever imprisoned in stone but aware, awake, utterly helpless?

And the wizard who had done this was still out there somewhere. I'd been so certain they were a part of the Liberation, yet I'd seen no sign of wizardry among Captain Porphyra's crew. And surely if there were rebel wizards, they would have detected Moppe's power long ago and trained her themselves.

So who had attacked Betrys and Pharon?

Who had sent the statues into the old ruins, and after Moppe and me?

I took a shaky step back, unable to bear looking into the petrified man's gaze any longer.

"If you're looking for Master Betrys, I'm afraid I've arranged for her to be transferred to a more secure location," said a man's voice behind me.

I spun round to find Imperial Envoy Benedict standing in the passage. He tilted his head, blue eyes twinkling. "But since you've gone to all this effort, perhaps you'd like to stay awhile and continue our discussion of magical theory?"

My throat seized. I couldn't have spoken a spell even if I had one. And I didn't. My mind was too busy trying to make sense of what was happening.

Benedict. The failed wizard. The imperial envoy.

"You needn't worry," he said, his resonant voice almost a purr. "I'm not here to arrest you. In fact, I admire your ambition. I'd thought Myra would have you bundled off on a ship back to the mainland by now."

I coughed, finding my voice. "She tried. But I—I couldn't leave. I had to do something. There must be some other way to set things to rights. Something other than war."

"You see, I knew from the moment we met you were a girl after my own heart," he said. "I agree completely. Far better to find a peaceful solution. Would you care to discuss the matter? Perhaps over some light refreshments?"

Benedict pulled something from his pocket and tossed it into the air. It looked like a plain white handkerchief and a few coins, but as the items arced downward he murmured something under his breath, and they began to change.

The two coins grew spindly, folding themselves into glittering brass chairs with graceful backs and clawed feet that clattered down onto the stones. The handkerchief rippled and fluttered between them, becoming a tea table complete with steaming pot, sugar, cream, and a platter of small cucumber sandwiches and frosted cherry cakes.

I gaped. I couldn't help it. It was a masterful display of enchantment and transfiguration. I wasn't even sure Master

Betrys could have managed it—not that she would try. She'd call it unnecessary frippery. Magic for the sake of magic alone, meant to impress and intimidate.

And it had worked. In spite of myself, my mind was buzzing with the puzzle of it. "How did you manage to heat the tea and chill the cream in the same spell?" I burst out, in spite of myself. "Doesn't the Rule of Opposites make that—"

"Impossible?" Benedict took a seat in one of the chairs, crossing his long legs. He began pouring the tea. "In a single spell, yes, but this is actually a series of nested incantations. I must say it's refreshing to encounter a young person with so strong an interest in magical theory. Usually it's all about the lightning bolts and fireballs at your age."

I sank into the other chair as the full weight of what I'd seen fell over me. "I don't see how you couldn't have earned your mastery if you can cast something like this."

"I never said I didn't *earn* it," he bit back. "I had to grind and scrape and study for every scrap of magic I learned, unlike some of my fellow students. There was one . . . I swear she was born with the voice of a god. It came so easily to her. It was *infuriating* to watch the Masters heap her with praise, when I'd practiced all night and she'd barely looked at the grimoire. To see her receive her mastery, while I"—he gave a hollow laugh—"I was sent home. Denied the one thing I loved most of all."

His eyes seemed to spark with the flames of longing and envy as he stared into the distance of memory. An expression so familiar it made my own heart jolt. I'd probably worn that same expression when I stood in Master Betrys's study, reading that letter. A ghost of it still haunted my heart, ready to come howling back if I wasn't careful.

But things were different now, and not just because the future of Medasia was at stake. A week ago I'd thought that if only I had Moppe's power, it would solve all my problems. But life was more complicated than that, just as Master Betrys had tried to teach me. If only she were here now!

"But they will see how wrong they were," continued Benedict, sounding almost wild now. "Because I'm the only one who can restore order to Medasia." His attention snapped back to me, so sudden it caught the breath in my chest. "And you, my dear girl, are going to help me."

20

THE TRUTH HIT ME square in the chest, making me gasp. "It was *you*! You're the wizard who sent the Furtive! The one who petrified Councillor Pharon! The one the mermaids saw poking around the sunken palace!"

Something flickered behind Benedict's eyes, but he only smiled, nodding as if acknowledging a hit in a duel. "Yes."

"You attacked me!"

"I was sent here to ensure the dominion of Regia Terra." He sipped his tea, looking in no way discomfited by the charges. "I discovered that Councillor Pharon was a Liberationist sympathizer. A danger to society. I couldn't risk him gaining the Medasian crown. A hard choice, but a necessary one."

"Then you can order the guard to set Master Betrys free," I said. "She can help stop this war!"

He gave a regretful shake of his head. "I'm afraid not. Julien's allegiance remains questionable. I need to know that those I'm working with will put the needs of Regia Terra first and foremost. I need an ally who understands what is at stake. Someone like you, Antonia."

"What do you mean?" I shook my head, disbelieving. "You don't need me. You can do all this." I waved at the enchanted tea table. "You could just magic the crown away from Moppe."

"Not easily," he said, swirling his cup. "It's rather more difficult when there's an enormous sea serpent protecting her. Not to mention the fact that there's no known magespeak for *crown*."

I gave a tight huff of laughter. "How do you expect me to help with that? I'm not even powerful. I'm—I'm just a middling wizard."

Benedict frowned. "If you can understand Therenval and the Rule of Opposites, you're hardly middling." His blue eyes transfixed me. "Unless *you* believe it. Do you?"

I should. I'd seen the words in clear black ink, in that letter of Master Betrys's I'd read what felt like ages ago. I'd witnessed my own failures, the faltering spells, the lack of potency. Especially compared to what Moppe was capable of.

And yet . . . deep in my heart, a small, defiant flame burned. I might not have raw power, but that didn't mean I wasn't skilled. I was the one who had come up with the spell to stop the Devastation, who had realized that Moppe and I could cast it jointly. Even on my own, I'd managed to trick the Black Drake, giving us this chance to find a peaceful solution. My power would never be as bright and fierce as the sun, but even a single candle could light the dark.

"No," I said. "I know my own strength. But that doesn't mean I'm going to help you. Moppe is my friend."

Benedict arched one dark brow. "Indeed? She betrayed you, cast you aside, and you still wish to help her? The girl who stole your apprenticeship?"

I swallowed. I couldn't deny the envy that still smoldered deep inside me. But that didn't mean it was right. That didn't mean Moppe couldn't also be my friend, if only we could find a way to navigate this storm to safer shores.

Benedict sighed. "If you truly do care for the girl, then all the more reason to help me. As I understand it, we have you to thank for ensuring that the Black Drake hasn't already caused considerable devastation."

"Er. Yes. I convinced it to take Moppe away, to keep things from getting any worse."

"You see?" He smiled. "You've already saved countless lives, Antonia. Now you have the chance to save even more. I have it on good authority that an imperial armada is on its way here with orders to destroy the Black Drake by any means necessary, and to apprehend and execute all the traitors."

"Execute?" I croaked. "Moppe can't be a traitor, not if she's actually Meda's heir!"

"Based on the say-so of some traitorous pirate? That's hardly proof." He made a *tsk*ing noise. "Perhaps, if we could end this now, obtain the crown, and persuade the Liberationists to surrender, then I *might* be able to call for mercy. But the moment Regian blood spills, this becomes war. And that moment is dangerously close."

He was right about that. I felt it, the tide of the future surging in, perilous and unrelenting. But that didn't mean I trusted the man.

I had to find out what his plan was. Most of all, I had to get to Moppe. Together, we could fix this. I was sure of that.

I used every trick Mother had ever taught me to control my expression. "There must be something we can do," I said carefully.

Porcelain clinked as Benedict set down his cup. "There is. We simply need to convince your friend to relinquish the crown. So," he said. "Will you help me?"

A muscle in my jaw twitched. I turned away to hide it, pretending to push back a loose lock of hair. "And what will happen to Moppe?"

"She's a child," Benedict said, waving his hand dismissively. "If she yields and gives up her claim to Medasia, then all will be forgiven."

It was a false promise, yet it gave me courage. There was hope. Those brief, tantalizing dreams I'd shared with Moppe could still come true.

The scent of paper and ink teased my nose, as if I already

sat curled in a corner of the Grand Library, bent over a grimoire. I could almost feel the weight of the heavy silken stole of mastery being laid across my shoulders as cheers rippled up from the crowd at my graduation. I turned to grin at Moppe, and—

I blinked, tugging myself free of the bewitching dream. I just had to play along a little longer, use Benedict to get myself to Caphos Lighthouse. Moppe and I could fix this. Together. We'd stopped the Devastation. We could stop this. Dragging in a steadying breath, I set the words on my tongue as if they were an incantation.

"Yes," I said. "I'll do it."

The thick air hung damp and gray as we arrived at the causeway. To the west I could see the fuzzy, pale disk of the veiled sun begin to sink toward the horizon. The plaintive cry of the foghorn echoed over the sea. I knew the drone was meant to warn nearby ships, but somehow it felt much more personal right now. I could be making a terrible mistake. Benedict was dangerous. He could petrify me if he suspected I wasn't wholly on his side.

"Are you prepared?" asked Benedict, as we advanced along the stone bridge out over the sea.

I forced myself to breathe, slow and deep. Soon this would all be over. But the drum of fear had settled into my bones. Not just fear of what Benedict could do, but fear of the drake itself. I had a plan, but no guarantee it would work.

If it didn't—if blood spilled and war broke out—I could

lose everything. I shivered, thinking of the streets of Port Meda clotted with wounded soldiers. The brilliant blue skies shrouded by the smoke of cannons. What would become of Moppe? And Betrys? Even my indomitable mother might fall, her reputation ruined by my failure. And deep inside, something else might break. This kindling ember of faith that I had the power to change things—I had to keep it burning.

"Yes," I said. "I'm ready."

We'd reached the end of the causeway, where it opened up onto the craggy island that held the Lighthouse itself. Benedict halted in the shadows of one of the stony outcroppings. "Excellent. I won't risk going farther. Best she see only you. She knows you. Trusts you."

That's what I was counting on. I forced myself to meet his slippery grin with my own false smile. Then I continued on, toward the Lighthouse.

"You're doing the right thing, Antonia," Benedict called after me.

Yes. I was. I knew it, deep in my bones, with every step that brought me closer to my friend. To the *only* person I could trust right now to do the right thing. I loved and feared my mother. I admired and respected Master Betrys. But that wasn't enough right now. I needed the person who had seen me at my worst. Who had forgiven me once already. Who knew my shames and fears and had shown me hers in turn. The person who'd nearly died with me, more than once. I needed Moppe.

The fog was breaking up. Ragged sheets of haze rose from

the sea like pale gray flames. I could see the rocky base of the Caphos Lighthouse. Or rather, I could see the creature coiled atop it.

The drake had twisted himself around the base of the lighthouse. As I drew closer, I heard his familiar hiss, scraping like metal chains over stone.

"But it is not safe, glorious queen."

"If you don't let me out of this infernal tower, I swear I'll transfigure you into a worm!"

"You ordered me to keep you safe above all else," the drake replied, sounding slightly hurt. *"I am only following your command."*

"This wasn't what I meant!" she exploded. "How many times do I need to explain it?"

"I will not fail my duty again," said the drake. *"I am bound to serve the crown."*

I had crept close enough now that I could see Moppe. She stood along the balcony that wrapped around the lighthouse, which put her eye-to-enormous-eye with the drake.

"I order you to take me back to the *Victory*," she said, in a voice ragged with frustration. "And look, I'm wearing the crown." She jabbed a finger at the pearly circlet perched on her black curls. "So obey my command! Please?"

The drake shivered his coils, the tremor running all the way to the very tip of his tail. He shook his head, as if she'd just told him that one plus one was three. *"It is not safe. You will fall ill of the spotted fever!"*

"There is no spotted fever! That was a trick!"

"There were spots." His massive head wove closer to her, with ominous certainty. *"I saw them. I have very good eyesight."*

"So you're keeping me safe, even from my own orders?" Moppe demanded.

His jaws curved into something that might have been a smile if his teeth had not been so very, very sharp. *"Of course. You mortals are very delicate and prone to self-destruction."*

I could hear Moppe's groan even from my hiding spot behind a boulder. The creature's devotion was charming. It did, however, present a problem if my plan wasn't enough to lure him away. I brushed off my trousers and stepped out from my hiding place.

Moppe saw me first. Her brows arched in surprise, but she smiled. It caught me like an arrow in my chest.

"Queen Agamopa!" I called out as I jogged forward. "Thank goodness you're alive!"

The drake gave a mighty growl, coiling so protectively around the lighthouse that the ancient stones creaked. *"Stay back! I will not allow harm to befall my liege!"*

It took all my courage not to quail as the monster's ravenous jaws snapped above my head. Small pale fragments of bone pattered on the stones around me. That horrible skull leered down at me, still impaled on the drake's tooth, a foreshadowing of my own fate if the creature realized what I was doing.

I set my fists on my hips, doing my best to match his fury. "Look at her!" Under my breath, I murmured the polka-dot spell.

The drake snapped his jaws closed and tilted his head in befuddlement. He gave a nervous rumble, turning his craggy snout toward the tower. Then a snort of horror. *"My queen? You have the spotted fever!"*

My spell had worked rather nicely, I had to admit. The bright crimson spots stood out ominously against Moppe's dusky olive cheeks, ears, neck, even her hands.

"Quickly," I cried. "You must find her the cure! Isn't that right, glorious queen?"

"Er, yes," Moppe said, thankfully catching on to my scheme. "Go now! Find the cure. Or else I will perish!" She swooned dramatically against the balcony. Honestly, I thought she was rather overdoing it, but it was clearly working. The spiny ridges along the drake's head quivered with dismay.

"Tell me what I must do!" the creature demanded. *"What is the cure?"*

Moppe froze, looking down to me with wide, desperate eyes.

"Chocolate!" I shouted. "It's well known that a cup of hot chocolate every day will ward off the deadly spotted fever."

"Where can I find this chocolate?"

Oops. I hadn't quite thought this part through. "Ah. Well, there's a shop right on the harbor called the Bee and Bonnet. But you mustn't attack it or knock it down. Just ask the woman who works there to make you a pot. And don't hurt anyone! Right, Queen Agamopa?"

"Yes," she called down quickly. "Ask nicely. Don't break anything. Or eat anyone!"

The drake bobbed his head eagerly. *"It will be done, Mighty Majesty, with the utmost haste! Do not die until I return!"*

Slick as oil, he unfurled his coils, slithering down into the waves to ripple away in the direction of Port Meda. I just hoped he would follow these commands as faithfully as his charge to protect Moppe. And that Mistress Bonnet would not run screaming in terror.

A drum of footsteps turned me back toward the tower. Moppe burst out from below, jogging to meet me and grinning like a loon. "It worked! I can't believe it. You saved me!" She charged forward, wrapping her arms around me in a desperate embrace. "Thank you," she whispered in my ear. "I knew you were a true Medasian. And a true friend."

"We don't have much time," I said. "I came here with Benedict, the imperial envoy. He thinks I'm here to help him get the crown, but he's up to something. He's the one who sent those statues after us."

Moppe pulled back, frowning.

A wave of power shivered through the air. A rich, resonant voice called out something in magespeak, too far away for me to make out clearly. Benedict.

"Antonia, I—" Moppe gave a gasp, the sound cutting off abruptly.

"Moppe?" I took a step closer, waiting for her to say something, to tell me how true friends like us could get through anything, how we'd make peace, make a brighter future for Medasia.

But she only stared, one hand outstretched, as if reaching

for me. Skin shading gray. Eyes going wide with fear, then blank as a statue's.

That's when I realized what the spell had been.

What Benedict had cast, once I had sent the Black Drake away and distracted Moppe.

Petrify.

21

THE SEA WINDS WHIPPED my hair, slapping it against my face as I stood there confronting the painful truth. She was . . . *gone*. I tried to step forward, but my legs wouldn't move. Horror gripped me tight. Her empty stone eyes held me transfixed.

Petrify was a solitaire.

A spell that could never be undone. She would be trapped in stone forever. Until the waves crushed her body and the wind ground her features away to a smooth nothing.

Would she know? Was her mind still alive, somehow, in there?

Oh gods. What had I done?

I might as well have killed her.

My knees went watery. I stumbled, falling against the gritty earth. I wanted to sink into it. Bury myself away from all of this. Maybe I was still in the Forest of Silent Fears. Maybe this was all just some test, a nightmare I could wake from with the help of a magic goat and a friend's voice.

But my friend's voice was silent now. Gone forever, because of me.

A scrape of sound tugged me from my misery. I looked up to find Benedict standing beside Moppe's stone form.

"Excellent work," he said, as if I were a child he'd just taught to swing a croquet mallet.

All my horror and guilt and sorrow boiled up at the sight of his hateful smile. "You!" Fury shook my voice. "You *used* me! You petrified her!"

"I'm afraid it was a necessary price to pay," he said, plucking the pearly crown from Moppe's stone curls. "You see, there's no way I could do this, otherwise."

He twirled the crown around his finger, then propped it on his own head, giving it a rakish tilt. "Besides," he said, "she was your rival. Now she's out of your way. The path is clear, Antonia. Straight to the Schola Magica and beyond. Everything you wanted can be yours."

The air in my chest huffed out. "I didn't want *this*!"

"No? You didn't want wizardry? Power? Acclaim? For the world to recognize your abilities?"

Curse it all. "Yes," I admitted, my voice raw and soggy. "But not this way!"

"You'll thank me, eventually," he said. "Or if not, then I suppose you never really wanted to succeed. Perhaps you've spent too much time with your dear Julien, and she's already smothered your ambition with her petty ethics and rules. She was the same way when we were at the Schola together. What a waste." His lip curled. "This is your chance to be someone who matters, Antonia. You can take it, or you can fade away to nothing. Like your 'friend' here."

He tweaked Moppe's stone nose, smirking.

Boiling warts were too good for him, but at least they were a start.

Just as I prepared to curse the insufferable man, a triumphant hiss interrupted, proclaiming, *"I have acquired the chocolate!"*

The drake coiled up from the sea. A barrel was tied around his throat, sloshing with promise. As he beheld the scene before him, his eyes narrowed in suspicion.

He looked between Moppe's frozen form and Benedict wearing the crown. *"Glorious . . . king?"*

"Yes, I am your king," Benedict called out. "And I command you, by the power of this crown, to serve me."

"But I am sworn to guard the queen from harm."

Benedict chuckled. "As you can see, Queen Agamopa is perfectly safe. Nothing can harm her now." He rapped his knuckles against her forehead.

The drake's coils shifted uneasily.

"And the crown compels you to obey me, is that not true?" asked Benedict.

"He's a liar!" I shouted. "Don't listen to him! Moppe is your queen!"

The drake shuddered in mournful agony. *"I must do as the crown commands."*

"Excellent. Then I command you to go forth, find the *Victory*, and destroy it."

The drake gave a miserable whistle that set gooseflesh over my skin. He struggled for a long moment, before finally dipping his great head. *"It will be done."* Then he slithered away into the waves once more.

"You're just going to kill them all?" I demanded. "Without a trial?"

"I meant what I said, Antonia. You have a promising future. One I'd like to encourage. But you'll never become a Master Wizard if you get caught up in treason."

I flinched back. "I don't care about becoming a Master Wizard!" The words burst out of me, unexpected, but so sharp I knew they were true. My voice twisted higher, pierced by agony. "You murdered my best friend!"

The briefest flash of disappointment crossed Benedict's face. Then he shrugged. "So be it. You aren't the girl I thought you were. Unfortunate."

He swept his hands through the air. I darted back a step, but he only chuckled. "Don't worry. I have bigger concerns than you, Antonia. And you've made it clear you don't have the will or the power to stop me."

He gave me one last taunting smile, then stalked down to the frothing waves, murmuring an incantation. Under the flourish of his fingertips, the waves spun up, forming a glittering craft of diamond-bright ice. He leapt out onto the enchanted boat, setting it in motion with another gesture. Without a backward glance he sailed off after the Black Drake, leaving me alone.

How had it all gone so wrong? To think the greatest struggle I was facing ten days ago was how to enchant a turnip to dance. To think I'd dared ask the Cave of Echoes how to make my dreams come true and expected an answer. Maybe this was it. Maybe Rhema's strange incantation had set this all in motion, to give me the chance to accept Benedict's offer.

Maybe the only way I could hope to attend the Schola was by betraying a friend. But I would never trade Moppe's friendship for that. It was so clear now. Now that she was gone.

I huddled against the cold stones, knees pulled to my chest. None of my magic could help now. There was no cure for *petrify*. Maybe the gods knew it once, but they were gone. Dead or slumbering, it didn't matter.

If only I knew the word to unwind time, to go back to that day in the Cave of Echoes. I'd give up the Schola Magica, everything, if it meant I could undo this.

That would be my dream come true.

"Please! Help her!" I screamed, not even knowing to whom I was begging. The gods were gone. Master Betrys was imprisoned. I was alone.

Help her. Help her. Help her.

The words echoed back from the stones around me.

Strange that I could hear them over the crash of the waves and the ragged edge of my own breath. Something fluttered in my chest. It wasn't strong enough to be hope. More like the scratch of a damp match in the darkness, a prayer the light would catch.

What if Rhema had given me the answer I needed? Maybe that was why the word hadn't worked yet. Because it was waiting for the day when my dreams lay shattered and only one spell could heal them.

I pushed myself upright. Shaky as a newborn foal, I made my way over to Moppe. Salt-tanged air filled my lungs as I spoke Moppe's name.

I drew another shivering, quivering breath of anticipation, filling it with all the intensity of my will. *Free her. Please.* Then I spoke the word I'd learned in the Cave of Echoes.

Seabirds circled high. Waves crashed.

And Moppe remained stone.

With a groan, I slumped back. I'd been so sure it would work. But I had failed again. Failed myself, failed Moppe, failed Master Betrys. My memory dredged up that last image of her being dragged away by the goldcoats, her fierce brown gaze transfixing me, expecting the best from me.

Wait.

I wasn't the only one who had asked a question in the Cave of Echoes. What had Master Betrys said? That she feared the return of someone dangerous from her past and needed a way to stop them. Benedict clearly despised her, and they'd been students together at the Schola. And he had sent the Furtive.

My heart began to thrum. In the fight after the gala, when I tried to interfere, Master Betrys had cast a counterspell on me that I didn't recognize. And when the statue had grabbed for me, there had been that moment when I was *certain* I was going to be petrified. When I survived, I assumed it must have been a different spell.

But what if it wasn't? What if the long-lost word Betrys gained from the Cave of Echoes was the magespeak to un-petrify someone, because she suspected her old rival had returned and knew what he was capable of? What if she'd used it on me, and that was why I'd survived the statue's attack?

I dug back into my memory, struggling to remember the incantation. I spoke it silently, twice, to practice. Then once, aloud.

Magic rippled through me, sharp and clear and powerful.

I held my breath, staring at Moppe, eyes stinging, unable to blink or look away. A faint tinge warmed the gray stone of her cheeks, so slowly I feared it was only the reflection of my own glow. Then darkness shot through her stone curls. They began to ripple, blowing in the breeze. Her throat shivered. Her lips quivered. Her eyes darkened. Blinked.

She gasped, and my entire world suddenly spun back into motion, like a freshly wound clock. "Moppe!" I cried, flinging my arms around her.

Cloth and hair and flesh and bone. "I'm sorry!" I chanted it over and over again.

Her arms squeezed back. "I know. I'm sorry too."

I don't know how long we stood there. But finally Moppe asked, "Am I really?"

"Are you really what?"

She pulled back, looking at me with an odd expression. "You told that pustule Benedict I was your best friend."

"You heard that? But you were stone!"

"I could hear everything. See everything." She shuddered. "Imagine being trapped that way, forever. But yes, I saw you standing up to that imperial pimple."

"Oh." I looked down to hide the flush on my face. I hadn't really thought about it. The words had just . . . tumbled out. But they felt true. In spite of everything, in spite of the jealousy and the betrayal, Moppe *was* my best friend.

"It's funny," she said. "I despised you when I first came to Master Betrys's. Every time I saw you I wanted to tear those ruffles off your gown and stuff them in your face. Arrogant know-it-all."

Strangely, her words didn't hurt. Instead they loosened something in my chest. I huffed, almost a laugh.

"I hated you, too," I admitted. "Do you know how hard it was for me to get a single turnip to even wobble? And then you came in and had them all dancing minuets with no training at all. You're so powerful, Moppe. It's—it's hard not to be jealous."

"I am pretty wonderful," she said, smirking.

"And you call *me* arrogant?" I snorted. "You declared yourself *queen*."

Moppe tucked her arms around her midsection at that, looking uncomfortable. "I don't really want to be queen. But Mama says it's the only way for Medasia to be free. If we can prove that Meda's bloodline is still here, the emperor will have to honor that. I don't want a war, but I do want all Medasians to have a fair life. Not just the ones who toady up to the Regians, who already have fancy houses and fancy manners."

"I guess my brother thought that too," I said. "And . . . and so do I."

Moppe bit her lip. "I'm sorry about Florian. I know that doesn't make it better, but I'm sorry."

I nodded, gulping down a tight knot in my throat. "Do you know what he asked the Speakthief?"

She shook her head. "I never met him. I asked my mother, but she said he never mentioned it. I guess he didn't tell anyone."

I squeezed my eyes shut. "It doesn't matter. My brother died fighting for a free Medasia, and I ruined it. If I hadn't tricked the Black Drake into kidnapping you, none of this would have happened. But I was afraid you wouldn't be able to stand up to your mother. I should have trusted you."

"She is a hard woman to say no to," said Moppe, giving me a wry grin. "I guess we both know something about that. I should have trusted you after we got the crown in the first place. I thought you only wanted the crown so you could turn it over to your mother and the council."

I snorted. "I guess we're even, then."

"Now we just need to stop Benedict before he turns this into an outright war," said Moppe, looking out ferociously across the harbor.

War. War. War.

I stared up at the craggy, echoing stones. Echoes again. Was it simply chance? Or was someone—something—trying to send us a message? Now I knew what Master Betrys's answer had been. My own answer was likely as useless as my question. But someone else had asked Rhema a question that day.

"Moppe, what did you say you asked in the Cave of Echoes?"

"I asked for a way to free Medasia without a war. But I told you, it didn't work. I said it about a thousand times: *Medasia*, and then the word. I must have not heard it right."

"Maybe it's more complicated than that," I said. "What if there's some other way we can fix this and free Medasia without a war, using your word?"

"Could we use it to get the crown back from Benedict?"

I drummed my fingers against my chin, thinking hard. "If it was the word for *crown*, I could try a recovery spell and—"

"Except that won't really solve the problem." Moppe grimaced. "Someone will always be trying to steal the crown, so long as it controls the Black Drake."

A bolt of understanding shivered through me. "What if it didn't? What if your word can set him *free*?"

Moppe's brows arched. "But—"

"What would you rather have?" I asked. "The Black Drake compelled to do Benedict's bidding? Or the Black Drake deciding for himself what to do?"

"But what if he goes on a rampage? Or just abandons us?"

"It's the risk we have to take. But he seemed rather nice. I mean, for a sea monster."

Moppe nodded. "Let's do it. It's worth trying, at least. How do I target it, though? Do I just say 'Black Drake'? Is that his name?"

"It's the only name I've ever heard him called. Even if it's not a proper name, if you say it in magespeak, it should work. He's the only black-colored drake around, so as a target identifier it should be enough. You already know the word for *black*, and drake is *drake*."

She groaned. "Another hundred-syllable word."

"It's not that bad. Only twelve. Can you remember it?"

I had her repeat the magespeak for *Black Drake* until she could say it without stumbling. When she finally got it, she did a small jig of triumph, punching the air. "Finally! Now we need to get close enough to use it, without that stinkfin petrifying us."

I grinned. "Let him try. *Petrify* isn't a solitaire. Not anymore! I'll counterspell us both before we get there."

"He's still out in the middle of the ocean, though," said Moppe. "Should I turn you into a dolphin again?"

"No!" I held up my hands hastily, warding off the suggestion. "I've got a better idea."

22

SALT SPRAY SPATTERED MY HAIR and dress, dashing up in my face with every cresting wave. I crouched in the shell-coracle beside Moppe as Nerine and the Ravager tugged us through the bounding waves in pursuit of the Black Drake.

"There," the mermaid queen called out, pointing. "I see the drake. He's attacking those drylanders."

Moppe craned her neck to see. "That's the *Victory*!"

The frigate was clearly in peril, listing to one side, masts snapped, sailcloth floating in the water. And yet they fought on. As I watched, smoke puffed along one side, followed by the boom of a cannon. Around it, the water frothed and spun as the Black Drake circled the ship.

He reared up, jaws snapping, to catch one of the cannons from the deck, shaking it like a cat with a mouse, before spitting it into the water. Gods, I hoped this worked!

"We need to hurry!" Moppe urged.

Nerine sang a wordless song. The Ravager beat her tail more strongly, whipping us through the waves.

"How close do we need to get?" Moppe asked, kneeling now, braced against the smoothly luminous shell.

"The closer, the better," I said. "Generally, just being able to see or hear or feel the target is enough."

"I guess it's good he's so enormous. *Black Drake*—oh blast it, he's gone under."

"Ware the drylander," called Nerine.

"It's Benedict!" I called out as I caught the glitter of ice on the horizon. "He's spotted us!"

The wizard's enchanted ship wove through the waves like a crackle of lightning. Benedict stood at the prow wearing an expression of disbelief as he stared at Moppe. "Impossible! The girl lives!"

A great surge of water rose up as the enormous dark serpent loomed over us. *"Glorious queen, you have returned!"*

"She's not your queen, you foolish creature!" spat Benedict. "I have the crown. I am your liege now, and you will do my bidding. Destroy that ship!"

The Black Drake gave an agonized whimper. With a great heave, he twisted and hefted his bulk back toward the rebel ship. Around and around he spun, coiling up and over the *Victory*, a terror of dark scales lashing round the vessel.

"This rebellion ends today," snarled Benedict. "I will bring order to this chaos. I, and I alone. Those fools thought I was too weak to be named Master. Now they will learn the truth! Now they will honor me as I deserve!"

"Black Drake!" shouted Moppe. And then, finally, she spoke the word.

But nothing happened. The Black Drake still coiled around the ship, snarling and snapping. In moments, the ship would be crushed. Screams echoed across the water. Sailors scrambled across the heaving deck, trying to arm the cannons. Captain Porphyra's purple scarf flashed among them as she fought to save the ship.

Moppe spun to face me. "Did I say it wrong?"

I shook my head. "No, you said it perfectly. Every syllable." Heavy dread dragged me down. I was missing something. Blast it! And if I didn't figure it out soon, we were all doomed.

Benedict threw his head back, laughing long and loud. "I'm sorry," he drawled, "was that supposed to be a spell? Foolish girls. If it were that easy, I'd have gained control of the creature long ago. Whatever it is you think you're doing, it will never work. The Black Drake has no name. The only power that binds him is this crown." He tapped the circlet. "But since you insist on interfering, we may as well end this now. Black Drake, I command you to kill the false queen."

The Black Drake made a horrible noise, somewhere between a groan and a bellow. *"As you command, my king."*

He was upon us in heartbeats. Nerine barely had time for a warning trill before a great scaly bulk crashed into the coracle-boat, spilling us into the water.

I sputtered, slapping at the sea and kicking. But with every movement I only sank deeper. Icy water swirled around my hands and legs, tugging me down. I reached out, grasping desperately for anything that could save me.

Something slid under my hands: smooth but grooved just enough that I could catch hold with the tips of my fingers. It heaved, flexing. With a thrill of horror, I realized what it was, but I didn't let go. It was still better than drowning.

I clung to the Black Drake's neck, tight as a barnacle, as the water suddenly fell away in heavy sheets. The creature had surfaced! I gasped, filling my lungs, then coughed to clear the salt from my throat.

I had never been this close to the Black Drake before. I could almost see my own reflection in the glossy dark scales. Dark as wine. Dark as the evening sky.

Dark. But not truly *black.* The color was richer and deeper. Like the heart of a velvety iris, or the dusky bloom of a ripe grape. It was only now that I was so close that I could see the truth.

A shriek above me shattered the fragile thought. I peered up to see Moppe dangling only a few feet above me. Gods save us, the Black Drake had her in his jaws! An answering scream came from the *Victory*, where Captain Porphyra clung to the railing along the stern, watching the horrible scene unfold.

Moppe struggled, beat against his muzzle, writhed and twisted. It was no use. Those terrible fangs imprisoned her tight.

I felt as if someone had petrified my heart. His great gold eyes were blank as a statue's. He was nothing but raw power now, his will utterly lost to the crown. To Benedict, and his schemes and hatreds.

Moppe was suspended above me, black curls spilling in a cloud around her terrified face. She reached out, hands flailing in the empty air. "Antonia!"

And finally, I knew what to do.

"Moppe!" I cried. "Remember how we stopped the Devastation?"

Understanding flared in her eyes, driving back some of the terror. "Yes!" She struggled against the clench of the monster's mouth, fingers straining to close the gap between us.

"Kill her!" thundered Benedict. "Now!"

The Black Drake tossed his head, clearly fighting the command. But with the crown's hold on him, he couldn't resist forever. Already his jaws were tightening.

Moppe screamed, but the drake's flailing had dipped her closer to me. Finally my fingers caught hers, tangling tight. She squeezed back. Our eyes met, holding steady even as the world fell to chaos all around. Then I spoke the word Rhema had given me, praying I had guessed its meaning, finally.

A tingle of magic coursed through me.

I spoke the second word. *"Drake."*

The tingle became a torrent, a tide of raw potential that

was like wading in starlight. Moppe's hand jerked, yanking me half out of the coracle.

I clung tight. I couldn't let go. Not until she finished this. Just a little longer!

Moppe shouted the final word of the spell.

A flood of magic broke loose, cascading over me. Everything seemed to stop. The screams, the sun, the heaving of the sea itself. The drake.

For a dreadful moment I was afraid Benedict had petrified the monster, but his scales were as sleek and black—or rather, dark *purple*—as ever. Then time spun back.

The Black Drake lowered his great maw, dropping Moppe gently onto the overturned coracle. I slid down beside her, collapsing in a boneless heap. We clung to each other, all rattled breath and triumph.

I looked up to find great golden eyes blinking down at us, no longer empty and enslaved.

"I . . . I am free."

He rose up, long neck unfurling, turning to face Benedict.

"I do not wish to kill. And I am not a foolish creature," he hissed with a trace of petulance.

Benedict's expression melted into wrath. He seized the pearly crown from his own head and shook it at the drake. "I have the crown! You have to do what I command!"

"No." The drake bared his terrible teeth, thrumming a low rumble. *"I do not think so. You are not my glorious king."*

Benedict's fierce gaze found me. "You. You did this." He gave a huff—half annoyance, half admiration. "You're more clever than I thought. Making me think the girl was petrified. What was it? An illusion? Some sort of transfiguration? Not that it matters. You'll soon understand that you made the wrong choice. *Antonia. Petrify.*"

The magic buzzed over me, a cold lick of power.

Then my counterspell pinged, bouncing the magic back and making Benedict wince. Now he looked more than simply annoyed. He looked . . . scared.

I crossed my arms, tilting my chin, enjoying his discomfort. "Here's a clue," I said. "It wasn't an illusion. And it wasn't transfiguration. Actually, I used your variation of Therenval's Technique to layer on the anti-petrify counterspells, so I've still got about ten of them active. In case you want to try again," I added, giving him my sweetest and most poisonous smile.

Benedict snarled, but I was faster. *"Benedict. Petrify."*

He had only enough time to look startled before his skin dulled to gray and his lips froze. The enchanted boat splintered to shards of ice beneath his weight. I had one glimpse of his blank stone gaze before he was lost beneath the waves.

The Black Drake gave a fluting cry and dived after him.

"Hey!" Moppe exclaimed. "I thought we set him free."

But the serpent rose up barely a heartbeat later, carefully clasping something small and luminous in his mouth. He swam slowly over to our upturned shell boat, dipping his great head down so we could see what he held so gently between those ravenous teeth.

It was the crown.

I nudged Moppe. "I think he wants you to take it."

She did, though her hands were trembling. The Black Drake gave a satisfied nod.

"Glorious queen, how may I serve you?"

"But you don't have to serve me," she said. "I set you free."

"Yes. And now I am free to serve you. Not by the words of the gods, but by my own choosing. What is your command?"

Moppe's anxious expression broke into a grin of pure relief. She smiled at me, reaching out to squeeze my hand as she said, loud enough so even the battered rebels aboard the *Victory* could hear, "Let's go negotiate a peace treaty."

It turns out that peace treaties take a lot less time to negotiate when one party has a giant, terrifying sea monster on their side. It took only three days for my mother, the rest of the council, Captain Porphyra, and Queen Agamopa to come to an agreement. Unfortunately, I was there for most of it, even the deadly boring bits about the spiny-snail territories and restrictions on harvest. I knew they were important, but honestly, the details had begun to blur together by the fifth hour of debate.

By the third day they had winnowed down the long list of grievances to a mere handful of issues. I was only half listening, more interested in searching my grimoire for the elusive counterspell that would free me of my glow. It had been quite useful in the past days, but I was more than ready to turn it off.

"No," Captain Porphyra was insisting, "that's not negotiable. Medasia must be reborn free of the taint of treason. We cannot risk another betrayal."

"It happened over a century ago," my mother replied, in

what I liked to think of as her "negotiation" voice, a decep-tively cool tone like a steel blade sheathed in silk. "He's long dead. You can't punish—"

"Be glad we're not demanding a blood price," Porphyra replied.

A pause. My mother pinched the bridge of her nose, then nodded. The day was already hot, even down along the shoreline, where tents had been erected to shelter the nego-tiations.

Beside me, Moppe groaned. "If I'd known being queen would be this boring, I never would have agreed to it. Maybe I should let Lyssa take over."

"Do you regret it?" I asked, lowering my voice, though I doubted either of our mothers were listening, busy as they were with negotiations.

"No," she said, rolling a slip of scrap paper into a crumpled ball. She'd been practicing in preparation for sign-ing her name to the treaty. "I mean, it's for Medasia. That's more important than what I want."

"What about magic?" I asked. "You can still study."

"With whom?" Moppe tilted her head.

"My mother said they'll release Master Betrys as soon as the treaty is signed," I said. "We can go back to being apprentices, assuming she still wants us. It can be like it was before."

"You mean with us hating each other?" She tossed the paper ball at me. It pinged off my scowling forehead.

I rolled my eyes.

"What about the Schola Magica?" Moppe asked. "I thought you were all fired up to escape Medasia and go off to get one of those fancy hats and capes."

"I don't think that's likely now," I said. "Just because the emperor agreed to the treaty doesn't mean he's happy about it."

A missive had come just that morning, bedizened with gold flourishes and silken knots, granting Mother the power to finalize the negotiations on behalf of the emperor. It seemed he was desperate enough to ensure his supply of Medasian purple dye that he chose not to escalate the conflict any further. Especially not after the broadsheets had published their blood-chilling accounts of the Black Drake.

"Very well," my mother was saying. "But only if you lower the tax on lemons another five percent."

"Done." Porphyra bent over the table, scanning the vast array of papers spread across the surface. "I think that's the last of it. All that's needed now are the signatures."

My mother took up her plumed quill, inscribing her name with a flourish before passing it along to the five other men and women gathered about the table. "And here's Councillor Pharon, just in time."

I squinted along the shore to see the older man making his way toward us, supported by a walking cane and the arm of a stout young man in a physician's smock. I had un-petrified him three days ago, but the curse had left its mark upon the poor man. He'd been recovering under close watch. This was the first I'd seen him up and walking.

Mother went swiftly to greet him. "Councillor Pharon, I trust you're feeling better?"

The older man coughed, rubbing a hand along his throat, as if unused to breathing. "Yes," he began, "I—"

He broke off as a scattering of shouts and anxious cries echoed from the harbor. We all turned to see a great slithering black serpent making his way past the fishing boats and trade ships toward our beach.

The Black Drake coiled up onto the shore, utterly heedless of the alarm his passage had provoked. He spat something onto the wet sand, then curled over it with an air of immense satisfaction.

"I have found the false king, effulgent one."

Benedict's stone body lay half-submerged, one fist frozen in defiance, his expression caught in that moment of painful realization just before my spell took him. I have to admit I felt not the least bit sorry, even as he began to sink into the wet sand.

"There he is!" Pharon croaked, waving his walking cane at Benedict as he marched forward. Before any of us could stop him—not that I necessarily would have—Pharon cracked his walking stick against Benedict's forehead. "Traitor! This is all your fault!"

"What exactly do you mean by that, Councillor?" asked my mother, a slight frown creasing her beautiful brow. "Envoy Benedict is certainly responsible for petrifying you, though he claimed it was due to your own Liberationist leanings."

"Oh, so he says," Pharon sputtered. "I'm no rebel. I just know the truth about why he was sent here in the first place. He shows up dandying around, acting as if it's some great mission, when really he's just a washed-up, washed-out wastrel with barely a scrap of honor left. The Schola Magica rejected him and he's never gotten over it. The emperor never ordered him to start a war. He did it out of pride. He thought he could prove himself by destroying the Liberation."

"Mmm." My mother made a slow circle around the petrified wizard. "Then we will trust the emperor to deal with him as he sees fit."

"We're going to leave him like this?" I asked. Not that I minded, of course, as long as I didn't let myself linger too long on his expression of mixed horror and awe.

"For the journey, at least," she said. "You can release him at the will of the emperor."

I started to nod, then caught myself. "Wait. No. I can't. We're not going back to Regia Terra."

Mother's brows arched mildly. "Of course we are, darling. Now that the treaty is settled, we have a week to pack our things and depart."

I shook my head. "But that was just because you were afraid there would be a war. Now there's a treaty. Everything's going to change."

"Yes," said my mother. "Everything is changing. And we have no place here. Not anymore."

"What?" Moppe demanded. "Why?"

"Because it's one of the terms," answered Captain Porphyra, crossing her arms as she regarded me. "All those who carry the bloodline of the traitors who murdered your great-great-grandfather are hereby exiled from Medasia. Forever."

"But that's not us," I said, turning to my mother. "Grandmama was from Regia Terra, so she couldn't have been involved. And Grandpapa was so traditional! He *loved* the old kings and queens. His family couldn't have been traitors."

"It wasn't *my* family." She was looking up into the hills, toward the billowy crest of Mount Turnip, her lips a fixed, implacable line. She gave a small shake of her head, then turned to meet my desperate gaze. "It was King Goros's steward who did it. Slipped the poison in the cakes the king had ordered for his daughters, to celebrate the Feast of the Red Moon. He loved the king, but he loved gold and power more. And he had both, once Medasia became an imperial colony. His family prospered from his betrayal. They moved to the southern shore to escape the rumors. Built new lives. But there is always a cost." Her voice caught.

I shook my head.

Her face went hard. "Your father's grandfather made his choice, but you, unfortunately, must bear the cost. We have no place here," she said. "We leave Medasia within the week. And we can never return."

23

"No!" Moppe's voice twinned my own as we both cried out in shock and dismay.

"That's ridiculous," said Moppe, setting her fists on her hips as she scowled at her mother. But Captain Porphyra's stern expression did not waver.

"You'll understand when you're older, Agamopa," said Porphyra. "You're queen now. Sometimes queens must do disagreeable things, for the sake of their land. This is one of those times."

"No, it's not! Antonia is my friend! I'd never even have found the crown in the first place without her help. She doesn't deserve to be punished for something her great-grandfather did!"

"It's not about punishment," said Porphyra. "It's about the precedent you set as queen. You have to show strength. You can't let them think they can destroy you, as they did Goros."

"Banishing my best friend isn't a sign of strength," Moppe said fiercely. "It's a sign of weakness."

Porphyra stifled a sigh, then looked to my mother. "It's too late. We've already decided things. Isn't that right, Councillor?"

My mother eyed me grimly, then nodded. "Indeed. And it's for the best. This island has brought our family nothing but sorrow."

"Sorrow?" I exploded. "You can't just give up on things when they let you down. You have to fight for them. Even when it's hard! Like Fl—" I gasped as the word slipped away. "Like my brother," I finished. Mother's brows arched in surprise at my tone. And yet there was something softer in her eyes. "What would he say, if he were here now?" I asked.

"We signed the treaty," began Porphyra, but Moppe interrupted, cheeks flushed.

"I didn't sign any such treaty. And in case you didn't notice, I'm the one with the crown." She jabbed a finger at the pearly circlet.

At the gesture, the Black Drake suddenly lifted his great wedge-shaped head, sinuous neck curving over us curiously. *My queen, are you certain you are well? You are turning very red. Shall I acquire more chocolate?*

"No, thank you," she told the creature politely, her gaze still fixed on our mothers. "I think I have everything I need right here." Then she glanced toward me, holding out her hand.

I took a step closer, reaching out. Our fingers twined fast, clasping tight against the world. We spoke no magespeak, but the current that ran through me then was as powerful as any spell. In that moment I felt the same *click*, as if the universe had suddenly shifted all around me, setting me in my proper place.

"Queens don't rule alone, Mother," said Moppe. "Not the good ones. And if you really want what's best for Medasia, you'll stop trying to rip people apart and accept that I need friends. I need help, Mother. From people I trust. And I trust Antonia. I couldn't have done this without her."

Warmth flared through me, as she squeezed my hand tight. She was right. Together, we could do anything. Even convince my mother to change her mind. "We can't give up, Mama," I said. "I know terrible things have happened here. But we have the power to make something better. I know you don't think much of my magic, but *I did this*. Me and Moppe. We stopped a war. We didn't have cannons or treaties or the writ of the emperor. We just had each other, and our magic. I'm not giving that up." I finished my speech breathless, bobbing up on my toes. It was all true, and somehow that filled me with the high, billowy freedom of the clouds above. If only my mother could understand.

She and Porphyra were both silent. But there was a spark of something almost like pride in my mother's green eyes. Had I finally reached her?

"You make a compelling argument, Antonia," Mother said. "I see you've learned something from me after all." The faintest of smiles curved her lips. "Well done. I believe we must reconsider, Captain."

"Very well," said Porphyra. "I only want what's best for my queen." She looked to Moppe, her frown softening. "And for my daughter."

My mother nodded, then turned back to the table of papers. "I'll start a new copy of the treaty, without the exile clause."

Moppe turned to face me. "You can stay! Think of all the adventures we can have now!"

Her smile shone as bright as the glitter of the sunset sea. I wanted to say yes, more than anything. I opened my mouth to agree.

"No," I said instead.

"What?" Moppe's fingers went slack. My hand fell from hers, loose to my side.

"I mean, not right now. I . . . I'm going to go to the mainland."

"But we just—you're not going to be exiled!" she sputtered. "You can stay!"

"I know," I said. "And I'm glad I have that choice. Medasia is my home. You—you're my queen. But I want to be a Master Wizard. I'm going to the Schola Magica. I'm going to find a way. And I'm going to learn everything I can."

The shock in Moppe's brown eyes hollowed my heart, but I pushed onward, trying to explain. "And then I'm coming back," I told her. "I'll come back. I swear it, by the First Word."

She tried to smile. "You'd better. You're my Lyrica Drakesbane."

"And you're my Queen Meda," I said.

Then I flung my arms around her, hugging her tight so that she'd understand everything I hadn't said, everything there were no words to express, not even in the language of the gods.

She hugged me back. "I understand," she said softly. "But I'm going to miss you."

I stood along the railing of the *Perseverance*, taking one last look at Port Meda. It was early, the stones of the city gleaming in the pale gold light of morning. Gulls wheeled above the dockside. The dark water slapped at the hulls of the fishing boats, matching the drum of my own heart. Only a slim gangplank still connected the ship to the docks, and soon even that bridge would be gone. We would be sailing away, out across the sea, to Regia Terra.

My trunk was packed below, crammed full of grimoires and gowns. I didn't know how long I would be gone. Mother had arranged for me to stay with my great-aunt Eglantine once I reached the mainland. Supposedly she had a friend who had a sister who might know someone who could introduce me to one of the Masters at the Schola. It was a long shot, but it was better than nothing.

I would make it happen, even if I had to sleep on the doorstep of the Grand Library for an entire year. It was my dream, and I wasn't giving it up.

And then I would return to Medasia. Because that was my dream too. I belonged here, to these deep blue waters and green slopes, to the scent of lemons and the stark majesty of the mountains. To turnips and goats and olive trees. To Moppe.

A sharp blade seemed to cut my chest. I hadn't seen her since Liberation Day. She'd been swept off by Porphyra and her people for ceremonies and feasts and meetings with various influential Medasians. I'd hoped she might come to see me off, but she was so busy now.

It didn't matter. Our friendship would endure. I knew that, felt it deep in my bones, in my breath. We had faced nightmares, enchanted ferrets, stone lions, the Speakthief, murderous mermaids, and averted a war together.

I slanted a sideways glance at the stone figure lashed to the deck a few paces away, then stepped closer so I was in the line of sight of his blank stone gaze. "I'm not sorry," I told him. "Moppe is my friend. I might always be jealous of her, but that's my fault, not hers. And I'm better than that."

"I'm glad to hear it," said a voice behind me. "And never happier to be proven wrong."

It was Master Betrys, looking as poised and scholarly as ever in her neat blue robes, her cap perched smartly atop the glossy coils of her dark hair. "You've made me very proud.

Both you and Moppe. I knew you were capable of great things, provided you recognized your own strengths."

Her eyes, shifting to Benedict, had an odd, faraway look. Almost sorrowful. "A shame that you never learned that lesson, Benedict," she said softly. "It did not need to come to this."

I frowned, trying to read the strange expression on her face. She shook her head, pacing away, and gestured for me to follow. She led me to the far side of the ship, away from the petrified wizard.

"He was the reason you went to the Cave of Echoes," I said.

She nodded. "I hoped it wouldn't be necessary. But I'm glad Rhema answered me. And that you're a clever, brave girl with a very good memory." Her smile was warm, but there was still a shadow on her face.

"I'm going to release him when we reach the mainland," I said. "He won't be petrified forever. Though I suppose they may throw him in prison for a rather long time."

"You hold a rare power now, Antonia. The power to petrify. And the power to undo it. Tell me, have you shared the counterspell with anyone else?"

"Moppe," I said. "Only Moppe."

"And what of your own answer?" One brow quirked meaningfully. "I know you asked a question at the cave. And I suspect it had something to do with how you and Moppe managed to free the Black Drake."

"Er. Yes. But . . ." I hadn't shared *that* word with anyone. Not even Moppe. It was, in some ways, even more powerful than a solitaire. If it became common knowledge, Medasia's purple dye would be worthless. And there might be even greater dangers. I coughed. "Is it true that the Imperial Treasury is guarded by purple doors, to protect it from enemy wizards? And that the emperor himself wears violet robes, to guard him against sorcerous attacks?"

Master Betrys frowned. "Yes."

"So it would be a bad thing if anyone ever learned the magespeak for purple."

A light of understanding flared in her eyes. "Yes, it would. We will simply have to hope that if anyone ever does learn such a powerful word, she's a sensible and thoughtful wizard who uses it wisely." She gave me a small smile, then continued. "Guard what you know well, Antonia. In our art, words are power. And you will need all the power you can muster, if you're to enter the Schola Magica."

I had started to nod along, but at her last two words my mouth fell open. "What?"

She cocked her head curiously. "I was under the impression you had an interest in attending. Or is there some other reason you doodled 'Schola Magica' and 'Master Antonia Durant' all over my copy of *Principles of Enchantment*?"

Heat flooded my cheeks, but she was smiling. She tugged a furl of paper from the folds of her robes and held it out. "Here. This should be sufficient to gain an audience with the headmaster. You'll have to pass the entrance exams, but I've no doubt you'll make top marks. You're a brilliant theoretical wizard, Antonia. You belong at the Schola. They will teach you far more than I ever could."

"Th-thank you." I stared at the paper in my hand. At Master Betrys's handwriting, forming the letters of my own name, words of praise, a glowing recommendation.

"I—I thought maybe you didn't think I was good enough," I managed to spit out. "They didn't give Benedict his mastery, and I've seen what he can do."

"The Schola didn't deny Benedict his robes because of any failing in craft or power, Antonia. Sometimes, when we want things too badly, they poison us."

I cringed, thinking of how I'd envied Moppe. How I still, deep in my heart, yearned for her abilities. "I wish I were as powerful as Moppe," I admitted. "But . . . I'm still a wizard. I'm still proud of who I am."

"As you should be." The corner of her mouth quirked. "Moppe is in her own class. She'll need careful instruction, and quickly. The last thing this island needs is a reckless, half-trained wizard-queen of unspeakable power."

I hoped her smile meant she was joking. It sounded a bit too believable for me to laugh.

"So you're staying here," I said, gesturing to the gangplank, the docks, and Port Meda beyond. "On Medasia."

"Yes."

I thought she was going to simply go then. But she

hesitated, brown eyes piercing mine deep. "Remember, Antonia. Power isn't the key. It's what you do with your power that matters. Choose wisely."

She fixed her gaze on something behind me. "I'll take my leave now. There's someone else who has come to say goodbye." She departed, boots clicking across the deck. I turned, a desperate hope clogging my throat, to see who else had come.

The early morning sun caught reddish glints in her black curls.

"So," I said, trying to grin, though it felt more like a grimace. "What's the polite way to greet a queen? Should I bow?"

Her own lips wobbled into something like a smile. "I'm not a queen right now." She tapped her head. "See? No crown. Mama had it locked up in the treasury."

"I don't think being a queen is something you get to take on and off," I said. "I think you're stuck with it."

Her jaw tightened. "It's not like in the storybooks," she said. "I tried to get them to bring me cakes for breakfast yesterday and Mama refused. And I—I can't stop you from going away."

"It's not forever," I said, my voice rough. I held up the paper from Master Betrys. "Master Betrys gave me a recommendation. I'm going to go to the Schola Magica."

"And become even more insufferable," she said, but with a smile. "You'll be brilliant, Antonia. I know it."

"So will you," I said.

We stood along the railing, elbows propped along the

smooth wood, shoulders brushing together, warm against the brisk ocean breeze.

"Write me," she said, with a high, desperate edge to the words. "I'm going to learn to read. Maybe I can get one of those fancy tutors. Whatever it takes. And I'll write every week. I promise. I won't forget."

"Good," I said, and now my throat felt tight as a vise. "I'll read them all. And I won't forget. Not ever."

Her hand slid along the railing, gripping mine tight. I squeezed back, sealing the promise. It wasn't a magical spell. And yet I believed it would hold fast.

We sailed from Port Meda later that morning. As the sails rippled taut, blowing us east to the mainland, I stood at the stern, looking back at the docks, and the small black-haired figure standing there. I waved and waved until my arm ached and Port Meda was merely a glimmer.

Then I breathed deeply, filling my lungs with the salt air of my home, and turned around, ready to face the new life ahead.

acknowledgments

As lovely as it might be for a book to spring fully formed from one's brain, that rarely happens. In this case, my story needed quite a lot of help to become what it is today. Thank you to everyone who provided helpful feedback on part or all of one of the many drafts along the way: R. J. Anderson, Lauren Bjorkman, Geoff Bottone, Stephanie Burgis, Melissa Caruso, Megan Crewe, Robin LaFevers, Anne Nesbet, Sarah Prineas, and Jenn Reese.

I remain endlessly grateful to my agent, Hannah Fergesen, for being my advocate and adviser, and for her thoughtful insights on the manuscript. Big thanks as well to the entire team at kt literary for their efforts and ongoing support.

Many thanks to my editors, Reka Simonsen and Julia

McCarthy, who pushed me to make this book the best I could and inspired some of the best and most fitting improvements. Thank you to everyone who helped produce this book, including Valerie Shea, Jeannie Ng, and Rebecca Syracuse. Many thanks to Saoirse Lou for the gorgeous cover art.

My family has provided invaluable support over the years, allowing me the security and energy to pursue my creative dreams. Thank you, Mom, Dad, and Dave!

And to the ones who stood closest beside me as I worked on this book: my amazing husband, Bob, and my dog, Charlie, who remind me every day that the most important thing we can do in this world is love and be loved.

Turn the page for a sneak peek at

NIGHTINGALE.

Maybe it was because my name was Lark, but I had always loved heights. The way everything small fell away, leaving me with the thrill of possibility. Even now, when I was about to do the most dangerous thing I'd ever done.

Perched on the roof of the Royal Museum, I could almost convince myself that the world was full of opportunity. The city of Lamlyle spread in glittering splendor around me like the spangled skirts of a fine lady's gown. Aether lamps sparkled their otherworldly light, tracing the patterns of streets and outlining the dark mystery that was Prospect Park. If I squinted, I could even make out the lights of the great barges on the river. Barges that could carry me away to grand and faraway lands, to find adventure, to be free.

But the truth was, I wasn't free. My debt to Miss Starvenger bound me tight and heavy as iron, and just as unbreakable. If I didn't escape it soon, I'd be trapped forever in a life I hated. A life my mother had died fighting to save me from.

That was why I was here. All I needed was to make this last leap over to the museum's west wing, then drop down to pick the lock on the window. A wiggle inside, and I was golden. Literally. There were enough treasures in the Royal Museum to pay off a thousand debts.

I probably should have felt guilty, but really, all I felt were nerves. Guilt could wait. No, guilt could go stuff it. Guilt was for people who had other options.

I breathed in cool night air dashed with the scent of smoke and sugarcakes from the nightmarket in the next square. The gap before me seemed wider now than it had a few minutes ago. But it was the only way to reach the west wing, to get inside and claim my prize. The great glass dome of the central observatory was too slick, and there was no convenient wisteria vine on which to climb.

Just jump, I told myself. I'd practiced it a dozen times. But my feet remained rooted to the roof.

A quaver of voices sent me hunching down, wary of being spotted by the patrolling watch below. Peering over the edge of the roof, I saw two girls on their way to the nightmarket. Girls like me, from the looks of it. Ragged around the edges, underfed, underloved. As they passed out from under the glow of the lantern, I blinked. Because the light seemed to chase after them. It wrapped around them, a faint luminous gleam that bloomed from their skin, their patched and faded smocks, even the long braids slipping down their spines.

Factory girls. People called the folk who worked in the

aether shops "haunts" for a good reason: they looked like living ghosts. The luminous aether dust seeped into their clothing, their hair, their flesh. Beautiful and terrible. The magical stuff might power marvelous works of artifice, but it was dangerous. Too much of it, and you truly did become a ghost. You couldn't touch things. Couldn't eat. Couldn't speak. Eventually, your body faded completely away.

Not that anyone seemed to care. The factories kept right on hiring, and there were always folk desperate enough for coin to answer.

A swell of fury rose in my chest, ember-hot and useless. If I could, I'd stick Mr. Pinshaw, the factory owner, at one of his own grinding benches to see how he felt after breathing in poison all day. But I was only twelve. An orphan. It took every scrap of my strength just to stay alive and whole. Wishing to do more was like wishing for a star to fall into my pocket. My mother had tried to change things, and she'd died because of it. I wasn't going to make the same mistake.

One of the girls below stumbled, coughing. Soundless gasps shook her frail limbs, nearly bending her double. Her friend tried to reach for her, but her hand slid right through the sickly girl's arm. My own body tensed in useless sympathy. Maybe it was just a momentary flicker. Please, let it just be a flicker.

Finally, the girl straightened, catching her breath. I sagged in relief as they walked on, slipping away like gleams of moonlight lost in the clouds.

That sad scene was my fate if I didn't find the gumption to make this leap and seize fortune by the scruff of its neck. Plenty of Miss Starvenger's other girls were already answering the whistle, trotting down every morning to grind raw aether ore into dust, coming home gleaming and flickering. That was Miss Starvenger's idea of "charity." Take in a clutch of young girls from the orphanage, then squeeze every scrap of copper and silver out of us that she could. Even if it meant sending us to the haunt-shops. We owed it to her, she said, for all the care she'd invested in us.

Not me. *Never.* The factories had killed my mother, but they weren't taking me. Even if I had to risk death and dishonor.

I tugged a bit of black cloth from my pocket and tied the makeshift mask across my eyes. Five paces back along the roof. A turn. My legs coiled tight and strong. I ran, straight toward the edge. Launched myself into the air.

Flew.

My feet slammed into the roof of the western wing. I stood, shaky but victorious, shoulders back, feeling the air fresh and triumphant in my lungs.

I would make my own fate, starting tonight.

I didn't belong here. Everything in the posh halls of the Royal Museum made that utterly clear. No matter how carefully I stepped, my footfalls rang like warning bells through the dim corridors. The displays full of lush velvet robes mocked my threadbare breeches and coat. But none of that was going to stop me. I needed coin, and no one was going to notice a few missing trinkets.

My pulse buzzed with anticipation as I crouched before a glass-fronted cabinet. A bevy of small gold trinkets lay within: a handful of rings, a toothpick, a thimble. Because of course when you already ruled an entire country, you couldn't possibly use a *brass* thimble. Or pick your teeth with slivers of wood like the rest of us.

Then my gaze caught on something even better: a set of silver hair combs shaped like songbirds. Larks! And silver was easier to fence than gold.

I tugged a thin bit of metal from my cuff. The lock didn't look bad. The moonlight filtering down from the skylights above revealed no protective runemarks, either. A moment of careful fiddling and the lock gave a satisfying click. I was about to pull open the doors and claim my prize when a distant scuffing made me freeze.

My breath burned in my chest as I held it, listening.

There it was again. Something, somewhere behind me in the hall with all the swords and armor, also known as my escape route. Wonderful.

I could leave the loot and run for it. I could take off my mask and make up some story about getting lost as the museum closed. If they caught me, I'd only be guilty of trespass. Given my age, it was likely I'd escape serious punishment.

But if I gave up, this entire escapade was a waste. All the planning. All the time I'd spent watching the guards, plotting my route to the roof. That final, perilous leap.

And, worst of all, if I didn't make my weekly payment to Miss Starvenger, she'd order me to the factories to work off the rest of my debt. Turn me into a haunt, like those girls I'd seen, coughing and fading away.

The silver combs glittered, taunting me. Stuff it, I hadn't come this far to give up now. I snatched them from the shelf and shoved them into my coat pocket, then added the golden thimble and a few other baubles. If I was going to dabble my toes in the water, I might as well jump into the sea.

I crept back past a collection of marble statues, then sidled behind a large display of spears. There was *definitely* someone else in the museum. A cool blue light spilled from somewhere on the far side of the room. A boy was speaking.

And he was blocking my way out.

He stood in front of a low, wide pedestal bearing a single artifact: a sword. His spindly body was bent nearly double, as he traced something—runemarks?—in an oval around the blade.

In spite of myself, I let out a low breath of wonder. I'd never seen someone doing aethercraft. The practice of artifice was rare these days. My housemate Sophie said that, in theory, anyone could do it—it was like cooking, you just needed to follow a recipe. But so many of the cookbooks had been lost during the Dark Days, and now only folks with coin could afford the proper ingredients. Which they only had thanks to folk without coin working themselves into haunts in the factories.

The boy shuffled along the pedestal, still intent on his work. What *was* he doing? Maybe he was a very young museum guard, working late to add new wards on a prize display?

He wasn't *dressed* like a guard. He wore dark blue breeches and a pale linen shirt. There was a matching blue jacket slung onto the shoulder of a nearby suit of armor.

Curiosity tugged at me, but I couldn't afford to linger. What mattered was getting past him unnoticed, to the windows that filled the wall behind him. In particular, the one on the far left, which I had left cracked open after scrambling down from the roof earlier.

His back was to me. It was my best chance. I adjusted my mask to make sure my face was covered. Then I scuttled forward, ducking behind a gruesome display of armored mannequins playing out some ancient battle, complete with splatters of gore.

But the blasted boy must have heard something. He straightened abruptly.

I froze as he searched the shadows, a slight frown on his narrow, pale face. He didn't look much older than I was. Maybe thirteen, at most. And he definitely wasn't a guard, not with that glimmer of gold around his neck, a medallion with an insignia I couldn't make out from this distance.

But the tight set of his shoulders and gleam of sweat on his brow seemed proof enough he wasn't supposed to be here any more than I was. He stared into the shadows near my feet for a few seconds longer before returning to his work. That's right. I was just a breeze. A creaky old floor settling. Nothing to worry about.

I should have made another go for the window then, but the mystery of the boy and the sword gnawed at me, tempting as a fat purse. He'd begun to intone some sort of invocation. I could make out only a few phrases.

". . . nightingale return . . ."

". . . new champion arise . . ."

". . . defend the land . . ."

I thought of all the stories I'd heard of the marvels of the Architect, who first taught the sorcerous craft of artifice. The wonders of the Golden Age, when all of Gallant glittered with enchantment, when diamond-bright airships raced across the sky, aetheric threshers harvested grain so that no one was hungry, and magical devices cured any injury.

My housemate Sophie didn't think it could really have been all that grand, or it wouldn't have fallen apart so easily. You couldn't fix the world with artifice, she said, because no artifice could turn human cruelty to kindness, or greed to generosity. That was why she was so fired up about making new laws to protect workers. She said that was the only way to actually change anything.

And she was probably right. It was foolish for me to linger here. What did I care about some rich boy enchanting a sword? It had nothing to do with me. It wasn't going to change my life. Only the trinkets in my pocket could do that.

Then I saw something that knocked every bit of breath from my chest: a vial of glowing blue liquid. The boy held it in his hand, brandishing it above the sword.

I gaped at it, my chest swelling with wonder. Aether was the most valuable substance in the entire world. A single drop could power a streetlight for days. That was why the factories churned on, eating up desperate folk to crush the poisonous ore into dust, then boil it into stable, harmless liquid aether.

The boy didn't seem to care that he held a king's ransom in one hand. He leaned out and poured the entire bottle's worth over the sword. There was a fierce intensity in his expression. It reminded me of Sophie when she was caught up explaining some bit of philosophy. Whatever he was doing, it was vitally important to him.

I crept forward in between two of the armored figures. I had to see what he was doing. How had a boy—even a rich one—gotten his hands on so much aether? And why? A buzz of excitement rippled over my skin, driving away all sensible thoughts. Hundreds of factory workers had turned themselves into haunts to fill that vial. What was worth such a price?

The gleaming blue liquid ran into a groove along the length of the blade, then into more runes etched into the steel itself. For a moment, the entire weapon seemed to glow, the runes blazing into my eyes, even when I blinked. The light flared, suddenly brighter than noon.

I gasped, jerking back, wary of being spotted.

And caught my pocket on the knee of the armor beside me. Cloth tore. Metal crashed down, an iron fist driving me to the floor and setting a horrendous clatter echoing through the air.

Ears ringing, bones jangling, I struggled to free myself. Finally, I slithered forward, escaping the armor's embrace, only to find the boy staring at me with a mixture of amazement and outrage.

"Who are you? Who sent you?" he demanded. "If you're here to stop me, you're too late!"

I held up my hands as I stepped to the side, putting the pedestal and the sword between us. It had stopped glowing, though its runes still held a faint blue gleam. "I'm not here to stop you. In fact, I'll just be going now, if that's all right with you."

"No," he snapped. "You need to explain yourself. You're not allowed to be here."

"Neither are you!" I spat back.

For one brief moment he looked uncertain. Guilty, even. Then he tossed back his floppy black hair and said, airily, "Of course I'm allowed to be here. It's my museum."

I blinked at him. "Aren't you a little young to be a museum director?"

"I'm the *prince*," he blurted out, sounding irritated. "This is the *Royal* Museum."

I cocked my head, looking him up and down. "You're not the prince."

"Yes I am!"

"Prince Gideon is seventeen. And blond."

"I didn't say I was Gideon," snapped the boy. "I'm Jasper. His younger brother."

"Oh." I squinted, trying to find the resemblance.

To be honest, I'd almost forgotten there *was* a second prince. Heir apparent Gideon was a constant feature in the ephemera-boards, his dashing smile beaming down from the sides of buildings and factories throughout the city. He always seemed to be winning a horse race, or saving a drowning kitten, or attending a charity gala. He'd been only sixteen during the last war, but he'd still managed to lead a small unit of the Bright Brigade to win a key victory over the neighboring country of Saventry. The whole city of Lamlyle was in a swivet over his birthday next week, when he would finally be crowned king.

All I recalled of Jasper was a hazy image from Queen Jessamine's funeral procession. A small, skinny boy blurring into the background.

But the person standing before me now was definitely not blurring away. He was vibrantly, distressingly present, his intent blue eyes taking in every detail of the scene.

He glanced at the floor a few paces away from where I stood. Something glittered there. Silver combs. I stifled a curse, slapping one hand to my pocket, only to find the cloth ragged, hanging empty and torn. Rust that rotting armor!

"Though I hardly need to justify myself to a thief," said Jasper.

Ugh. Why had I let myself get distracted? Now I was deep in the pot and the water was starting to boil. I tried to lift my chin to feign nonchalance under his accusing gaze. "I'm no thief. Those just got knocked out of their displays."

"And, what, you're just wearing that mask because you're shy?"

Oops. I had forgotten about the mask. Rust it. Well, at least he wouldn't be able to recognize me. You know, next time I got invited to tea at the palace.

He held up a glittering palm-size box. "You'd best surrender now."

"Or you're going to throw a snuffbox at me?"

He gritted his teeth. "It's not a snuffbox. It's an aethercom. All I have to do is trigger it and there'll be a dozen soldiers from the Bright Brigade here before you can blink."

I smirked at him, even though my heart was battering my chest. "Why are you skulking alone around here if you're the prince? What are you up to that's so secret?"

A rich flush burned into his pale cheeks at my words. "Nothing that a thief need worry about," he snapped back. "Now are you going to surrender, or do I need to summon the Bright Brigade?"

I drew in a steadying breath. There was no way I was surrendering. And I saw only one source of leverage in the room. So I grabbed for it.

The moment my fingertips closed around the hilt of the sword, everything shifted. A brilliant light fell over me, sharp and bright as diamonds. I heard something like music being played in a room very far away, but so beautiful it made me want to cry. Even the air smelled different, blown in from some faraway meadow full of flowers I had no names for.

A hum ran through me, starting in the hand that held the sword, arcing up my arm and into my chest, then spreading out to every other limb. What was happening? I tried to let go of the weapon, but my fingers only spasmed, clutching it tighter. A voice—or maybe it was several voices, speaking in unison—said, *Greetings, Nightingale.*

Then, suddenly, it was over. The light was gone, the air smelled musty, and I was standing across an empty pedestal from an angry prince, clutching a sword that might have just spoken to me.

Looking for another great book?
Find it
IN THE MIDDLE.

Fun, fantastic books for kids
in the in-be**TWEEN** age.

IntheMiddleBooks.com

 SIMON & SCHUSTER
Children's Publishing   /SimonKids   @SimonKids

Isaveth and Quiz must solve a magical murder mystery....

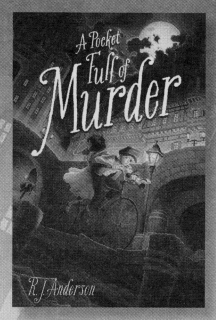

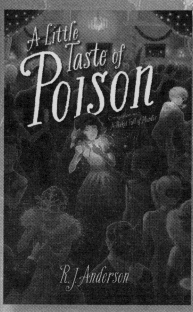

✱ "From the dynamic cover ... to the twisty ending, this has fullness and depth unusual in middle-grade mysteries. ..."
—*Booklist* on *A Pocket Full of Murder*, starred review

"Thoroughly entertaining."
—*Kirkus Reviews* on *A Pocket Full of Murder*

Atheneum

PRINT AND EBOOK EDITIONS AVAILABLE
simonandschuster.com/kids

ALONG A LIVELY RIVER LIVES A GIRL NAMED LUNA.

All her life she has heard about the old days when sprites danced in the waves and no one fell ill from a mouthful of river water. Luna thinks these are just stories, though—until her little sister gets sick. Now, Luna is determined to find a cure, no matter what it takes. Even if that means believing in magic . . .

★ "[A] delicate fantasy of sisterly love tested by separation and illness."
—*Publishers Weekly*, starred review

★ "A quiet story of perseverance and hope, exquisitely written with words and images that demand savoring."
—*Kirkus Reviews*, starred review

★ "Highlights the power of sisterly love in a truly enchanting way."
—*School Library Journal*, starred review

PRINT AND EBOOK EDITIONS AVAILABLE
simonandschuster.com/kids

TAMORA PIERCE'S BELOVED SAGA...

ALANNA
THE FIRST ADVENTURE

IN THE HAND
OF THE
GODDESS

THE WOMAN
WHO RIDES LIKE A MAN

LIONESS
RAMPANT